The Siege of
White Deer Park
&
In the Path of
the Storm

TWO FARTHING WOOD STORIES

by

COLIN DANN

RED FOX

A Red Fox Book
Published by Random House Children's Books
20 Vauxhall Bridge Road, London SW1V 2SA
A division of Random House UK Ltd
London Melbourne Sydney Auckland
Johannesburg and agencies throughout the world

The Siege of White Deer Park first published by
Hutchinson Children's Books 1985
Beaver edition 1986, Red Fox edition 1991
Text © Colin Dann 1985
Illustrations © Terry Riley 1985

In the Path of the Storm first published by
Hutchinson Children's Books 1989
Red Fox edition 1991
Text © Colin Dann 1989
Illustrations © Trevor Newton 1989

This edition specially produced for School Book Fairs
by Red Fox 1993

Reprinted 1993

Printed and bound in Great Britain by
Cox & Wyman Ltd, Reading, Berkshire

RANDOM HOUSE UK Limited Reg. No. 954009

ISBN 0 09 937511 7

The Siege of White Deer Park

Colin Dann

Illustrated by Terry Riley

RED FOX

Contents

For Sarah, Rachael, David
and Ruth

—1—
What Sort of Creature?

In the Nature Reserve of White Deer Park the animals were looking forward to the bustle of Spring. It was the end of February and dead Winter's grasp was loosening little by little with each spell of sunshine. The survivors of the band of beasts and birds who had travelled to the haven of the Park from their destroyed home in Farthing Wood had passed their third winter in the confines of the Reserve. Only a few still survived. The short life spans of most had run their course. But now their descendants populated the Park, and they knew no other home. These voles and mice, hedgehogs, rabbits and hares mingled and mated as natives with others of their kind whose forefathers had always lived within the Park's boundaries. Yet they were still conscious of a sort of allegiance to the few stalwarts of the old Farthing Wood community who remained alive.

Foremost among these were the Farthing Wood Fox and his mate Vixen, venerated almost as mythical beings to whom the animals turned for advice and counsel. They were the doyens of the Park's inhabitants, along with the aged Great Stag who was still supreme among the deer herd. Fox's oldest companion, Badger, was also a counsellor who tried to promote harmony between birds and beasts where it was feasible within their own natural order. Badger was very ancient now and never strayed far from his own set. He was slow, dim-sighted and rather feeble, but his kindly ways made him, if less respected, more loved even than Fox.

Tawny Owl, Adder, Toad, Weasel and Whistler the heron still lived and were occasional companions of Badger's extreme old age. But the old creature missed Mole, who had been his special friend. Mole's offspring – the result of his union with Mirthful, a female born in the Reserve – tended to live their own lives. So Badger suffered the loss of the wonderful bond that had existed between the two underground dwellers. Mole's allotted span of existence had reached its end during the winter. As he had lived, so he died – underground. His home had become his grave, and his tiny body went unnoticed in the labyrinth of tunnels. But he was remembered and mourned.

The descendants of Fox and Vixen now stretched almost to the fourth generation, for in the spring the cubs of their grandchildren would be born. From their own first litter Friendly and Charmer survived. Their cub Bold, who had left the Reserve and died outside it, had mated with Whisper who had journeyed to the Park for the safe birth of her own offspring. Now they, too, would become parents. So each season the Farthing Wood lineage was extended.

Badger and Tawny Owl had never paired off in their second home. They were too old and set in their ways – at least, so they said. As for Adder, who vanished altogether for long periods – well, no one was quite sure about him . . . .

It was dusk on one of the last days of February when the first signs of some strange influence in their lives appeared to one of the old comrades from Farthing Wood. Tawny Owl had been quartering the Park's boundaries where these adjoined the open downland. He noticed an unusual number of rabbits converging on a hole scraped under part of the fencing. The timid animals were jostling and bumping each other in their attempts to reach this entrance to the Reserve before their fellows.

'Hm,' mused Owl. 'This is odd. What's their hurry, I wonder?' He was not thinking of the possibilities for himself in this sudden abundance of food. His first thought was for the cause of their fright. He flew out of the Park a little way, following the rabbits' trail backwards – all of the time expecting to discover what was driving them. But he saw nothing, however much his night eyes scanned the ground.

'*Something* scared them,' he murmured to himself. 'Yet why haven't they dived for their burrows?' Tawny Owl knew all about the behaviour of rabbits.

He flew back and hooted a question at them. 'What's all the fuss about?'

Some of the animals looked up but, when they saw the owl, they scuttled ahead even faster. They were certainly not going to stop still to talk to a hunter! And, by the time Tawny Owl remembered his stomach, they had disappeared into the undergrowth.

He perched in an ash tree and pondered, his great round eyes staring unseeingly through the bare branches. He rustled his brown wings.

'No point brooding on it,' he muttered. 'Things reveal themselves eventually.' He flew off on his noiseless flight into the gathering darkness.

A few days later, again in the evening, Fox and Vixen were emerging from their den to go foraging. In the winter months there was often carrion to be found and recently they had been subsisting chiefly on that. Fox paused as a clatter of wings broke the stillness of their home wood.

'Pigeons,' he remarked.

But there were other noises. Birds' cries, and the sounds of sudden movements in the tree-tops as many took to flight, made the pair of foxes listen intently. There was a general disturbance that went on for some minutes.

'The whole wood's been alarmed,' said Vixen. She stayed close to her bolt-hole in case of trouble.

Fox gazed fixedly at the night sky. At last he said: 'I think I see what it is.'

Vixen waited for him to explain. He was still looking up through the fretwork of naked branches.

'Yes,' he said. 'I'm sure of it.'

'Well – what?' Vixen prompted, a little impatiently.

'There are a lot of birds flying in from beyond the Park. They seem to be wheeling about, uncertain where to go. They must have unsettled those at roost here.'

'They sound very panicky,' Vixen observed.

The foxes watched a while longer. Eventually many of the birds from outside found perches in the Reserve.

Others flew onwards, and gradually quietness was restored. Fox and Vixen went on their way.

Occurrences such as these became more frequent in the ensuing weeks. All the inhabitants of the Park became aware that something, as yet unknown, was bringing change to their little world. Animals from all over the countryside came flooding into the Park. Sometimes the creatures stayed; sometimes they passed right through or overhead; sometimes they returned again whence they had come. But it was obvious that the wildlife around was in a state of real alarm, and these continual movements to and fro brought an atmosphere of disquiet to the Nature Reserve. Weasel, running through the carpet of Dog's Mercury under the beech trees, noticed a sudden increase in the numbers of wood mice. These mice appeared to have thrown their inbred caution to the winds – most of them were running about quite openly, inviting themselves to be taken. Weasel was not one to refuse the offer and he had quite a field day or, rather, night. It was only later that he realized that the mice had been thrown into a state of panic by the arrival of dozens of hunting stoats and weasels like himself, who were closing in on their quarry from every direction. The poor mice simply did not know where to run next. But where had these hunting cousins of his suddenly appeared from? They were certainly not the ordinary inhabitants of White Deer Park.

Squirrel and his relatives found themselves competing for their hoards of autumn-buried acorns and beech mast with strangers from elsewhere who watched where they dug and stole where they could.

Hare's first-born, Leveret, who was still called so by his Farthing Wood friends from old association (though he had for long now been an adult) saw more of his own kind running through the dead grass and bracken than he had ever done since his arrival in White Deer Park.

Finally the friends began to gather to compare their opinions. It was now March and a shimmer of green was slowly spreading through the Park. New grass, tentative leaves on hawthorn and hazel, and ripening sycamore and chestnut buds gave glad signs to the animals that Winter was over. But they were puzzled and a little worried by the recent influxes.

'Where do they come from?' asked Squirrel.

'What's bringing them here?' asked Leveret.

Badger had no comment to make. He was only acquainted with the facts by hearsay. He had seen nothing himself.

'It's as if they've been driven here,' Tawny Owl said.

Fox had been doing a lot of thinking. 'You could be right, Owl,' he remarked. 'Birds and beasts are being driven here to the Reserve in the hope of shelter and then – '

'Finding themselves cornered?' Vixen broke in.

'Exactly! Then they'd be ripe for rounding up. It's like part of a deliberate plan by some clever creature.'

'Or creatures,' Weasel observed.

'Yes,' said Fox. 'It couldn't be just one. Unless . . .'

'Unless of the human variety,' finished Whistler the heron drily.

'Wouldn't make sense,' Tawny Owl contradicted him. 'What purpose could there be in this for Man?'

'How should we know?' asked Friendly, Fox's son. 'Who else is so clever?'

'I don't like this rounding up idea,' Leveret said nervously. 'It stands to reason – *we'd* be caught up in it too.'

They fell silent while they digested the implications of this.

'From what you say, Fox,' Badger wheezed, 'it sounds as if some animal or other is planning to use the Park as a sort of larder.'

Fox looked at him. 'You've gone straight to the point, Badger. But what sort of creature . . . .' he muttered inconclusively.

'A sort of creature *we* know nothing about,' said Owl.

'The deer are very uneasy,' put in Vixen. 'You can tell they sense something.'

'It's horrible waiting around,' said Charmer, her daughter, 'for this . . . this . . . *Something* to make an appearance. There are young to be born and looked after.'

'We mustn't get too jittery,' said Fox. 'Perhaps there *is* no "Something". There might be a more simple explanation. And a less alarming one.' But he could not convince himself.

Tawny Owl said, 'We mustn't fool ourselves either, Fox. We should prepare for the worst.'

'That's very helpful,' remarked Weasel sarcastically.

'I meant it for the best,' Owl defended himself. 'We don't want to be caught napping, do we?'

'No, but there's a reasonable chance in your case,' Weasel murmured wickedly. It was well known that Tawny Owl spent most of the daylight hours dozing. Owl pretended not to hear.

'Oh!' exclaimed Fox. 'How I wish our brave Kestrel was still around to do some scouting for us!'

'Yes,' said Whistler the heron. 'If anyone could have spotted the danger he could have done. But can I be of any service? I don't have Kestrel's piercing vision, but I *do* have wings, and there's a deal to be seen from the air which you creatures would likely miss.'

'Of course,' said Fox. 'Thank you. Any help is most welcome.'

'You know long flights are awkward with your bad wing,' Tawny Owl pointed out to the heron. He referred to the bird's old wound from a badly aimed bullet, which had caused him more trouble as he grew older. 'It had better be me.'

Whistler, whose name derived from the noise this wing made as it flapped through the air, knew perfectly well that Owl felt he had lost face by not offering his services first. But he was too polite to mention it. 'That's all right,' he said. 'I know you night birds have to catch up on your sleep while my sort are active.'

His intended tact misfired. Tawny Owl's feelings were hurt. He was very conscious that his advancing age made him sleep longer than he used to. His feathers ruffled indignantly.

'Nonsense!' he said. 'I'm quite capable of flying by day. And more accurately than you, I might add.'

'As you say, old friend,' Whistler said readily with his constant good humour. He was quite unaffected by Owl's sharp retort.

'We'll share the search then.'

'Very well,' replied Owl huffily.

Weasel looked at Owl with distaste. 'He gets worse as he gets older,' he murmured to himself.

—2—

The Pond is Deserted

The two birds made long flights over the surrounding area; the heron by day, the owl by night. Neither was able to see anything that might explain the recent developments. But some of the creatures who had taken refuge within the Reserve talked to the animals they met there. Word spread of a large, fierce beast who made raids in the night. No animal had seen it and survived, so none of the refugees could give even the vaguest description of it. There were rumours of terrible slaughter. Tales of its unnerving hunting skills were rife. It could climb; it could swim; it could catch creatures underground. Some even suspected it could fly, since

birds also suffered from its depredations. Soon the whole
Park was in a state of suspense.

But it was Spring and, despite the suspense, the
activities of Spring went on. Pairing and mating, nest-
building and preparing dens for imminent births
overrode any other consideration. For a while the threat
of the unknown seemed to recede. Then, with startling
suddenness, a change in the usual absorbing routine
shocked the animals out of their preoccupation. In the
midst of their mating season, the colony of Edible Frogs
made a mass exodus from their pond. They were not
content to hide themselves in the waterside vegetation.
They hopped away in all directions as far as they could
go, apparently desperate to get right away from the pond.
Other aquatic creatures such as newts were seen in great
numbers leaving the pond, and the ducks, coots and
moorhens who had built their nests on or near the water
deserted them entirely. It was obvious that something
very alarming had happened to drive them away. The
animals and birds did not need to ask each other what
this could be. They knew. The Beast had arrived in the
Park.

Toad, who had acted as guide to the Farthing Wood
animals on their long journey to White Deer Park, was
eager to talk to Fox. He had not been in the water himself
when the eruption of the Edible Frogs from the pond had
occurred. But he had witnessed their panic.

'It was pandemonium,' he told Fox. 'They couldn't
scramble away fast enough from that water. There was
something *in* the pond.'

'Did you see what it was?' Fox asked quickly.

'No, no. It was too dark for that,' replied Toad. 'But I
didn't want to stay around myself to find out!'

'Of course not. I can well see why.'

'I don't know what the Frogs will do now,' Toad croaked. 'The pond is their gathering point. How can they carry on their lives now – and in the middle of the most important time of the year?'

'I wonder how any of us will cope,' Fox returned. 'You can't deal with something unseen.'

'I'd like to stay around here for a while if I may?' Toad murmured. 'There's comfort in company and I haven't seen Badger in a long while.'

Fox spoke quietly: 'I'm afraid he's failing, Toad, little by little. We're all much older than we were, but Badger seems to live in his own little world. He only does what's necessary – can't be bothered with anything else.'

'I think Mole's sadly missed,' Toad murmured. 'And Kestrel too. What an acrobat *he* was in the sky! But our old life, back in the Wood, and the great trek here that seemed as if it would go on for ever – doesn't it seem so long ago?'

'An age,' Fox agreed. 'Vixen and I often talk about the past. A sign of *our* age, no doubt,' he mocked himself.

'Yes. We always overcame troubles together before, didn't we?' Toad went on. 'But, you know, this new menace – I have a feeling it may be too much for us.'

After this, life in the Reserve went on as if on tiptoe. The whole community held its breath – and waited. One morning the remains of three adult rabbits were found close together under some blackthorn. It was obvious this was not the work of a fox. The other rabbits spoke of a hint of soft footfalls around their burrows. As usual they had seen nothing. But each of them seemed to have been aware of a Presence.

At intervals other carcasses were discovered. Their killer had great stealth and cunning. It was never seen during the day, and at night, although every animal and bird stayed alert for it, nothing positive was heard.

The inhabitants of White Deer Park, many of whom were chiefly nocturnal in their habits, began to feel as if they were under siege. Yet they had to eat. They went about in fear and trepidation, trying to stay as close to their homes as possible. But deaths still occurred. The mystery continued to hang balefully over the Reserve.

The creature's amazing silence was a constant talking point. The hunters among the Park's population began to feel a sort of grudging respect for its expertise. Some of the young foxes harboured ideas of emulating its methods.

'That sort of skill would make any animal the most respected of predators,' remarked one youngster, a nephew of Friendly's called Husky.

'Do you admire it?' his uncle enquired.

'Of course. Don't you? If I were like that I'd be the envy of all.'

'You'd have to learn a little more quietness then,' Friendly chaffed him. The point was not lost on his young relative who was something of a chatterer. 'And,' he went on, 'can you climb trees?'

'I can climb a bit,' the youngster declared. 'I'm not sure about trees.'

While this conversation was proceeding, the elders of the Farthing Wood community were meeting specifically to discuss the threat from the super-predator. The talk seemed to go round and round in circles, without anything being resolved. At last Badger, who had held his peace for most of the time, murmured, 'I can't help thinking of cats.'

'What? What did you say, Badger?' Fox asked sharply.

'Well, you see, Fox,' Badger went on in his rather quavery voice, 'I'm reminded of Ginger Cat. I spent a lot of time with him in the Warden's home after my accident. You'll remember that winter when I hurt my –'

'Yes, yes,' Fox cut in hurriedly. He knew how Badger was apt to wander off the point. 'We all recall Ginger Cat. Now what about him?'

'Well, the thing that struck me most about *him* was his stealth,' Badger explained. 'He could be so quiet in his movements, you wouldn't know he was about. And . . . and . . . he could *climb* like anything. So I wonder if this stranger in our midst might be a cat?'

'Oh, Badger, don't be absurd!' Tawny Owl scoffed. 'How could a cat have slaughtered as this beast has done? It wouldn't have the strength.'

'I didn't necessarily mean a cat like the Warden's cat,' Badger continued doggedly. 'But – er – another sort of cat : . . .'

Weasel said: 'It makes sense, doesn't it, Fox?'

'I don't know,' said Fox. 'What other sorts of cats are there?'

None of them had an answer to that.

'It's *not* a cat,' Tawny Owl declared peremptorily. 'It's a larger animal altogether.'

'But if it's so large, Owl,' Weasel said cheekily, 'why haven't you been able to spot it?'

Tawny Owl looked awkward. 'I don't know,' he said, and shuffled his feet. 'But Whistler looked too,' he added quickly as if that helped his argument which, of course, it did not.

'The fact is,' said Toad, 'we're all completely in the dark. And we shall remain in the dark until one of us – or another animal – comes face to face with the creature.'

'If that should happen, he won't live to tell the tale,' Fox reminded him.

'He might – if he had wings,' Toad suggested.

'Wings haven't been of much use so far,' Whistler said. 'Birds have been taken from their nests.'

'Then the bird in question should remain in the air,' Toad answered.

'I think Toad has something,' Vixen remarked. 'Another search should be made. Tawny Owl and Whistler didn't actually search the Reserve itself because the beast was believed to be outside it.'

'Very true,' said Fox. 'No use looking by day, though. It keeps itself well hidden. Owl, if you were very clever and very quiet, you might catch a glimpse of it. It has to hunt.'

'Oh, I can match the beast itself for quietness,' Tawny Owl boasted. 'No question of that. My flight is utterly noiseless. You see, my wing feathers – '

'Yes, we're all aware of your abilities,' Weasel cut in, rather sourly.

'Will you have another try?' Fox asked hurriedly, before Owl reacted.

'I certainly will,' the bird answered at once. He was delighted to be relied upon, and flattered by Fox's confidence in him.

'I still think it's a creature of the feline type,' Badger muttered obstinately.

Tawny Owl stared at him. His hooked beak opened on a retort, but he closed it again without speaking. He would very soon prove Badger wrong about that.

The gathering began to break up, when Fox suddenly asked: 'Has anyone seen Adder?'

It appeared that none of them had. Toad was usually the first to set eyes on him in the spring, for they often hibernated together. But even he had no idea where he was.

'I don't like to leave him out of our discussion,' Fox remarked. 'But he knows where *we* are so it's easier for him to seek us out.'

'Perhaps now it's warmer he'll turn up soon?' suggested Whistler.

'Huh! I suppose he might deign to show himself,' Weasel retorted. 'But as time goes by Adder gets crustier and crustier or, perhaps I should say in his case, scalier and scalier.'

'He'll be around,' Toad affirmed. 'I think I know him better than you do, Weasel. You've always taken his offhand manner too much to heart. It's just his way. After all, he is a snake, not a warm-blooded mammal. And I can tell you, he's just as loyal as any of us.'

The little group split up and went about their own concerns. As it turned out, talking about Adder seemed, though quite by chance, to hasten his arrival. The very next day Vixen found him coiled up by the entrance to her earth.

'Ah, Vixen,' said the snake. 'Another spring and yet you look just the same.'

Compliments from Adder were few and far between. Vixen was conscious of the unusual distinction. 'How nice to be greeted in such a charming way,' she said graciously. 'And how good to see you after all this time.'

Adder uncoiled himself and slid towards her. His thin body was blunt at the tail where some time ago he had lost about two centimetres of his length in a tussle with an enemy fox.

'The Reserve is alive with frogs, it seems,' he remarked with his infamous leer. 'I must try to work up an appetite and make the most of them.' His tongue flickered in and out as he tested the air.

'That won't be very difficult after your long fast, I should think.'

'Oh, my cold blood needs time to heat up properly,' he

answered. 'I'm always a bit sluggish at first.'

Vixen explained what had happened at the pond.

'Yes, I've heard rumours,' the snake drawled. 'There seem to be all kinds of strange stories about. Some monster or other on the prowl, I believe?'

'I think that's an exaggeration,' Vixen said. 'But there *is* a fierce creature roaming the Park. None of us feels safe. And the worst of it is – we don't know what this creature *looks* like.'

Fox, hearing Adder's voice, had emerged from the earth. 'Tawny Owl is keeping a lookout on his night travels,' he added, after he and Adder had exchanged greetings.

'Hm. Well, I've seen nothing,' the snake said. 'Except –'

The foxes waited but Adder seemed to have forgotten what he was going to say.

'Except what?' Fox prompted.

'Oh, it's of no importance,' Adder hissed. He had quickly decided that something he had detected might alarm them further. 'Have you seen Toad?' he asked to divert them.

'Oh yes. He steers clear of the pond too,' Vixen told him.

'Mmm. I hope I come across him,' Adder murmured. 'Well, I'm off to sun myself,' he added abruptly. 'Then I'll be ready for those frogs.'

He disappeared rather hurriedly and Fox and Vixen looked at each other with wry expressions.

'He doesn't change,' Vixen observed.

'No, he doesn't,' Fox concurred. 'And I wouldn't want him to. But he's keeping something from us. I know him.'

*****

Adder *was* keeping something back. Before he would say more, he wanted his suspicions about what he had seen confirmed or allayed. Toad was the one to do that. So the snake went in search of him.

He had not been misleading the foxes about sunning himself. He needed the warmth from a long bask in the sun to get his muscles working properly in case there should be a bit of travelling for him to do. He found a patch of dead bracken which faced into the spring sunshine. The spot was dry and the ground felt quite warm. It was ideal for him. While he enjoyed his sunbath Adder reflected that it was just the opposite of the sort of place Toad would be seeking. Toad liked dampness and shelter from the sun's rays, and preferred to move about after dark.

When Adder felt thoroughly warm and sufficiently lively, he moved off. He was still in the part of the Park originally colonized by the band of Farthing Wood animals, and so he hoped he might meet some old companions. As he rippled through the dry dead stalks of grass he saw an animal rise from the ground a few metres in front of him. It was Leveret who, in a typical attitude, was standing on hind legs to look about him. Adder hastened forward, calling in his rasping way. He knew that if Leveret bounded off there would be no hope of his catching him again. No animal in the Park could move so swiftly. Luckily Leveret detected the snake's movement and dropped on all fours to await him.

'I thought it must be you,' he said when Adder came up. 'Well, it's a sign Spring has really and truly arrived when you are seen moving about.'

'I'm looking for Toad,' Adder stated bluntly, without offering a greeting.

'Yes. I see.'

'Well, can you help me?'

'I hope so, yes. What's the problem?' Leveret asked.

The snake's tongue flickered faster than ever, a sure

sign of his exasperation. It was always the same with this maddening animal, he thought. Everything had to be said twice. 'Can you help me find Toad?' he hissed slowly and emphatically.

'If you wish it, Adder. Now where shall we begin?'

'Oh, don't bother!' said the snake angrily. 'Perhaps I'll manage better on my own.'

Leveret looked surprised. 'But I thought – ' he began.

'Look,' said Adder. 'I'm going towards the pond. If you see Toad tell him to meet me there. I need his advice.' He slid away in a bad humour. 'Mammals!' he muttered.

Leveret watched his departure. 'Funny he should be going *to* the pond when everyone else has been moving away from it,' he said to himself.

—3—
Footprints and Eyes

Adder took a roundabout route to the pond. Always one of the most secretive creatures in his movements, he now used extra care in view of the new air of uncertainty in the Reserve. It was a while before he reached the pond and his progress had been arrested twice on the way by two plump frogs who had presented to him irresistible reasons for delay. But once near the water's edge in the early dusk, Adder was still able to see the strange signs he had detected before. He settled himself down amongst the reeds and sedges for what might prove to be a long wait. The surface of the pond was undisturbed in the evening calm and no sound – not a single croak or chirp – arose from the vegetation clothing its banks.

Toad had soon been rounded up by Leveret. He was puzzled by Adder's message but, since he well knew that the snake was not prone to seek another's company without a definite purpose, he agreed to set off for the rendezvous. It was with some considerable misgiving that Toad found himself returning to the scene of so much recent agitation. He decided to run no risks – even though he suspected a small creature like himself might be beneath the notice of the mysterious fierce hunter. He covered most of the distance to the pond in daylight, but as soon as he got close to the danger area he hid himself in some thick moss to await darkness. Then, with the benefit of its screen, he continued rather more confidently. However, he was still wary, and he paused often to listen. He reached the pond without noticing any evidence of an unusual presence abroad that night.

Toad gave a muffled croak once or twice in the hope that only the waiting Adder would recognize it. The snake had expected him to arrive after dark and had remained alert, so the ploy worked.

'Well, you've taken a chance,' Toad said in a low voice as he pulled himself into the waterside screen from which Adder hissed his position.

'Only a slender one if there's no chance of discovery,' Adder observed wryly. 'I want you to look at something, Toad, I'm at a bit of a disadvantage.'

'What do you mean?'

'That patch of mud,' Adder indicated in front of them. 'What do you make of it?'

Toad looked where he was bidden. After a while he said, 'Nothing much. Unless you mean – oh!' a little croak of alarm escaped him involuntarily.

'You see them then?'

'Paw prints!'

'I thought as much,' hissed the snake. 'But, you

understand, Toad, someone who relies on my sort of locomotion can't claim to be an expert in such matters.'

'I take your point,' said Toad. 'But there can be no doubt. The frightening thing is – '

'I know – the size of them. I suppose they've been made by a mammal?'

'Oh yes. No frog or toad in existence could make marks like that.'

'I first saw them a day or so ago,' Adder said, 'and didn't pay much attention. It's only now I realize their significance.'

'Do the others know?'

'*I've* said nothing. I wasn't sure. Well, Toad, this will put their fur into a bristle.'

'I wonder if we should tell them? I mean, LOOK! What size must the creature be?'

'Big enough to kill a deer. No, we can't leave them in ignorance. They should be prepared.'

'Prepared for what, Adder? What can they do?'

'Nothing, I imagine,' the snake answered bluntly, 'except – keep their wits about them.'

Toad recalled the birds' mission. 'The animal might have been seen by now. Tawny Owl is combing the park.'

'This creature's too clever to be found by an owl,' Adder remarked with a hint of contempt. 'It's a master of concealment.'

The notion entered Toad's head that the Beast might be lying hidden nearby at that moment, and keeping them under observation. He became very nervous. 'I – I –think we shouldn't stay here,' he chattered. 'It might come back at any moment and – and – we know it's active at night. Let's separate.'

'I think we're safe enough,' Adder drawled affectedly,

'But all right, Toad. Thanks for your advice. My fears were well founded.'

Toad muttered something about seeing Adder again 'in the usual place' and hopped hurriedly away. The snake made up his mind to stay awhile in case he might be able to add some more evidence to the existing clues.

In the meantime Tawny Owl was on his second reconnaissance flight. He combed the park methodically, concentrating on the areas most fitted to an animal who wanted to hide itself. But, like the first, this second night of searching produced nothing. Before dawn, Tawny Owl flew wearily to a favourite perch in a beech copse. He was very tired indeed, but was pleased with the way he had carried out his mission. He felt he had left, as it were, no stone unturned. He settled his wings sleepily and, little by little, his big round eyes closed.

The Moon shone brightly over the countryside. White Deer Park shimmered in its glow. Once or twice the owl shifted his grip on the beech bough. It was a bright night, and each branch of the tree was picked out sharply in the moonlight. Tawny Owl dozed. But something – some influence or other – prevented him from sleeping properly, despite his tiredness. He opened one eye and, from his high perch, looked down towards the ground. What he saw nearly caused him to fall from the branch. A huge face, with eyes glinting in the moonlight like live coals, stared up at him.

Tawny Owl lost his grip, overbalanced, flapped his wings frantically and just saved himself from plunging downwards head first. He let out a screech and fought his way awkwardly up through the branches, at last gaining sufficient height to feel safe. He veered away from the copse· and steadied himself as he recovered from his sudden shock. The Beast!

As Tawny Owl calmed down he wondered if any other creature had seen his frightened reaction. He looked all round to see if he was watched and then alighted elsewhere, far enough away from his first spot to be comfortable. Now he wondered if he had imagined what he'd seen. It was so sudden – had he been dreaming? He did not think so, but he knew he ought to go back for a second look. After all, he was quite safe in the air. He thought about it for a while, trying to find valid reasons for not going back. But he could not think of any.

'Still. It's probably moved by now. Not much point,' he told himself unconvincingly. Then he thought of his friends. He owed it to them to make a proper report. He hesitated. Tawny Owl was not lacking in courage, but he really had had a bad fright. The Beast had been so close! At last he stiffened his resolve and took to the air once more, flying on a circular course which eventually brought him back to the borders of the beech copse. He fluttered to and fro uncertainly. Actually to enter the little wood again was extraordinarily difficult.

When he finally did fly in, he went cautiously from one tree to another, stopping each time before moving on. When the tree from which he had seen the Beast came into view, of course there was no sign of any animal, large or small, in its branches. A feeling of great relief flooded over the owl and now he flew right up to the tree for a closer look. Nothing!

'I shouldn't have delayed,' he muttered. 'It was wrong of me. Two great eyes – *that's* not much to go on. Now I suppose the thing's got well away from this place.' He flew about the copse, examining everything that might yield a clue. But there were no clues, not even footprints,

for last year's dry leaves were still thick on the ground.
And not the slightest rustle disturbed them.

Tawny Owl left the copse and directed his flight
towards Fox's earth. He began to feel quite proud of his
news. He, alone of all the Park's inhabitants, had had a
glimpse of the stranger who had come to dominate their
lives. It made him very important.

Day broke as he arrived. He called to Fox and Vixen
peremptorily. Already his mind was beginning to
exaggerate the little he had seen. There were stirrings in
the foxes' den. Vixen peered out.

'Oh, hallo, Owl,' she murmured and went promptly
back inside again.

'Wait!' cried the bird. 'I've news that – '

But Vixen was not listening. Tawny Owl could hear
voices inside the earth. He hooted with frustration. He
was bursting to tell them of his experience. Then Fox
emerged on his own.

'Have you had any luck, Owl?' he asked nonchalantly.

'Luck!' spluttered the bird. 'I – I – I've SEEN it!'

Fox looked at him sharply. 'The Beast? The hunter,
you mean?'

'Yes, yes. I came to tell you. I was in a tree and – and it
was *enormous*.'

'Did it attack you?'

'No. Oh-ho, no. I was too quick for that,' Tawny Owl
boasted. 'I was asleep, you see, Fox. I awoke and – there it
was.'

'You were asleep? Oh, I understand. And what did the
creature look like?'

The suspicion in Fox's voice was unmistakable and
Tawny Owl noticed it at once. Did he think he had
imagined it? Well!

'If that's your attitude,' he said resentfully, 'why should

I continue the story?'

'Now don't get in one of your huffs,' Fox pleaded. 'But sleep's a funny thing. We can all – '

'*All* doesn't come into it,' Owl interrupted haughtily. 'I alone have seen this thing. No one else was around. I was merely dozing after tiring myself out looking for the creature. I tell you I looked down and saw a massive head with gleaming eyes just below me. It was watching me! Do you think I invented it?'

'No, of course not,' Fox assured him. 'But – what was the rest of it like?'

'Ah well,' Owl mumbled, 'now you're asking. I wasn't able to see the *rest*.'

Vixen joined them. 'I overheard most of it,' she said. 'There's to be a meeting in the Hollow. Why doesn't Tawny Owl tell *everyone* about it then?' She was addressing Fox.

'A wise idea. It's tomorrow at dusk, Owl. Friendly and Charmer will come, and Weasel and Badger. And Whistler, of course. Perhaps he might have seen something too.'

'I doubt it,' Tawny Owl remarked jealously. 'The Beast doesn't reveal itself in the daylight.'

The Hollow was the traditional meeting place of the Farthing Wood community. It had been their first resting point on their arrival in the Park after their months' long journey. They had returned to it ever since when important matters were to be discussed, as a place of significance to them all.

The party assembled as darkness began to fall. Leveret and Squirrel were among the numbers. Toad arrived last, unwittingly bringing news to corroborate Tawny Owl's statement.

When Owl finished giving his description, which by

now he had embellished with all sorts of additional dramatic references, Toad croaked out what he and Adder had seen.

'I can vouch for the truth of Owl's remarks about size,' he added afterwards. 'The prints we saw could only have been made by a monster. Your feet, Fox, would have fitted into one corner!'

There was a silence and some of the animals looked at each other in consternation. Tawny Owl felt that his experiences were not getting the attention they deserved.

'Pooh,' he said, struggling to find words to bring his own experience back into the limelight, 'what are marks in the mud compared to a sight of the entire beast?'

Fox and Vixen looked at each other with wry amusement at the bird's childishness. But Toad wished Adder had been there to supply one of his caustic retorts. Owl could be very trying and silly at times. He had already admitted that he had seen only the head of the Beast clearly.

Badger asked if the prints had been like a cat's.

'Neither Adder nor I are qualified to tell you that,' Toad told him.

Badger turned to Tawny Owl. 'What about the head? Did it resemble a cat's?'

'Not in the least,' the bird answered immediately, without thinking about it. 'I told you you were on the wrong track.'

'But what other creature can climb a tree?' Badger persisted. 'Apart from our friend Squirrel.'

'None I know about,' Squirrel remarked.

The young foxes, Friendly and Charmer, were becoming impatient with the obtuseness of the ageing comrades.

'What does it signify whether it's a cat, a dog, a – a –

horse or a giant rat?' cried Charmer exasperatedly. 'It hunts. It kills. And it's very dangerous. Surely all that matters is what we can do to protect ourselves?'

Her brother Friendly supported her. 'Charmer's quite right,' he agreed. 'Whatever it is, we've got to think of a way to get it out of the Park.'

'But that's impossible,' Leveret said nervously, 'if we never know where it is.'

'We can track it,' Friendly declared. 'We foxes. It must have a scent.'

His father intervened. 'You're getting carried away, Friendly,' he said. 'Even if the scent could be picked up and then followed – which I doubt – what would the object be? What would you do if you came up against the creature?'

'Er – well, I – er – *we*, that is, would, I suppose – ' Friendly stopped in embarrassment. What *would* they do?

'You see, you haven't thought it through, have you?'

'All right, Father. But we must do *something*, mustn't we? Otherwise we could face extinction.'

'I only know what we mustn't do,' Fox returned, 'and that is confront it. This is a cunning, powerful animal quite beyond our experience. We're not dealing this time with rivals of our own kind.'

Now the attention of all the animals was fixed firmly on their old leader. Fox was the one to whom they had always turned when in trouble or danger. They respected him and trusted him. He had never yet failed to find a solution. They waited for him to go on. But the words of wisdom they expected to hear were not forthcoming.

'I'm afraid I've nothing to add to that,' he said finally.

The animals looked crestfallen.

'We have to defend our home – don't we?' Friendly whispered uncertainly.

'We can't,' said his father. 'I told you – it's beyond us.'

The little group exchanged glances unhappily. This defeatist Fox was unknown to them. They depended on him so much and he had never let them down before. Fox knew what they were thinking.

'I'm no longer a young animal,' he told them. 'We've all grown older. We can't indulge in the sort of escapades we used to do in the old days. We're no match for this Beast.'

'It's true,' sighed Badger. 'It's as much as I can do to get myself out of my set to feed sometimes.'

The young animals – Friendly, Charmer and Leveret – felt like intruders into an assembly of veterans. Friendly began to realize his father was, as always, trying to be realistic about their abilities. Perhaps it was time for the younger generation to take up the fight. But Fox was speaking again.

'To be blunt,' he said, 'there are some animals more at risk in the Reserve than others. Rabbits and, I'm afraid, hares, too, are the most vulnerable, as well as the smaller game such as mice, frogs and so forth. Foxes and badgers and snakes are not generally hunted for food. Birds, of course, have the perfect escape mechanism. So what I'm saying is that most of us are safe if we ensure that we don't antagonize the Beast.'

'That's a lot of comfort for me,' Leveret said morosely.

'I'm certain Fox didn't mean we'd turn our backs on you,' Vixen reassured him. 'The Oath of Mutual Protection still survives.'

'Of course,' said Fox. 'All of us are available to help another animal who gets into danger. But that's rather different from setting out to court it.' He looked meaningfully at Friendly.

Friendly said nothing, but he was eager for the meeting to break up. After what his father had said about foxes not being so much at risk, he had started to formulate some ambitious plans of his own.

—4—

A Waiting Game

The animals did not stay together much longer. The
meeting had been inconclusive and the only message to
come out of it was that they each needed to take extra
precautions for as long as the Beast chose to make White
Deer Park its hunting ground.

After Tawny Owl's fright no more was seen or heard of
the stranger. Adder had seen nothing more, although he
had waited for a long time at the pool's edge. This state of
affairs continued for quite a while, and once again the
Park's population returned to its main concern – the
business of raising families. Even the Edible Frogs forgot
their alarm and, in dribs and drabs, returned to the
water.

Friendly had been down to the Pond in the meantime to see the reported footprints for himself, and to use his nose in the hope of finding a scent. But the stranger had moved on. The fox could find nothing useful and the mud where the stranger had left its pug marks now betrayed no hint of the unusual.

The animals started to hope again, although they still dared not believe that they were to be left in peace.

Then the Beast announced its presence with an emphasis that ruled out all their hopes. An old and infirm member of the deer herd that roamed the Park was killed. Its remains – and they were scanty – were found some time afterwards, lying under a screen of budding elm scrub. It chanced to be Friendly who came across them. He was shocked at the discovery but, in a strange way, excited too. For it meant that the heroic plans he had laid might still be adopted. At first he told no one about the evidence except his contemporaries. These younger foxes and their descendants formed quite a large group, all of whom were related to each other through the blood of their common ancestor, the Farthing Wood Fox. Whilst the females amongst them were occupied at the moment with their new offspring, the males had time to gather and listen to Friendly's news. The older animals were kept in ignorance for the time being.

'There was no mistaking the odour all round the carcass,' Friendly told them. 'It was a sharp, thin smell – quite detectable above the smell of the rotten meat. And it was an animal smell I've never picked up before in this Reserve!' He brought the last words out with an air of triumph.

'Did you try to trace it?' asked one of his own male progeny, who was now entering his second season.

'Yes, Pace. I followed it for a way back. Then the trail

lost its scent. But, between us, we should be able to pick it up somewhere else.'

'Then what would we do?' asked a nephew, one of his dead brother Bold's cubs.

'I want to trace it back to its lair,' Friendly explained. 'Once we've found that, we can choose our time to assemble together and corner the Beast. We'll make it understand it's not wanted around here. It can't fight all of us, however big it is.'

The other foxes were quiet. Friendly allowed them a while for his words to sink in. Some of them did not appear to be very comfortable with this plan. Others, the more adventurous among them, were enthralled at the possibility of routing such a remarkable predator.

'When would we begin this tracking down?' one asked.

'We'll let the Beast make the first move,' Friendly answered. 'Let it show itself. If it's too clever to allow itself to be seen, let it reveal its whereabouts by its activity. That carcass was an old kill. What we want to find is a fresh one. Then *that* would be our starting point.'

The foxes dispersed, most of them enthusiastic about the venture. The days passed. It seemed as if the stranger had an inkling of the plan, for no carcass was found. The Beast was taking great pains not to advertise itself.

There had been births in the White Deer herd, just as there had been births amongst all the other species that inhabited the Park. The stranger, having tasted deer flesh, was particularly interested in the new arrivals born to the herd. These babies promised an even more succulent meal than the first victim. So it had been stalking the deer in its silent way, waiting for the right moment to strike.

The moment arrived. The opportunity was taken. In the darkness the fawn's mother knew little about her loss.

The stealth, the swiftness of the stranger worked with a sweet harmony. It was a harmony that was also ruthless. The fawn was taken, carried off and devoured with a quietness that was bewildering. The tenderness of the hapless young deer enabled its killer to leave very little evidence in the way of remains. So it was easily overlooked by the foxes who were searching for clues while they hunted for themselves and their mates.

Friendly was baffled. He had expected the Beast would have given a hint of its hideout by this time. Now the animals were back to wondering if it was still around.

But now the Reserve Warden began to suspect that something was amiss. He was the last to become aware of the existence of a fierce killer in the vicinity. He knew how many births had taken place that season in the deer herd, and when he discovered the loss of one and, later, a second, he became suspicious. There was no sign of their bodies. So their deaths were not from natural causes. When on his rounds he discovered the rotting remains of the old animal that had first fallen prey to the Beast he knew at once a killer was hunting his deer. His first conclusion was that it was a dog, and he was well aware that such an animal, having once killed deer, will return again and again to the attack.

From that time on, the Warden kept a careful watch on the herd, making regular evening and early morning circuits near the deer's position. He saw and heard nothing at all. This puzzled him because he knew that a dog is not the most silent of animals, and he was an experienced and careful observer. What he did not know was that he had become watched: the killer the watcher.

So long as the Warden continued his daily rounds, the killer wisely contented itself with smaller game. But it had inexhaustible patience, and it knew that eventually there would be another opportunity to eat raw venison. The Warden had patience too. He expected the creature to strike again, and that this lull was a temporary one. He was quite sure it was still close by and he waited for its return. He carried a gun while on his rounds, since he had the authority to use it if necessary to ensure the protection of the rare white deer. And so a waiting game developed that was played by both sides.

Naturally the other animals were also interested in the frequent appearance of the Warden. They realized that human endeavour was now ranged against the intruder and the older ones were comforted. Friendly and the more daring young foxes had mixed feelings. They were heartened by the man's presence, but really they wished to have the glory of defeating this unknown enemy all to themselves.

Fox and Vixen had gone one day, as they sometimes did, to talk to the Great Stag, the leader of the deer herd. Like them, he had suffered the changes wrought by Time. It was a matter for speculation how long he would continue to lead his kind. By now Fox had heard of the deer losses.

'Can you add anything to the little we know of the killer?' he asked.

'I only know of its speed and its strength,' the Stag answered him. 'It's approach was unnoticed and its retreat unmarked.'

'What *can* we be up against?'

'An extremely efficient predator,' observed the Stag. 'Certainly one to worry our human friend as well as ourselves.'

'I have a sneaking feeling,' Fox declared, 'that he will meet with the same lack of success.'

'I can't comment on that,' was the reply. 'He has his

methods, I believe. But we must certainly hope otherwise. Because *we* have no defence against it.'

'None at all,' agreed Fox. 'I've already accepted that.'

'Oh, it won't be any concern to you,' the Stag went on. 'I think it unlikely it will show any interest in foxes.'

'We're only worried about some of our young friends being foolhardy,' Vixen told him. 'I'm sure Friendly sees himself as a sort of successor to Fox. He has a lot of confidence and courage.'

'Well, it must be in his blood, I suppose,' commented the Stag. 'But it would be a foolish enterprise, I fear, to attempt to tussle with this supreme hunter.'

'Yes. I prefer to respect it from a distance,' said Fox.

'And hope that before we're all much older it'll choose to go away,' Vixen added.

'I wouldn't hold out a lot of hope for that,' the Stag returned. 'The creature has had no opposition so far. I feel that, as long as there is a deer herd here, it will choose to stay. That is, unless it is persuaded otherwise.'

'It's a sobering thought,' Fox said solemnly.

'My hinds are in a proper turmoil about it. Their nerves are all strung up. And I can offer them no assistance.'

'Not while the Beast remains hidden,' Fox acknowledged. 'But you stags are about the only animals in the Reserve who might successfully oppose it in a fight. Surely one day it's going to make a slip and be seen?'

'Don't count on it,' the Stag advised him.

The three talked more. Then, with the Warden once again coming into view, Fox and Vixen departed.

*****

Adder had returned to his home area after quitting the pondside, using the secluded route that was habitual to him. He liked to enjoy as much of the spring sunshine as he could, and he lay amongst the bracken very often, sleepily absorbing the sun's rays. The first new fern shoots were just pushing their heads above the surface and the pale green tightly-curled heads carried a promise of the fragrance that was to come in the summer. One day Adder was lying in this way, his red eyes glinting in the sunlight. He was thinking about his next meal but he was in no hurry to look for it. His reptilian stomach did not require to be filled with the mechanical regularity of a bird's or a mammal's. Because of his proximity to the stream that ran through the Park, he happened to be the first recipient of news brought by a very flustered Whistler.

It was early morning and the heron had been standing in the shallows in his usual sentry-like posture. As he watched for the rippling movement of a fish, out of the corner of his eye he saw an animal move slowly along the bank away from him. It was some twenty metres away and appeared to be looking for the best spot to descend for a drink. Whistler's immobility had kept him unobserved. He noted the animal was large, with sleek brown and black fur in blotches of colour which merged into stripes on its back. Its body had a powerful but streamlined appearance, with a long, thin, furry tail. It got down to the water's edge and, leaning on its front legs, lapped thirstily. As it drank, it maintained a watchful eye on its surroundings. It paused two or three times to look about. When it was satisfied it raised itself, shook one front paw in a kind of fastidiousness, and moved away with an unhurried, loose and undulating motion. Whistler was impressed by the creature's graceful movement. It looked round once more and he caught just a glimpse of a round whiskered face with two green eyes, and small ears and nose.

Whistler had held himself quite still during this entire episode. But now he hastened to fly off. He flapped his long wings and, with his stilt-like legs trailing beneath, he gained height and turned in the direction of his friends. A few seconds later he spied Adder sunbathing. He dropped down briefly to tell him what he had seen.

'What do you think it was?' he asked the snake.

'Oh, the creature we've all been looking for,' Adder answered nonchalantly, without even shifting his position. 'No question about it.'

'I wondered the same myself,' Whistler replied. 'I must go and spread the word.' He gave a farewell 'krornk' and flew away.

Adder's feigned lack of interest turned into action as soon as the heron was gone. He slid furtively from his couch in the bracken and made for the stream side. There would be footprints by the water and he wanted to compare them. He went along the bank and his eyes soon picked out the place where the animal had drunk. Yes, there were the marks! He examined them for a while to make quite sure.

'Just as I thought,' he lisped to himself. 'Identical.'

Now his curiosity was aroused. He wanted to see the creature for himself. He debated whether it was safe to follow in its wake along the bank. There was very little cover at that spot and he wanted to remain undetected. Only in that way could he hope to have a chance of surprising the stranger. He slithered hastily into the nearest patch of vegetation. As he lay hidden his mind began to concentrate itself on a grand scheme.

Some seasons ago, Adder had been the chief victor in a battle that the Farthing Wood animals had fought against some foxes. These had resented the animals establishing

a new home for themselves in the Reserve. The snake had
a weapon more telling than any of his friends possessed –
the weapon of poison. He had used it before to rid them
of a dangerous enemy. Now he began to entertain
thoughts of doing so again – and with much more
purpose. For the stranger who had come to dominate
their lives was more powerful and dangerous than any
fox. And, as long as it lived amongst them, it was a
potential enemy of every animal in the Park. Adder had
no way of knowing if his poison was sufficiently potent to
immobilize such a big hunter. So there was only one way
of finding out.

The snake glided through the plant stems, intent on
his secret pursuit. Surprise was everything. There was a
patch of bare ground between the clumps of vegetation
he needed to cross. But, once across it, the cover was
thick and tangled again. He slid into the open. All was
quiet. His head was about to enter the next mass of
growth when the breath was driven from his body. A
heavy weight came down in the centre of his back along
his vertebrae. He was pressed against the hard ground so
tightly that we was unable even to wriggle his tail. Adder
was securely pinioned.

—5—
Strangers

Whistler sped on, his great steel-grey wings beating rhythmically. He began to call as he neared Fox and Vixen's earth.

'News! News! Sensational news!'

He made such a noise, and the noise was so unexpected from the normally dignified heron, that animals and birds came out of their burrows and holes and boughs, or stopped what they were doing, to look up at him. He hastened to land.

Fox and Vixen were all agog and an indignant and sleepy Tawny Owl flew to a nearby perch to hear what all the unwarranted (in his opinion) commotion was about.

'The Beast is seen!' Whistler cried by way of a preliminary. 'Drinking, as boldly and openly as you like, from the stream.'

More animals and birds were gathering to listen. There was a chorus of demands to know what it was like, in voices of many varied pitches and registers. The heron waited for the hubbub to die down. He was familiar with the ginger cat belonging to the Warden and so this was the obvious comparison to make.

'It was like,' he told them, and at once there was a hushed silence, 'a much larger version of the cat our Badger got to know so well.'

Tawny Owl blinked his great eyes in disbelief.

'The colouring was quite different,' Whistler added. 'But there was the same litheness of movement, the same suppleness, the same silent gait.'

The owl prepared himself to give a sharp retort if Badger should start saying 'I told you so.' He looked around, but Badger was not in the throng. Owl was glad – but felt he would have to defend his own argument sooner or later.

'Where did the creature come from?' Fox wanted to know.

'I didn't observe its approach,' replied Whistler. 'It was already on the bank when I first saw it. Then it drank and made off towards the nearest cover – thankfully in a direction away from this part of the Park.'

Friendly had been listening eagerly. He knew where Whistler preferred to fish and now at last he had the evidence that he needed. He did not wait to hear any more but ran off at once to round up his confederates.

'So we're dealing with a large, powerful cat,' Fox summed up. 'Well, it could be worse. But what kind of cat can it be? Certainly not a human's pet. It's something none of us have ever seen or heard about before.'

'Excuse me,' Tawny Owl interrupted in his pompous way. 'Aren't you jumping to conclusions, Fox? How do we know this is the animal that has been doing the killing?'

There was a pause while his words were considered. Tawny Owl felt he had produced an effect and he was much gratified.

'We don't *know*,' admitted Fox. 'But everything points to it.'

'Adder was quite clear about it as soon as I told him,' Whistler remarked.

'Adder?' Owl scoffed. 'Adder? What would *he* know about it?'

'Its very size, as Whistler describes it, must be a sufficient clue.' Squirrel said. 'And it's an animal that's quite new to us.'

'Just how big *was* it, Whistler?' Tawny Owl demanded, enjoying his position as the cautious dissenter.

The heron tried to give as vivid an impression as he could of the powerful body, the shape of the head – even the eyes. 'They had a cold gleam in them,' he said, 'just as you would expect to see in the eyes of a calculating, ruthless killer.'

'Stuff and nonsense,' Tawny Owl returned. 'There's a lot of your imagination gone into that description, Whistler. They don't sound a bit like the eyes *I* saw in my tree. It's certainly not the same beast.'

Tawny Owl had caused quite a stir, which is what he had intended. Were there *two* powerful strange animals roaming the Park? The animals started chattering all at once in a nervous way so that it was quite impossible for Whistler to make himself heard. Fox tried to think constructively, but that was impossible too.

Vixen said to him quietly, 'At least none of us is immediately threatened. We've got the time to think more about it, but now's not the right moment.'

'Just so,' agreed Fox, and they indicated to the heron that they were returning to their den.

'Someone should tell Badger your news,' Weasel said to Whistler. 'No one should be kept in the dark.' He ran off towards Badger's set.

Leveret mentioned that Toad was not present, but Whistler thought it likely that he might be found near the stream.

'And that takes care of everyone,' he summarized. He had no more to add and flew back to his usual haunt, though with the necessary circumspection.

Tawny Owl found himself surrounded by a miscellany of birds who bombarded him with questions about his experience with the Beast. He did not much relish this position, now that his close companions had gone on their way. It was daytime, he was sleepy, and he was never very comfortable in the company of a host of songbirds who sometimes chose to mock him during his periods of inaction in the daylight. Whilst he was trying in vain to disentangle himself, Weasel arrived at the entrance to Badger's home.

The first thing he noticed as he went in was the sound of voices. Badger lived alone and Weasel wondered to whom he was talking.

A voice, very like poor Mole's, was distinguishable. Weasel paused some way down the tunnel to listen to the conversation.

'You don't know how happy you've made me,' next came the gruff sound of Badger's voice. 'I really had given you up for lost.'

'But, you see, Badger, you're getting muddled,' said the Mole-like voice.

'Muddled?' Badger repeated. 'Oh yes, at my age – I

suppose you're right. I expect I do get muddled. But what does all that matter? What's important to me is that my dear old friend has come back. I *have* been rather lonely, Mole. Now we can have our cosy little talks again just like we always did. And I – '

'No, no,' the shriller voice interrupted. 'I'm not who you think. Oh dear. What can I say?'

Weasel detected a tone of helplessness in this voice and he began to put two and two together. He went on towards Badger's sleeping chamber. It was very dark deep inside the set so he could not see either of the other animals. He hurriedly announced himself.

'Oh! Weasel,' said Badger. 'What brings you here?' He did not wait for an answer but went on immediately with unmistakable excitement: 'This is a wonderful moment. Mole has returned! We've just been — '

A wail from the animal cut him short. It was a sound Mole had never been heard to make in *his* life. 'I am a mole,' said the unhappy creature. 'But not the one you want. *He* was my father!'

Weasel was glad he could not see Badger's reaction. He would have found it too distressing.

'I – I blundered into your set through one of the passages. I know my father used to use these tunnels,' the young mole explained. 'I can be company for you, and willingly, if you wish it. But I can't be the mole you want – only myself!'

Weasel thought he had never been witness to such a pathetic encounter before and he heartily wished he was elsewhere. He tried to divert the conversation.

'I've come to tell you, Badger,' he said awkwardly, 'about a discovery. Whistler has seen a great cat, and we think it must be the Beast.'

There was a deep silence. Weasel wondered if he was understood. Then Badger said, 'Cat? A great cat? Well, I wonder what we should do about it. What do you think, Mole?'

Weasel stared into the darkness in disbelief. Was Badger's mind wandering? He seemed not to have grasped what the little animal had told him. And this time the young mole remained quiet. Perhaps he had decided it was futile to make a further denial. Or perhaps he was too stunned to speak.

'You suggested, didn't you, Badger, that the stranger seemed to have feline characteristics?' Weasel prompted.

'What? Oh, oh yes, Weasel,' Badger murmured. 'I did. I recall it. But I don't think I can do anything for you, you know. I'm really getting very feeble now . . . .'

'No one expects you to do anything,' Weasel assured him. 'I merely brought you the news. It helps to know what we're up against.'

Suddenly Badger's mind seemed to have a moment of startling clarity. He said, much more briskly, 'No doubt Tawny Owl has refuted the notion of a cat, straight away?'

Weasel was impressed. 'Well, yes, he did, in a way. How did you guess?'

'Oh, Weasel,' Badger chuckled, 'don't you think I know our Owl after all this time?'

Badger's shrewdness did not tally with his previous confusion. Weasel began to realize that the old creature had wanted to believe Mole had returned and was rejecting the truth. He had shut out the idea that Mole was gone and was going to use his youngster as a substitute.

'Well, where's the harm in it, if it gives him comfort?' Weasel said to himself. He had an idea. He whispered to the young mole whose velvety fur his whiskers had located nearby, 'Go along to the outer tunnel. I'll join you there.'

When Weasel was sure they were alone he said to Badger, 'I haven't any more to tell you for the present. I'm sorry you've been lonely. We can't expect you to go visiting so much now, so we must come to you. And I, for one, promise to do so.'

'Thank you, Weasel. How very kind,' said Badger joyfully. He seemed to be quite moved. 'Do, please. I should enjoy it.'

They bade each other farewell and Weasel made haste to find the perplexed young animal who had, quite unintentionally, got himself into such a pickle.

'Come to the set entrance,' he said to him.

The youngster obliged.

Now Weasel was a last able to see him properly. When he had a good look he was astonished to note just how much the young mole resembled his father. 'What do they call you?' he asked him.

'My father used to call me Mossy,' was the answer. 'I'm not quite sure why, unless it had something to do with the texture of my coat.'

'Well, listen – er – Mossy,' Weasel said. 'From now on you can allow yourself to be called just plain Mole. It's for the old badger's sake, of course. He won't know the difference, as you must already be well aware. It'll mean such a lot to him, and what does it matter? Will you mind?'

'Er – well, no, I suppose not. But won't it be confusing?'

'Not at all,' Weasel answered. 'I can soon explain the situation to the others. Thank you, my young friend. And, by the way, do drop in to Badger's set now and then. I know you offered.'

'I will. I meant what I said, Weasel. I feel sorry for him and he's always been such a kindly creature.'

'Good. Well, I'll leave you. Oh, and remember, if he

starts to talk about 'The Old Days' – which you know nothing about – just agree with him. That's all he expects, really.'

Mossy watched Weasel's pencil-slim body make its retreat and sighed. 'Ah well,' he murmured, 'I suppose it's not much to ask.'

Tawny Owl had managed to disengage himself from the attentions of the other birds and was now trying to doze, away from interference, in a hollow tree. But since all of his friends knew this favourite place, the exasperated owl was disturbed again by Weasel.

'I just dropped in to tell you I've seen Badger,' Weasel explained.

Much irritated, Tawny Owl snapped, 'Is that all you've woken me up for? How kind of you!'

'No, no, there's something you should know. I'm passing the message to everyone.' He went on to describe the scene in Badger's set involving Mole's offspring.

'Humph! So his mind's addled,' was Owl's comment on Badger. 'I might have known – the way he kept on about the strange animal being like a cat!'

Weasel refrained from pointing out that it looked as if Badger was correct in that. He contented himself with saying, 'I don't think his mind's addled at all. He's playing a sort of game with this young mole and I think we all ought to play along with him.'

'Pooh!' scoffed Tawny Owl. 'I'm past playing games. Badger ought to see sense. At his age too!'

'That's just it, Owl, "at his age". He's very old. I really don't think we'll have him around much longer. So why can't we humour him? I'm sure Fox and Vixen won't mind.'

'Oh, I can't be bothered with all that nonsense,' said Tawny Owl. 'Haven't we got more important things to think about?' He ruffled his feathers, re-settled his wings and closed both his eyes in a very determined sort of way. Weasel knew that he was dismissed.

As he had expected, Fox and Vixen and, indeed, all of his other friends whom Weasel managed to find, were agreeable to keeping up the pretence for Badger's sake. They were upset by the idea of Badger being in his dotage, and they tried to push to the backs of their minds the thought that it might not be long before they were without him.

Weasel's message did not get to Adder or Toad that day. But Whistler found Toad in the early evening and quickly told him of his important news, as well as that of Badger.

'And I have some news for *you*,' Toad said, 'while we're on the subject of the Beast. One of the frogs told me and *he* had been told by another and that one by another and so on. You know how fast news can travel through the Reserve. The upshot is that, despite the Warden's patrols, another deer has been killed.'

—6—
The Trail of the Beast

Adder could see nothing of his attacker. He was unable to turn to look behind, and the pressure was so great on his body that he thought his bones might break. There were no animals in the Park who ate snake and so Adder was in no doubt that he was trapped either by a human foot, or, more likely, by the very creature he had intended himself to surprise. There was a momentary easing of the pressure and Adder at once tried to turn. As soon as he moved, a huge paw swung round and patted at his head. Luckily for him the claws were retracted.

For the first time in his life Adder was really scared. He was scared in a way that he would not have been if the

beast who was attacking him had been one he understood – such as a fox or a hawk. Fear of the unknown
coursed through his sluggish blood. He felt he had no
hope of escape. Then, abruptly, the great weight bearing
down on his back was removed.

For a moment Adder's fear kept him frozen into
immobility. He awaited the great blow that would crush
the life out of him. But his paralysis lasted only a
moment. Then he squirmed away painfully, in a
desperate bid to reach the patch of vegetation. He was
not permitted to. The paw descended again and knocked
him back. The Beast was toying with him.

Adder kept moving – first this way, then that. Each
time he was knocked back into place. Once a blow lifted
him up into the air. He landed awkwardly. Pain racked
his body but still he strove to get away. The Beast
prodded him, tapped him and, finally, he felt its claws
sear through his skin. He imagined he was going to be
killed slowly in a form of torture, just as a cat will torment
a bird or a mouse before the final kill. He wriggled in
vain, like a creature in its death throes. Then a particularly heavy blow hooked him up high above the
ground, over the vegetation, and suddenly Adder's scaly
coils landed with a plop in the shallow part of the
stream.

Like all snakes he was a good swimmer and, before he
quite knew where he was, he instinctively rippled away
into the deeper water. Only his head protruded above
the surface. He looked back towards the bank and saw his
assailant for the first time quite clearly. The Beast was
staring out at the stream in an attempt to discover where
its plaything had gone. Adder kept himself well hidden.
After a while the Beast got bored and slowly padded
away.

For a long time the snake dared not approach dry land,

although the water felt as cold as ice. He had to keep moving to avoid sinking to the bottom, but he merely swam through a cluster of weeds and then back again, until he was convinced the Beast would not return.

He made his way to the bank and slowly, painfully, drew his battered body into a cluster of rushes and reed mace. Here he rested and nursed his wounds. He was scratched, bruised and some of his scales were torn, but his bones were sound and for that Adder was profoundly grateful. All his grandiose ideas of performing the heroic act of ridding White Deer Park of this menace, seemed now to him piffling and nonsensical. A paltry creature like him trying to meddle with this great hunter from an unknown world! Why, he was no more than a worm who afforded a minute or two's distraction as a toy for such a powerful beast. Any animals who had made their homes in the Park had about as much chance of diverting it from its intentions as of learning how to walk on two legs. Adder would have chuckled at the absurdity of such a notion if he had been capable of it.

When he had recovered a little he moved carefully away from the stream, always keeping himself well screened, and slid with the utmost caution towards that quarter of the Reserve where his friends maintained their community. He had to make them understand about this Beast in no uncertain manner. But it was not until dusk that he approached close.

Toad was the first to hear of Adder's horrible encounter. He was full of sympathy.

'Oh Adder,' he croaked, 'my old friend! What a pounding you have had. Do come and rest yourself a little. There's a clump of moss I frequent which is as soft as thistledown. I'm sure if you lie there a while – '

'I'm much obliged, Toad,' Adder interrupted, 'and I'll take you up on your offer later. But I really feel Fox, at least, should know what we have to contend with.'

'I think he's aware of it already,' Toad returned.

'No. How could he be? He hasn't seen the creature. I tell you, Toad, we're all at its mercy. We're minnows by comparison.'

'Yes. Even the deer are suffering. Another one has been pulled down. I've just been telling Whistler. So despite the Warden's efforts – '

'Oh, the Warden!' hissed Adder. 'What can he do? Can he live amongst the deer herd? No. This hunter will take what it likes without hindrance. First it's at the pond, then it's by the stream or in a wood or choosing its prey in the open. It moves at will.'

'Is it the same creature?' Toad enquired.

'The same? What do you mean?'

'The same creature who caught you – did it make those footprints we saw?'

'My dear Toad, identical marks are all along the bank of the stream. That was how I was caught. I went to look.'

'It seems that Tawny Owl holds the view that there are two different beasts.'

Adder did not reply at once. Then he said in his driest lisp, 'If there are two, then our days are truly numbered. But I don't believe it. And now I must carry my warning.'

The snake's body was aching all over but he moved on. Fox's earth was empty. It was dark and, as usual, Fox and Vixen were on their evening quest for food. Their absence, however, at least gave Adder a chance of taking a proper rest. He awaited their return with patience.

As he lay, sleepily coiled up near the den entrance, another animal blundered into his path. There was an exclamation of surprise in a gruff, wheezy voice.

'It's only me, Badger,' Adder said evenly.

'Oh! So it is. I'm sorry. My sight was never very good and it seems to get worse. But I'm glad to see you. We don't often – '

'I'm glad to see *you*,' Adder butted in, 'because I'm bringing a warning.' He described his alarming tussle in dramatic terms.

'Goodness!' said Badger. 'You're lucky to be in one piece. But are you all right? Are you in pain at all? I can't see you very well . . . .'

'I shall survive,' Adder replied grimly. 'But I warn others – don't meddle with this creature!'

'Oh, I'm sure there is no question of it,' Badger said at once. 'That was Fox's advice before this happened. I doubt if anyone is contemplating such a thing.'

Adder said drily, 'It might surprise you to know that one was.'

'You?' cried Badger. 'But why? I mean, what could you have done?'

'That's immaterial now,' Adder drawled. 'But if *I* had the idea, another might too. That's why I'm here.'

Badger pondered this. He could not imagine any of the elders of the Farthing Wood community being so foolish. But he thought it would be tactless to say so, and, to change the subject, began to talk about the Warden and the recent deer killing.

Eventually Fox and Vixen appeared, and Adder told his story to them with his attendant warning.

'This is timely advice,' Fox said, 'because I already have a sneaking suspicion that something might be afoot. Vixen and I have seen no other foxes around this night, although we covered quite a lot of ground. Usually we come across at least one or two of the youngsters out roaming. I wonder if they are up to something?'

*****

Friendly had three young foxes in particular who looked up to him. There was his own son Pace, so called because of his speed; and there were two of his nephews. One was the son of Bold, known as Husky, who had his dead father's stout appearance. The other was Charmer's son, Rusty. Friendly's endearing qualities which had given him his name had attracted these youngsters and they were easily led by him. There were others, too, who had ties of one sort or another: Ranger, Charmer's mate; and a cousin of Ranger's, called Trip. Many of the vixens were fully occupied just then with their new litters, but Friendly had managed to gather together these five males – a substantial group – to join him on his expedition against the stranger who still threatened the peace of the entire Reserve.

He lost no time in leading them to the stream where the Beast had at last been seen in the open. None of these foxes knew anything of Adder's narrow escape, for that had happened while they were gathering.

Friendly soon noticed the Beast's spoor in the damp, soft ground at the edge of the stream. Working from there, he detected a scent and began to follow it along. The others ran behind. The youngest of them were both excited and frightened. Friendly had told them they were to track the stranger to its lair. He had not enlarged on what then was to be their purpose, but they were happy to be on an adventure and eager to prove themselves. Ranger and Trip brought up the rear of the party. They were about the same age as Friendly and of a cooler temperament.

The trail led through vegetation and then seemed to take a direction away from the water. The scent was fainter but Friendly was still certain of it, and it led them eventually into a wooded area.

'Now we must go very, very carefully,' he said. 'There's plenty of cover here and any scrub or undergrowth could be a hiding-place.'

A greenish light pervaded the enclosure. The young, newly-opened leaves made a thick screen which filtered the sun's rays. Last year's dead leaves and fallen twigs snapped and rustled underfoot, despite the animals' cautious movements. After a while Friendly lifted his head to listen, twitching his ears. He could find no unrecognized sound and bent his wet nose once more to the ground. He lost the scent and circled for a while before he picked it up again.

'Over here,' he called softly to the others, who had waited where they stood.

Friendly was moving slowly towards a mass of bramble which surrounded the base of an ancient hawthorn. Ranger had a sudden premonition.

'Take care!' he barked.

Friendly turned at the sharp sound and, as he did so, something stirred in front of him in the depths of the undergrowth. There was a muffled snarl and then the thing was gone, through some bolt-hole known only to itself, and with just the slightest disturbance of the low-lying foliage on the briars.

Friendly plunged after it, without stopping to think of the consequences. The other foxes hovered nervously, trying to peer in amongst the brambles. But they could see nothing. They could only hear their companion as he crashed through the undergrowth.

Now the youngsters turned to Ranger. 'What shall we do?' they asked. Pace said, 'Shouldn't we follow him? He's put himself in danger.'

'No. Stay together,' Ranger advised tensely. 'We're safer in a group and we might have to fight. We can't risk being picked off separately.'

'But what about Friendly?' asked Rusty.

Ranger did not answer.

The young foxes looked hesitantly from one to the other. They looked at Ranger and Trip who seemed uncertain of themselves. Without Friendly around, none of them had much confidence. The moments passed. A silence had fallen on the wood. The quietness seemed to them to be sinister.

'Sh – shall we wait a bit longer?' stammered Husky. It was obvious the way his mind was working.

'Yes. I think so,' Ranger answered, trying to sound calm. But their thoughts were all taking the same direction.

'I – er – don't see the point . . . .' Trip began, and then his voice petered out. He had caught a sound in the distance – a mere whisper, as of a brushed leaf. There was a soft swish of vegetation, nearer this time. The foxes' legs quivered. They were on the verge of scattering.

Then they heard Friendly's voice. 'It's no good – we missed him this time,' he called. They saw him approaching, but from another corner of the wood.

'There was just a glimpse,' he said as he came up. He was panting. 'A tail, I think.' He looked exhilarated. 'Anyway, we found its hideout – or one of them.'

'I don't think that's much help now,' Ranger said to him. 'Whatever was in there won't use it again, now it's known. The Beast is far too subtle for that.'

'*Was* it the Beast?' asked Pace in a whisper.

'Oh yes, I'm sure of it,' answered Friendly. He turned to Ranger. 'You're quite right, of course,' he said. 'No good looking here again. But the significant thing is – the creature ran! It didn't care to face all of us.'

The young foxes looked very pleased at this. They felt proud that Friendly had included them in the achievement, although they had not actually done anything definite.

'We can foil this beast,' Friendly continued confidently. 'We can drive it away from here.'

'Maybe we can,' said Ranger. 'But how do we ever get close to it? It's vanished again now, so I suppose we must start our search anew?'

Friendly considered for a moment. 'We could at least stay around this area for a while,' he said. 'It might not have gone far.'

The foxes stationed themselves at widely-spaced points so that they could cover quite a stretch of that part of the Park. They settled down for a long wait.

It was while they were waiting that the stranger killed its third deer. It was another fawn: only a few days old. The kill was sudden, silent and swift, just as before. Once again it seemed the Great Stag and all the adults of the herd were powerless to prevent it.

The meal was devoured in quite another corner of the Reserve and, by nightfall, the foxes themselves were feeling hungry. Ranger left his place and moved over to Friendly.

'I think we might as well call it a day,' he suggested.

'But it's the night when we should have the best chance,' Friendly replied. 'That's when this beast is most active.'

'Think of the youngsters,' said Ranger. 'Do they have the endurance? It could be a trial of nerves.'

'We shall be nearby – and Trip too,' returned Friendly. 'But perhaps I am expecting too much,' he added as an afterthought.

'I'm sure they must be famished,' Ranger remarked, 'if they feel anything like me.'

'Yes, very well. Let them refresh themselves,' said Friendly. 'But we'll wait on – shall we?'

Ranger looked glum, but his expression was hidden by

the dark. He kept his feelings out of his voice. 'Of course, if you think it will do any good.'

'It's worth a try,' answered Friendly. 'Will you tell the others then? And when they've fed they can come back. I have a feeling that, between us, we might be able to do something really worthwhile tonight.'

—7—

Trouble in Store

Fox and Vixen wondered what trouble Friendly and his followers could be getting themselves into. Then they discussed what, if there were to be trouble, *they* would be able to do about it. It did not take long for them to accept that there was nothing they – Fox and Vixen – *could* do. Friendly was no young cub to be reprimanded by seniors. He was a mature male into his third season who had strong ideas of his own and who, although he might listen politely to advice, would not necessarily act upon it. As for the younger foxes of a later generation, they were so remote in age from the elders that they might not even be prepared to listen.

'They must go their own way,' Vixen summed up.

'Yes,' said Badger who had remained with his old friends. 'Our day is done. All *I* hope for is sufficient peace and quiet to last me out.'

'I'm afraid we can't look forward to much of that at present, the way things are,' Fox said realistically. 'The Beast is still very much in evidence, as the latest deer killing shows. And Adder says it was done in daylight, so now there's a new dimension. The creature grows bolder. It seems to think nothing of stealing what it requires from under the nose of the Warden.'

'The problem does seem insoluble,' Badger agreed. 'But we know quite well humans are not fools. This brave hunter is likely to go one step too far.'

This notion comforted them all a little. Adder had left them to take advantage of Toad's proffered couch of moss. He had, so far, been the only surviving victim of an attack by the feared stranger. The others stayed talking a while, but Fox and Vixen were all on edge. They waited only for one of the younger foxes to put in an appearance. Eventually Badger went on his way. No fox came near.

Adder had barely made himself comfortable, after following Toad's directions, when he caught the vibrations of another creature moving along the ground nearby. His forked tongue flickered from his mouth as he tried to detect what sort of scent was given off. He was hoping for a tasty titbit in the shape of a frog, or maybe a shrew. His empty stomach felt like a cavern inside him. The leaves disturbed by the creature's progress crackled faintly. It was evident that it was something not very large. Adder was philosophical. Snails or large earthworms were all grist to the mill when you had not eaten for days.

The one thing he had not expected to come into view was another snake. But that was exactly what it was – and another adder, too. The snake came up quite close, slithering smoothly over the moss with an air of preoccupation. It did not speak to him.

Adder wondered if it meant to slide on past without appearing to notice him. For some reason, of which he was not quite sure, he felt indignant.

'I am alive,' he said sarcastically, 'not just part of the leaf litter.' Then he wondered why he had said it.

The other snake stopped and looked at him with the unwavering stare of their kind.

'Oh – yes. I see you are,' it replied phlegmatically. 'Have you been in a fight?'

'Well, I have. You're very observant.' Adder had not realized his scars were so obvious. Then he remembered his blunt tail. 'It's an old wound,' he added. 'It doesn't bother me.' He was a little surprised to discover that he was addressing a female.

'You're an old warrior, it seems,' returned the she-viper. 'There are scratches all over your body.'

Adder suddenly felt proud of his scars. For the life of him he did not know why. 'You're not often in this neck of the woods?' he ventured to enquire.

'Not very often. I've been looking for frogs. This is a good terrain for them when they're not in the water. But I was about to rest.'

'I'm doing the same myself,' said Adder. 'I can recommend this spot for comfort.' (What *was* he saying?)

'Well, since you recommend it, then,' said the female, 'I suppose I'd be a fool to ignore you.'

Adder did not know what to say next. He was quite unaccustomed to making pleasantries.

'There's been an abundance of frogs about this season,' the female went on. 'I've found them in all sorts of places.'

'Yes,' said Adder. 'And there's a reason for it.'

'A reason? Oh, I suppose you mean there was a glut of tadpoles last spring?'

'No, I don't mean that,' Adder hissed at her confidentially. 'It's a reason to do with a change of habitat.'

The other snake did not know what he was talking about and did not seem to be especially interested anyway. She made no reply.

Adder waited in vain. He was disappointed. He had been hoping to show off the depth of his knowledge. At length he said: 'You see, they took to the land at a time when they should have been in the water.' (He had an inkling this sounded rather foolish.)

'Really? Do tell me more,' came the toneless reply. It was obvious the she-viper was quite bored by the topic.

'You see, they were forced to leave the pond by a strange and powerful hunter.' Adder drew the words out slowly to heighten the dramatic effect.

'You mean the Big Cat? Oh yes, I know about that,' said the female. 'Have you only just heard the news? I should have thought every beast and bird in the Park would know by now.'

Adder was taken aback and, indeed, a little affronted. She had made him feel small and he did not think she was trying particularly hard to be polite.

'Er – yes,' he muttered. 'But how do *you* know about it being like a cat?'

'What a funny question,' she commented. 'Because I've seen it, of course!'

Her manner really was very abrupt, Adder decided. He did not know why he was bothering with her. Politeness was not something he normally cared very much about, one way or the other. He was preparing himself for one of his most sarcastic retorts when the female snake spoke again.

'I've just had a thought,' she hissed. 'Those scratches of yours. They couldn't be – '

'Yes!' Adder cried triumphantly. His attitude changed at once. 'I was mauled by the "Big Cat", as you call it.'

'I guessed as much,' she returned. 'You must have been very careless to have got in its way. It couldn't have been chasing you, because it doesn't feed off snakes!'

Adder had been mistaken in thinking his scars had impressed her. Now his anger began to kindle. Who was she to make comments about his carelessness?

'I'm afraid you're speaking from ignorance,' he said sourly. 'The stealth of this beast is more than enough to annul the most painstaking efforts at caution any other creature could make.'

The female snake looked at him for a few moments. She could tell she had annoyed him. 'Now don't get in a coil,' she said easily. She seemed to be preparing to rest, for she slithered away for a few centimetres. Adder heard her murmur to herself, 'Goodness, what a pedantic reply!'

His red eyes glared into the darkness. The mossy couch no longer seemed so soft and comfortable. He had not realized how offended he had been. He – the Farthing Wood Adder! What had *she* done to compare with his exploits? The more he thought, the more irritated he felt. In the end he could not bear to remain any longer in her company. Without another word he slid away, and it was not until he had put a fair distance between them, that he stopped again.

Before he quite sank into his usual nocturnal state of dormancy, Adder considered his reaction. *Why* had he been so irritated? What was this female to him that he should care so much as a fern-frond for her opinions? He was not sure he knew the answer. But he had half a mind, when daylight should arrive again, to return to Toad's clump of moss to see if she was still around – even if only to tell her what he thought of her!

The news of the deer killing was brought to Friendly by his young companions. Husky, Pace and Rusty had gone in search of food as had been suggested. They had kept close together to give themselves courage. Because of this they did not feel they had to restrict themselves in their range, and they wandered quite far. It was Husky who found the body. As usual, most of it had been consumed. The remainder was lying amongst some undergrowth, and there was no mistaking the freshness of the meat. The blood around it had hardly dried. Husky did not delay in bringing it to the attention of the other two.

'How could it have done that so quickly after escaping from us?' Pace asked rhetorically.

'Us?' Rusty echoed with a wry look.

'Well, Friendly, then . . . .'

'It moves as it pleases, doesn't it?' Husky said. 'It chooses its victim. It stalks it. And then it snatches it with the utmost ease.'

'I wish I had such confidence and such skill,' Pace remarked. 'I'd like to see the Beast in action. I can imagine the whole sequence – the smoothness, the stealth . . . .'

Husky was looking at the remains. 'Well, are we going to waste this?' he demanded of the others.

There was a silence. Then Rusty said, 'But we – we – *daren't*.'

'Why not?' Husky returned cockily. 'Can you see old "Stealth" around, or hear him?'

'No, but that's not to say he's not in the vicinity. How should *we* know?'

'We don't,' Husky declared. 'But I'm hungry – and there's more than one of *us*.'

'I – I don't think it would be wise,' Pace cautioned. 'The Beast might be planning to come back and finish this.' But as he looked at the meat and smelt again its freshness, he began to drool.

'Come on,' Husky urged him. 'We might not get another opportunity like this.' He bent and took a small piece of flesh from the carcass. 'You'll regret it if you don't,' he pronounced. 'Trust "Stealth" to choose himself the finest game.'

Pace did not need any more persuasion, and eventually Rusty too joined in the meal. It was an act of bravado, really, by these youngsters urging each other on. None of them were at ease as they ate. Their ears twitched to and fro constantly, trying to pick up the faintest of warning sounds. They chewed the meat stiff-legged, ready to dart away at the first moment. All the time their spines tingled and the hair on their backs rose slightly in a sort of awareness at the risk they were taking. But they were not interrupted and, when they had finished, they were all in agreement that they should return at once to the wood where Friendly and the older foxes awaited them.

They ran quickly, without any deviation from the route. They looked forward excitedly to Friendly's surprise when they would tell him of their audacity. As they loped along in high spirits, they were watched from a low branch of an oak by a pair of unblinking, gleaming eyes. Not one of them went unheeded. Not one of their actions was unperceived.

Friendly's reaction was not entirely as they had expected. He looked concerned at their news, and they thought they were about to be reproached for their daring. But he reminded himself how faithfully they had followed him and he had not the heart to issue a rebuke.

He even went so far as to remark that he liked their cheek.

Ranger, however, make them understand that he thought they had been very foolish. 'You don't know what trouble you might have stored up for yourselves,' he told them. 'If the Beast takes it into its head to teach you a lesson, don't come running to *me*.' He was ravenously hungry and the young foxes' foolhardiness only aggravated his general feeling of discomfort.

'You know you don't mean that, Ranger,' Friendly reasoned with him. 'We all stand together on this. We formed our group for a purpose and we can't back down now.'

'Well, there's no more to be done tonight,' Ranger asserted positively. 'We can't go off hunting now, we adults, and leave the juniors unattended. Not after what they've just told us. What do you think, Trip?'

'I agree with you,' said his cousin. 'There's always another day.'

'Of course there's another day,' said Friendly. 'But on another day we'd have to start from scratch again trying to pick up a trail. I still feel our best chance of success is *now*. I'm willing to ignore my stomach for the rest of the night if necessary.'

'Well, I'm not,' said Ranger bluntly. 'The situation's changed. We've lost the element of surprise. We might find that the Beast will decide to come looking for *us*.'

'Perfect!' was Friendly's reply. 'It would find it had made a grave mistake. How could it cope with the entire group of us?'

Trip decided the matter by siding with Ranger. 'It's too clever for that. Now let's go and feed. We can meet again tomorrow.'

Friendly saw he must succumb. 'So be it,' he said, trying to mask his exasperation. 'You youngsters must take us at dusk to this latest kill, and we'll begin to track it from there. We may find it easier next time, for we'll be following the taint of blood.'

—8—
New Measures

Toad returned to his mossy base later that night. He had fed well on slugs and insects, and he was in a good humour. He was keen to see if Adder had found the spot because he was feeling rather talkative. When he saw the mosaic coils of the snake at rest on his soft bed, he was delighted.

'Well, you've certainly made yourself comfortable,' Toad began, 'and – goodness! – it really looks as if your scratches are healing already!'

The she-viper raised her head and regarded the small amphibious animal who addressed her. Her eyes glared greedily, for she thought at first she was looking at a frog.

But when she realized it was a toad she lost interest. She knew how unpalatable toads were and, without saying a word, settled herself once more.

Toad was surprised and a little disappointed at the snake's reaction. But he knew how unpredictable Adder was. You could never be quite confident that he would be in a friendly mood. Then he remembered his recent experiences and wondered if Adder were in pain or feeling unwell.

'Are you all right, Adder?' Toad asked with real concern.

The snake looked up again. 'I'm perfectly well,' she answered smoothly, 'though I must confess I'm somewhat puzzled at your interest.'

Now Toad realized his mistake and, quite unconsciously, hopped a little further away. A strange snake was always a potential enemy. 'I – I took you for another,' he muttered and began at once to move off.

'I think I met him,' was the unexpected reply. 'He won't be far off, I should say. He *was* here, but somehow I seemed to upset him.'

Toad was most intrigued, but his discretion kept him moving. He would have dearly loved to have known what had happened at the meeting. Adder had never been known to consort with females, though his private activities were largely a mystery. But Toad was well aware that, even if he found his friend, the snake would give absolutely nothing away. He plodded on in a reflective mood.

From his solitary resting-place Adder heard the toad's rustlings through the leaves. He waited until he was closer and then made himself visible.

'You needn't have come looking for me,' he hissed.

'I didn't,' said Toad, 'I've had to abandon my little roost temporarily. I expect you can guess why.'

Adder's face was a mask. His impassive features did not show a flicker of comprehension. He remained silent. Toad said no more, but started to dig himself down into the leaf litter. His back feet worked vigorously.

'Are you burying yourself?' Adder asked curiously.

'Oh no. But I never squat quite on the surface,' Toad explained. 'You don't know what creature might come along.' He shot a sly glance at the snake but Adder made no response.

Later, when it was still dark but in the early part of the morning, they were aroused by the sound of running feet. They soon discovered the cause. It was Friendly and his group of followers.

'They look as if they have some purpose in mind,' Toad commented.

'Yesss,' drawled Adder. 'And I don't think it's a hunting trip.'

They watched the band of foxes move on their way.

'They don't often travel together like that,' Toad said. 'They've been on some errand or other.'

They had seen five of the foxes. Ranger had broken away to search for much-needed food. Some time afterwards he came right past the two animals, quite oblivious of their nearness. He was not one of the Farthing Wood community of creatures, but Toad and Adder were both impatient for information. So they halted him.

'Oh,' said Ranger, when he saw them. 'I hadn't realized. My mind was on other things.'

'We've just seen Friendly with a group of youngsters,' said Toad. 'Quite a bunch of them. We've been pondering the meaning of it.'

Ranger had no qualms about waiving secrecy, particularly as he had lost a lot of enthusiasm on this night for the idea of cornering the stranger. 'Yes, we made a party,' he told them honestly. 'We've been tracking the Beast.'

'I suppose you had no luck then,' Adder lisped, 'since there is no sign of any injuries?'

'We did and we didn't,' Ranger returned cryptically. 'It's all Friendly's idea. He wants to get the Beast away from here and he thinks a group of us can do it. I doubt if he's right. It escaped us easily. But I agree with him that *something* has to be done.'

Adder displayed his wounds in an elaborate exhibition of what could happen to them too. But they were lost for the most part on Ranger who, even in the moonlight, could scarcely see their severity.

'Do you mean to go on with this?' Toad asked the fox.

'Friendly wants to. I'm beginning to have doubts,' Ranger replied. 'But I'll stay with him a while and see what turns up.'

'I've just shown you what will turn up,' Adder hissed acidly. 'You won't be warned. So try and think of your offspring.'

'Oh, I have done,' Ranger assured him. 'But I have no control, you must understand. They're not cubs – any of them.'

'You're all cubs in temperament,' Adder told him bluntly. 'Playing around with something that could be lethal.'

Ranger objected to Adder's tone of superiority. He – Ranger – was no refugee from Farthing Wood who was obliged to respect the foibles of his comrades. 'You're entitled to your opinion,' he told the snake, 'for what it's worth. But I think the subject of tracking and out-manoeuvring a mammal is best left to those who know about these things.'

'Yes, yes. It wouldn't hold it,' Fox agreed. 'Something much more subtle would be needed for that cunning character.'

'It's not – er – something that all of us could be put into, is it?' Leveret asked hesitantly, afraid he would sound a fool.

The others were amused at the idea but tried not to show it.

'There would be no point in that,' Fox reassured the hare. 'Don't worry Leveret.'

A familiar hoot sounded and they looked up to see Tawny Owl flying towards them. He seemed to be in a great haste about something. He landed awkwardly, bumping into the heron's long legs and making the tall bird rock.

'Sorry, Whistler,' he muttered in a flustered way. 'The deer – the deer — ' he started to say. Then he stopped. 'I must remember my age – shouldn't fly so fast,' he murmured to himself.

'What of the deer?' Fox asked eagerly. It was obvious something of import had occurred.

'They're being – rounded up,' Owl told them with an effort. He had tired himself badly.

'So that's it!' the others cried simultaneously.

'Yes, there are men on horseback and – and – a couple of dogs,' Tawny Owl went on. 'I don't know where they mean to take them.'

Fox enlightened the bird. Then he continued, 'The men must want the whole herd in one place. Easier to look after them, I suppose.'

'They'll have to feed them as well,' Vixen pointed out, 'if they're not left free to forage.'

'Well, one thing's for certain,' said Weasel. 'It will call a halt to our silent friend's activities.' He spoke with great satisfaction.

'Yes, indeed,' said Whistler. 'But wait – this Beast could *still* get at them.'

'I think we should give the humans credit for a little more sense,' Fox said wryly. 'They're not likely to leave a herd of penned-up deer unguarded, are they? They're to be protected from its ravages, not left at its mercy.'

'Of course,' said the heron. 'How silly of me.'

'*And*,' Fox emphasized, 'there's another aspect. The deer might also act as bait to lead the Beast on. Then our clever Warden and his friends will pounce and – the threat is gone!'

'Poor deer,' murmured Vixen, 'to be used in such a way. I hope the Beast will show its cleverness again by seeing sense and leaving this hunting ground.'

As soon as Vixen had finished speaking she and all the others realized at once the implications of what she had said. They looked at one another with serious faces. The thought had occurred simultaneously to them. The Beast might decide not to leave, but simply to change its diet!

Leveret knew that he was the most vulnerable of the group then present. 'The likes of me and the rabbits will be its fare again,' he said in a whisper, looking ahead with frightened eyes as if he could visualize this nightmare. 'None of you are at such risk from it – nor have you ever been.'

'We must try and look on the bright side,' Fox told him earnestly. 'If the Beast has developed a taste for deer, then it might not wish to forgo the treat. So, what happens? It is captured – or destroyed.'

'I'm not convinced,' Leveret replied. 'Thank you for your encouragement, Fox. I know you mean well. But, you see, there's something about this creature – a kind of – er – invincibility.'

'Well, we'll see about that,' Fox said grimly. 'In the

meantime, you and your family must lie low and not stray too far.'

'Oh, we've been doing that all along,' Leveret said. 'But *that's* no defence.'

'Leveret's right,' said Tawny Owl. He turned to the hare. 'I don't know why you can't take a lesson from your rabbit cousins and get yourself underground. You lie out in the open with no more than a depression in the ground to hide you.' He never was the most tactful of beings and Weasel gave him a glare that told him just that.

'We're not diggers, Owl,' Leveret explained simply. 'We have to rely on our speed.'

Tawny Owl stared back at Weasel, quite unrepentant. Then he went on in the same vein. He made a virtue of bluntness. 'You'd need some speed, too,' he commented, turning once more to the hare, 'to get away from the creature *I* saw.'

Weasel was exasperated. 'What do you know about it?' he demanded. 'Was the Beast running when you saw it?'

'Er – no, but I – '

'Well, don't talk such nonsense then,' Weasel interrupted him. 'Leveret's a timid enough animal as it is.'

Tawny Owl did seem to feel a twinge of regret. 'I just think it's better to know the facts,' he excused himself. 'I'm sure Leveret understands. I wasn't trying to frighten him.'

'It's all right,' said the hare. 'Don't let's argue – that won't help. We're all in this together, aren't we?'

'Of course we are,' said Tawny Owl promptly. 'If I can be of any assistance at all you know you can always count on me.'

'Except for any diplomacy,' Weasel muttered.

'Tell me, Owl,' Whistler said hastily, 'are you still of the mind that there is more than one strange beast about?'

Tawny Owl had forgotten his own theory on that matter. 'Oh – er – well, I can't be certain about it, Whistler. The facts are beginning to point, I suppose, to there being – er – perhaps just the one.'

He had been caught off guard and felt a trifle awkward about it. He tried to retrieve the situation. 'Anyway,' he said, 'I'll keep an eye open tonight by this – um – deer pen and see if I can discover anything.' The animals watched him fly away.

'Well,' said Fox. 'The next few days should tell us if the Warden's plan will work out or not. The craft of the Beast will really be put to the test.'

—9—
Captured

Before dusk, Friendly was ready and waiting for the evening's action. The three younger foxes – Pace, Rusty and Husky– arrived just as darkness began to steal across the Park. Ranger and Trip came last. No word was spoken. They all knew what they were going to do.

Husky took the lead, with Pace and Rusty behind him. They made straight for the fawn's remains they had found the night before. As they neared the place they slowed and went much more carefully. As usual, they paused periodically to listen. They reached the carcass. There were only bones and skin left. Friendly sniffed vigorously at the carcass and then at the ground all about. The others followed suit.

'The smell of blood is very strong,' Friendly said in a low voice. 'And there's something else – something recognizable.' He was thoroughly absorbed. 'Yes, it's the same as before. It's the creature's scent all right. The question is – where does it lead?' With his muzzle bent low, he moved about, this way and that, making patterns over the ground. Then he gave a bark of excitement. 'Come on,' he whispered. 'This way!'

He was following the strongest scent; the one made most recently. The other foxes followed him through the undergrowth. The youngsters' hearts were beating wildly.

'Keep your eyes and ears at full alert,' Friendly turned to say. 'Leave the tracking to me.'

They went on slowly. The undergrowth gave way to open grassy ground. Much of it was still soft from the frequent spring showers of rain. Suddenly, Friendly stopped. He turned round. His eyes were glistening. 'Look!' he said triumphantly.

Amongst the short grass there was a small patch of bare earth dotted with plantain. In the centre of it, almost as if left deliberately to assist them, was a huge pawprint.

'We're really on to something, this time,' said Friendly. 'Here's an unmistakable clue.'

They all stared at it. It seemed obvious that it had been made quite recently. Only Ranger seemed unhappy. 'I don't know,' he said. 'It could be a trap.'

'A trap!' cried the young foxes together.

'What are you getting at, Ranger?' Friendly asked him quietly.

'Isn't it too obvious a clue?' he returned.

'Nonsense!' was Friendly's immediate reaction. 'Do you mean it's trying to lure us –' He broke off. He looked at Ranger and considered. 'There may be something in that,' he murmured. 'How are we to tell?' He was pensive for a while. Then he shook himself out of his reverie. 'Anyway, if you're correct,' he said, 'then so be it.' Friendly looked determined. 'Our friend will find he has more than he bargained for.'

The foxes proceeded on the trail but with noticeably more caution. They crossed the open ground and now the scent led them under some trees. They found themselves in a small copse. It was not one they had been to before. Pace, Rusty and Husky were feeling the strain of having their eyes and ears as it were stretched to their limit. Ranger and Trip showed no sign of their feelings, but they all were expecting something to happen. Friendly came to a stop at the foot of a tree. He went round the tree, trying to trace where the scent led. Then he sat down, looking puzzled. The rest of the group regarded him, but could not find their voices. The skin on their backs began to crawl. Slowly they raised their heads.

Friendly followed their eyes and, as he did so, a most unearthly snarl ripped through the stillness of the copse. In the next instant a huge creature leapt from the tree and landed directly beside Husky. With a vicious blow from a front paw it tumbled the fox over. The beast's jaws fastened on the scruff of his neck and he was lifted helplessly, legs dangling, as with one bound the creature whirled around and vaulted back into the tree. Its claws raked the bark as it raced up the trunk to its vantage point in a broad lofty branch. The five foxes barked furiously from the ground. Their fur was raised, their lips curled back to reveal their fangs, while their eyes gleamed with anger. But they were helpless. The beast retained its grip on the struggling Husky as securely as if he had been no more than a rabbit. There was a look of malevolence about the creature as it glared down at them which made their barks sputter into silence. The foxes were helpless and they knew it.

'It was – a trap,' Ranger muttered almost inaudibly. They stared up through the darkness, aware of their utter powerlessness in the face of this monster. All they could see was its shining eyes – eyes that seemed to mock their weakness. For some time they remained rooted to the spot. They were unable to think of any action they could take. They felt as if the Beast's influence had frozen their limbs into immobility.

At last Friendly said hoarsely, 'We must get help.' He had no idea what help they could look for, nor where they could look for it. It was a blind reaction from their situation put into words.

'But we can't leave . . . .' began Pace. His voice faltered and he lapsed into silence.

None of the others spoke. They dared not look at each other. Then, with drooping head, Friendly began to move away. He knew that, even if they should stay there until dawn, they could achieve nothing. The others followed him forlornly. From his terrifying height Husky witnessed their departure with the keenest agony.

As soon as the Beast was satisfied that the foxes had gone on their way, it released its grip. Husky fell like a stone to the ground.

When they were some distance from the copse the foxes began to give vent to their feelings. The natural course was to look for a culprit to blame for what had happened. So it followed that Friendly became the target.

'It was very foolhardy to come on this venture,' said Trip. 'It was your idea, Friendly. You might have known it could only end like this.'

'I guessed it would be a mistake from the start,' Ranger

concurred. 'Now see what you've led us into.'

'How shall we tell Whisper?' murmured Rusty.

Only Pace, Friendly's own son, forbore to comment. Yet his thoughts matched the others'.

'Don't you think I regret it now?' Friendly said miserably. 'But how could I have foreseen what has occurred? I did this from the best of motives. And – you didn't have to accompany me; none of you.'

'It's true,' said Pace. 'We must be fair. And it's too late to regret our actions.'

'We have to think of finding help,' Friendly said. '*I* don't know where to turn. Perhaps my father – '

'Your father,' Ranger cut in, 'would have had more sense at the outset!' (Now he recalled Adder's words.)

'You're right,' Friendly said unhappily. 'He gave his advice, at the beginning. "Don't meddle," he said.'

'Grandfather is very wise,' said Pace. 'He may think of something that can be done.'

They carried on their way in silence. In their minds was the picture of Husky clenched in the fierce jaws of the Beast – the powerful beast they had tried to tamper with! For Friendly the image held the most horror, for he did feel responsible despite what he had said.

Ranger and Trip left the group as they came near the earth of the Farthing Wood Fox. They were of a different parentage and had not the same allegiance.

Fox and Vixen were absent. Friendly gave a yelp of frustration. Just when he needed them most! Of course, they were hunting. However his call of distress brought another animal's answer. Friendly knew it was Badger's cry. He dearly loved the old creature but – ironically – he was the one friend who was really too old and feeble now to be of any assistance.

'What is it, Friendly?' Badger asked after greeting him and the two youngsters.

The fox explained with a woeful expression. Badger was aghast.

'Oh dear, oh dear, oh my word!' he muttered continually. He swung his striped head to and fro. 'Oh, Friendly!' he said. 'Oh dear, oh dear!' He was trying to think how he could help. 'Poor Husky. Has he a mate?'

'No,' Rusty answered.

'Well, that's a blessing,' Badger murmured. 'But Whisper will be so upset! Vixens are all the same when their cubs are in danger.' A though struck him. 'She mustn't be told – not yet,' he said hurriedly. 'She might do something foolish, and we've had enough foolishness already.'

Friendly took the implied reproof without demur.

Badger was beginning to think of an idea. It depended on what the Cat would do with its victim. If it intended killing Husky, then it was already too late for any animal to act. But if it merely meant to keep him captive, there perhaps was a way out. Badger made up his mind. He knew he could not tell the foxes his plan. They would be sure to prevent it. So he gave no sign.

'I think you must wait and speak to your father,' he told Friendly. 'No doubt you intended to do that anyway. You must all stay here. I'll see if I can find him and then I'll send him back to you. Now, you mustn't stray – do you promise?'

'We promise,' said Pace and Rusty. Friendly was too dispirited even to answer.

Badger shambled away, his head full of what he must do. It was some time before the realization struck him that he did not know where he was going. He did not know where Husky was!

'Oh, you old fool,' he castigated himself. 'You forgot to

find out where it all happened.' Now what could he do?
He could not traverse the entire Park in search of the
elusive hunter. And he could not go back to Friendly with
the all-important question. He would be suspicious at
once and then his plan would come to nothing. He had
not meant really to look for Fox. He only wanted Fox's
three relatives to remain where they were, out of the way.
He knew that Fox and Vixen would return eventually of
their own accord. But now he could think of nothing
better to do than to consult his old friend himself. So he
shuffled about, going to all the places he thought most
likely to find him, and calling at intervals in his gruff,
wheezy voice. He even went up to the stream and along
the bank for a stretch in case Fox was after a meal of
water-rat. But he saw nobody, not even Whistler, who
was comfortably at roost in a tall tree at that time.

Badger, thoroughly disheartened, made his slow way
back again. He hoped to find all the foxes together now.
He was so wrapped up in his thoughts on the matter that
he did not see a small creature move quickly out of his
path. But he heard it squeak.

'Mole?' he mumbled automatically.

'No. Er – yes. Here I am, Badger,' was the answer. It
was Mossy.

'Oh Mole, what trouble,' Badger said. 'Things have
taken a turn for the worse. Husky has been captured by
that awful Cat.'

Mossy did not know who Husky was, but he remembered Weasel's advice and made a pretence. 'Poor
creature,' he commented, wondering for what sort of
creature he was showing sympathy.

'Yes,' said Badger. 'They shouldn't have gone near it.
And he's only a youngster.'

'I know,' fibbed Mossy.

'If this had to happen to one of us, why couldn't it have been me – or – or – somebody like me,' said Badger. 'My life's as good as over anyway.'

'Don't say that, Badger,' shrilled Mossy, more genuinely. 'Your friends would be heartbroken.'

'Well, thank you, dear Mole,' Badger said warmly. 'But – oh! I must leave you now. There's no time to waste.'

Mossy watched Badger lumber away and he felt a surge of affection for the old animal. 'He was the truest of friends to my father, I know,' he murmured to himself. 'Perhaps I can help repay the debt.'

As soon as he was within sight of Fox and Vixen's earth once more, Badger noticed that they had come back. All five foxes were in conclave – Friendly, Pace and Rusty anxiously explaining what had happened. Badger paused awhile in order that the bad news would have been grasped, with all its implications, before he joined them. When he did do so, Vixen turned a miserably worried face in his direction. Fox was deep in his own thoughts. Only when Badger was amongst them did he see Tawny Owl looking on from a nearby perch. He wondered if Owl had had something to report too. Now he felt he must ask his question.

'Where is Husky? Where did it take place?'

In a low voice Pace described the copse. Badger pumped him for more information. What quarter of the Park? Was it near the boundary fence?

'Nowhere near that,' Tawny Owl chimed in. 'The Warden is in that area, guarding the deer. So the Beast is keeping well away. In any case, it would have no need to risk being shot.'

'No. There's other food,' Badger agreed. Then he wished he had not. He had been thinking of rabbits and such like, but now he wondered about Husky.

'Not only other food,' Owl continued, 'but its preferred food.'

Badger was puzzled. 'Preferred food?' he repeated.

'Oh yes. Not all the deer have been penned, you know. I've seen two hinds wandering free, quite on their own. They must have wandered off and become separated. Probably old ones past breeding.'

Now Fox looked up. 'You see, human ingenuity has failed too, Badger. What hope have *we* of ridding ourselves of this pest?'

'Well, we can't live life as if we're under siege,' Badger declared. 'And first of all we must rescue Husky.'

'Do tell us how you propose to do so,' Tawny Owl begged. He was convinced Badger was becoming senile and he waited to hear a stream of nonsense.

'I do have a plan,' said Badger uncertainly. 'But I – I – can't tell you it.'

Tawny Owl made derisive noises. But Fox was interested.

'Why can't you tell us?' he queried.

'You wouldn't approve,' Badger explained.

'He's got some madcap notion of challenging the Beast to combat, I suppose,' Owl remarked scornfully.

Badger remained silent. There was a grain of truth in what he had said but he had not quite hit the mark.

'I hope that's not – ' Fox began urgently.

'No, no, don't worry,' Badger assured him. 'I'm not quite the old idiot Owl takes me for.'

'I didn't say that,' Owl remarked, a little embarrassed.

Badger now pretended to have taken great offence. It suited his plan. 'And you're so sharp, aren't you, Owl?' he growled. 'You couldn't even recognize the creature as being a big Cat!' He made a great play of looking very hurt and indignant and turned his back on them all.

'Now look what you've done,' Fox said angrily to Tawny Owl. 'Do you have to make even more trouble? As if we haven't enough to contend with!'

'Well – I – I – never intended . . . .' the bird spluttered.

When Badger was sure he was hidden by the darkness, he put on speed. He knew he had to act quickly, because he was sure Fox would eventually demand that Friendly lead him and Vixen to the scene of Husky's capture. He could not simply do nothing. It was not in Fox's nature. So, armed with only the scant descriptions Pace had given him, Badger trundled forward in search of the copse. His idea was a simple one – to offer himself in exchange for the release of Husky.

—10—
A Common Aim

Fox had, indeed, accepted that there was no alternative
but to go to help, and at length the four male foxes went
on their way. Vixen left Tawny Owl for Badger's set. She
wanted to console him for the hurt she supposed he had
taken. The set, of course, was empty. As Vixen emerged
from Badger's dark labyrinth she found Mossy apparently
on his way there.

'Is Badger there?' he asked. He knew who Vixen
was.

'No, Oh – you must be – '

'I'm to be known simply as "Mole",' he twittered
informatively.

'Of course.'

Mossy began to ask Vixen about Husky. He soon discovered he was another fox. Then he told her what Badger had said about his life being almost over, and how it would have been better if *he* had been the captured animal. Vixen went cold. She recalled Badger asking Pace for directions. Yes, there was no doubt of his intentions – it would be typical of him. She must stop him!

She raced away. Her first idea was to use Tawny Owl as her messenger. Wings were faster than legs. But Owl was nowhere to be seen now and she had to trust to her own speed. Vixen was no longer the swift-footed, lithe creature of her youth. She loped along for a while, then eased down to a trot. If she could catch up with the other four, one of the young foxes could be sent on to forestall Badger. But her breathing became laboured and soon she had to stop altogether, her sides heaving, to bring it under control.

Badger's lead had been cut considerably by Friendly's faster pace. But the old animal lumbered on persistently, full of dogged determination. He was not absolutely sure of his destination and, because of this, the foxes on their direct course arrived at the scene first. Friendly led them, with much trepidation, towards the tree where the killer had lurked. Husky's body lay where it had fallen, all life crushed out of it. Friendly stared at it in horror and disbelief. The others surrounded him.

Fox looked at his dead grandson. He remembered, with a sharp pang, another occasion when he had found one of his own cubs in just such a state. The only difference this time was that the body was full grown. And there were no marks on it.

Pace and Rusty were looking fearfully up into the tree. No sound, no sign hinted at the presence of the hunter.

The Cat had done its work and had moved on – who knew where?

Vixen was next to arrive. Fox looked at his mate without speaking.

'Are – are we too late?' Vixen whispered. Then she saw the still form of Husky.

'He never had a chance,' Fox rasped. He was racked by helpless, impotent anger. 'I will get even,' he intoned in a growl to himself.

Vixen understood. She could find nothing to say. Her heart ached.

'It was a desire to get even that began it all,' Friendly muttered. 'I didn't think – oh how ignorant I was!'

'Let's get away from here,' Rusty suggested. The sight of Husky's body frightened him. He knew how easily it could have been himself lying there.

'Yes – it's a hateful place,' said Fox.

'We must wait for Badger,' Vixen said hurriedly as they began to move.

They looked at her questioningly. 'He – he thought he could help,' she explained lamely. There was no need now to go into detail.

'So that was why he wanted the directions,' Pace remarked. 'Dear old Badger – this is no quarrel of his.'

'Of course it is,' Fox told him surprisingly. 'Any quarrel of mine has always been Badger's too. He'll soon tell you that.'

Badger came at last, grunting, and out of breath. He saw, in his turn, the young animal he had set out to save. 'It really has gone too far now, hasn't it?' he muttered.

'But what are we to do, Badger?' Friendly wailed.

'Wage a war,' was the old animal's reply. His voice suddenly seemed to have lost its wheeziness. It sounded crisp, assertive and younger.

'*I* tried,' said the fox. 'Look what I've achieved.'

'You should not have acted alone,' Badger admonished him. 'There are those who are wiser and more experienced than yourself. They should have been consulted.' He named no names.

The Farthing Wood Fox spoke. He was unaccustomed to finding himself put in the shade by Badger and he admired his resolution. 'Well, old friend,' he said, 'this isn't the first time we've faced danger. Where do we begin?'

Vixen did not like the tone the talk was taking. She saw the cause as hopeless. 'How can you begin anywhere?' she cried. 'How can you fight an enemy you can't see and know nothing about? None of us, separately or together, is a match for this beast.'

'Are we to wait about then, all of us, to be picked off one by one?' Fox demanded. 'Is that what you want?'

'No, no,' said Vixen. 'But I don't want any more deaths either.'

'Deaths are inevitable,' Fox declared. 'There will continue to be killings until this threat is eradicated.'

'Oh, you've changed,' she told him. 'You said yourself, before, we shouldn't meddle . . . .'

'Yes, I've changed,' Fox admitted coldly. 'That pathetic sight at the foot of the tree changed me.'

Vixen knew her mate. His mind was made up. Now, she feared, there would be no end to their troubles. She clung to one faint hope. Human intelligence. Somehow the Warden would find the Big Cat before they did.

The animals left the copse. Fox was already formulating ideas for a campaign. He would need all the help and support he could muster. – not just from the old community of Farthing Wood, but all their dependants;

all the birds he could find willing to scour the Reserve by day and night; the other larger mammals of the Park – every creature who could play a part. Before anything else they *had* to locate the Cat and note its movements; otherwise there might be a massacre. How he wished he could count on the strength of the white deer herd. The stags, with their antlers grown, would be formidable contestants. But they were out of the reckoning now, bottled up in one corner in a fruitless attempt by Man to frustrate the Beast's activities.

They reached their home territory. 'Put the word about,' he told the other foxes. 'All the animals in the park must be united in this. I want to have any slightest clue reported. Whistler and Owl must speak to the birds. We ourselves must assemble in the Hollow tomorrow at dusk – every one of us. That includes the vixens. Every animal will be needed. We *must* involve everyone from the largest to the smallest. We all know the risks. But risks are preferable to subjection. And that's what we're experiencing.'

Fox was his old self. Like Badger, he seemed suddenly to have thrown off the seasons. He was a leader again. The younger foxes marvelled and ran off unquestioningly to do his bidding. Fox waited for Tawny Owl to put in an appearance and, when he did, told him what he wanted. Owl recognized the urgency in his voice and the note of command. He respected Fox above all others and bowed to his authority. He noticed Badger watching and regretted that they were at loggerheads.

'Oh – um – Badger,' he hooted, 'you know, I never meant to – um – give the impression – er – well, that you – '

'It's all right, Owl,' Badger called up to him. 'Think nothing of it. We're all apt to say things at times.'

'Thank you, Badger,' said Tawny Owl in an unusually humble manner. 'Are we still friends?'

'Oh, Owl,' said Badger. 'Have we ever been anything else?'

Tawny Owl gave a hoot of pleasure and flew away.

At dusk on the following day the Farthing Wood animals gathered with their kindred. Whisper, Husky's mother, had been told of his death and was near the front of the gathering. The other vixens, among them Charmer and Russet, Friendly's mate, were there too. Fox explained how the entire Reserve must be alerted. Together they could drive the stranger from their home. Whisper's loss was alleviated a little by the proposal for action. She wanted to have a leading role in avenging her cub.

Over the next few days and nights, the animals and birds of White Deer Park became aware that all of them were to be part of a concerted move to restore their habitat to safety. Despite day-to-day differences which arose from the natural order of things, they realized that on this issue they were as one. All of them knew of the existence of the stranger and feared it. They had needed something to be done and had only lacked a leader. Now in Fox they had been given one: a co-ordinator for their scheme. They were glad – and relieved – to be doing something positive. So all over the Reserve the animals and birds kept watch at all times for a sign of the Cat. They waited for it to make a move, some by day and some in the darkness.

Each night the Warden or another man patrolled near the deer pen, unwitting allies of the animal community. For a while there was nothing to report. There were no more killings. This lapse was unexpected. Had the Beast gone away of its own choice? Or was it using its cunning again to lull them into a false sense of security?

The deer still at loose in the Park were aware of their vulnerability and kept constantly on the move, never staying in one area for long, and ranging through the whole of the Reserve. One of them was found near the pen one night and persuaded, with the use of a stick, to join its fellows. Then the gate was securely fastened again behind it.

The deer herd did not relish their confinement. They had no escape route if their attacker should decide to put in an appearance by day. They suspected that the Cat could vault the enclosure and create havoc amongst them if it should choose. They felt unsafe and had no faith in the humans' ability to protect them. They would have preferred to take their chance and roam free when they at least had the use of their legs to run from danger. However, it was soon proved that *they* were not to be the target, but the one deer still at large.

Somehow the Cat had eluded every effort to locate it. Of course there was nothing to stop it going in and out of the Park at will, and none of the animals was quite sure just what its movements were. It never allowed even a hint to come their way. Then at last the solitary hind was stalked and pulled down as she drank by the stream in the evening. The Beast was hungry and ate a hearty meal, leaving part of the deer well hidden amongst a mass of waterside vegetation for its return later. The kill was not witnessed, but the carcass was discovered by a moorhen paddling about amongst the reeds. Whistler was soon made aware of it and gradually the Park heard that the Beast was back in action. They tried again – keeping eyes peeled, ears open for a clue.

Meanwhile the Warden had come to the realization that the ruse of penning the deer was not going to work. The hunter was too clever to come near and there was no benefit to the deer themselves, who were becoming

fretful and difficult to feed. So the barricades came down
and the nightly vigils were ended. The deer ran free again
and exulted in the feeling. The Warden was reduced to
tramping over the Reserve again in daylight hours. He
was becoming convinced that the threat was over. Fox
and his associates knew better.

'It's beaten us again,' he complained to Vixen. 'How
does it manage it?'

'It's a superior creature,' she answered. 'Superior in
cunning, superior in hunting, superior in every way.
Husky's name for the Beast was "Stealth", and stealth is
the essence of the animal. It has a sort of stealth that we
cannot begin to understand.'

'And with all of us – every animal around – out looking
for it! The humans are beaten too. Where *does* it go?'

With the deer herd available again as an unlimited
food source, the Cat had no need to return to the place of
its last kill. So the motley collection of birds and animals
who had that corner under special scrutiny had no
reward for their pains. However, at last a sort of clue did
emerge from an unexpected source.

Adder had not encountered the surprising she-viper
again. After their first meeting he had not felt that he had
given a very good account of himself and he wished he
could put that right. He felt she had somehow got the
better of him and he could not feel comfortable about it.
As time went on he did not think a lot about her but when
he did she still intrigued him.

The weather was now quite warm. All the trees were in
leaf; there was new greenery everywhere. Adder had his
favourite spots for basking and one of these was a piece of
sloping ground, not a great distance from the stream. It
was well screened by fronds of bracken. The bed of last
year's brown dead fern fronds underneath him made the
ground warm and, among the new fast-growing green

shoots, Adder delighted to indulge himself, particularly after eating. He had thought this place was his and his entirely. But one day, after swallowing a vole and feeling very sleepy, he had slid into the spot, only to find another occupant. This did not please him and he said grumpily, 'How long have you been coming here?' He was talking to the she-viper.

She stared at him in the snake's usual unblinking way. But her tongue tested Adder for smell. 'Oh – the scarred one,' was her response. 'But no,' she added. 'Am I mistaken? Or have the wounds healed?'

'Of course they've healed; they were only scratches,' Adder hissed. 'And you haven't answered my question.'

'Coming here? Not very long. I found this spot by chance.'

'Did you though? Well, I might tell you that I've been sunning myself here without interference from another for as long as – '

'I'm not going to interfere with your habits,' she interrupted. 'There's plenty of room for both of us.'

'I like solitude,' Adder asserted. (As soon as he had said it he wondered why he had.) 'And I have a prior claim.'

'You make yourself understood,' the female replied drily. 'I take the hint. There's plenty of room in the Park.' She uncoiled herself and began to slide away. Before she disappeared she said, 'You may like to know, Solitude-lover, that this isn't necessarily the safest of places for you.'

Adder checked her departure. 'How do you mean?' he lisped.

'I mean that, in view of your previous tussle, you possibly wouldn't want to risk another one.'

'Are you referring to the Cat?'

'Indeed I am,' she answered. 'I know for a fact that it

sometimes uses a large hole in the bank by the water's edge for concealment. The hole is well covered and not many know about it. Who can say if the creature is there now?'

'How do you know all this?' Adder asked, thinking of the way all the inhabitants of the park had been baffled by the stranger's secrecy.

'Quite by accident,' the female snake informed him. 'It can only be seen from the stream and I happened to be following a frog.'

'But why haven't you told anyone?' Adder demanded. 'I assume you've been involved in the general alert?'

'But I have told someone now, haven't I?' she answered disarmingly. 'Because I thought you needed to know.'

Her final remark had scarcely registered its message before she was gone. Adder was left to brood in his solitude, unsure whether he was glad or sorry she had left. He felt strangely restless. He had never experienced uncertainty about himself before.

—11—

United

Adder did no sunbathing that day. He pulled himself
together and set off for the stream, but with the she-
viper's caution very much in his mind. He wanted to
investigate the lair in the bank. Once in the water, Adder
felt he was safe. He swam in one direction, close to the
edge of the stream, looking for places where the
vegetation was thickest. He saw no hole large enough for
the Cat to get into so, despite his feeling of chill, he swam
across to the other bank and reversed his direction. He
was becoming colder and colder and his movements
slower and slower. He knew he would soon have to
abandon the stream and search for warmth. Then he saw

it – a dark opening in the bank almost obscured by reeds and rushes. He could see at once that its cavernous depths would easily accommodate a whole group of animals. Adder swam on by. He was not such a fool as to approach any closer. The darkness of the hole would comfortably hide whatever creature might be inside it.

When he was far enough away from the lair, the snake slid from the stream and up the bank. He was quite torpid from the cold, and allowed himself to revive in the sun's warmth, only a metre or so from the water. When he was ready, he rippled away at his swiftest pace to carry the news of his sighting. He was hoping to find Whistler the heron before anyone else. The bird could act as his messenger.

He found him without difficulty, and quickly explained about the hole in the bank and of its importance. He said nothing of the she-viper, but only that 'another animal' had given him the clue. It seemed that Whistler had no idea that the hole was there.

'I look downwards at the water, you see,' he told Adder, 'so I'd be looking the wrong way.'

'Yes,' said the snake. 'The hole faces the stream so, unless you could swim, you wouldn't discover it.'

'Well,' said Whistler, 'at last we've got something to get to work on. I'll tell Fox.'

Adder composed himself to wait, while the tall bird spread his wings. Fox received the information with grim satisfaction.

'Good,' he said. 'Now we'll gather as many together as we can and we'll have the resources to beard our friend in his own den.'

Once again Vixen was wary. 'I wish we could leave this to the humans,' she said. 'The Cat is sure to kill another deer sooner or later, and then they'll be combing the Park for it.'

'We can't trust to that,' Fox answered. 'It would almost certainly elude them again. Anyway, we know what they don't know. We've found its hidey-hole.'

'From what Adder told me, this lair seems to be used only periodically,' Whistler said.

'That's enough,' said Fox easily. 'We're bound to catch him at home some time.' Then he turned to Vixen again and said softly to her, with all his old affection, 'You've been a wonderful mate to me – no fox could have asked for a better one. I've always listened to your advice. But we've always looked after our own and our age doesn't alter our obligations. Husky's death makes it necessary for us to take some action now, when before we might have stood aloof. I have been thinking of Bold. Remember how he wore out his own life to ensure that Husky and his other offspring should be born here – in what he believed was a haven. I feel we owe his memory something.'

Vixen's eyes melted as she looked at him and, for a brief moment, she and Fox were lost in their own private world. Whistler stepped awkwardly away on his long thin legs. Neither of the foxes spoke any more but Vixen had given her answer.

It took some time for the animals to gather, for word of the discovery had to be taken around from creature to creature. By the evening, however, there was a large assemblage outside Fox's earth, while new arrivals swelled the numbers all the time. There were creatures of all sizes – foxes, badgers, stoats, hares, rabbits, squirrels, hedgehogs, weasels, even mice and frogs. In the nearby trees there were owls, rooks, magpies, crows, thrushes, jays, blackbirds, starlings and tree sparrows. The Farthing Wood animals and their kin kept in a group together. All of them had come, including the smallest – Toad and Mossy. Whilst none of these assembled animals would have had the temerity to act of their own accord, they felt safe in the heart of the gathering, and even appeared to be enjoying themselves. Only the deer herd had stayed apart. The deer were convinced that they were the true quarry of the hunter, and therefore served their own purpose best by staying together and trying to protect each other.

During the night there were more arrivals. Fox was content to wait until dawn. He knew the Beast was active principally by night. So the most likely time to catch it unawares was by day when it would probably be resting. In the darkness many of the animals slept. At first light, Fox was ready to move. With Vixen alongside, and with all their relatives behind them, he set off for the stream. After the foxes came Badger, Weasel and Leveret. The rest of the creatures followed them, the largest at the forefront. Overhead the birds flapped, with Whistler at their head.

Adder's first realization that something was happening was the sight of the heron accompanied by Tawny Owl, with birds of all sizes strung out in their rear.

'It's begun,' was Whistler's announcement to the snake. 'You never saw such a collection.'

Adder made no comment. He was waiting for Fox. When he saw him approaching he slid forward. It was still early morning.

'You've chosen a good time,' the snake remarked. 'A short while ago I saw the Cat slaking its thirst downstream.'

'How far?' Fox asked at once.

'Oh, not far. About as far as the lair lies from here.'

'Then the game is on,' Fox murmured.

The animals moved on at their varying paces. The most timid of them experienced a feeling of security in the company of fiercer creatures that was quite unlike the normal pattern of their existence. For they all knew that there was but one aim in all their minds.

Adder guided the leaders as far as he dared. He indicated the mass of vegetation that clothed the entrance hole. It was indeed perfectly hidden from observation. Fox went down the bank and stepped gingerly into the water. Keeping near the shore he paddled out just far enough to see the lair for himself. Nothing could be detected inside. No sound issued from the den. He returned to the bank.

'Well, we must assume our friend is there,' he said. 'We have no proof.'

Many of the animals began to question him about his tactics. Would he go in? Would he wait for the Beast to come out? What were *they* to do in the meantime?

'There's nothing to do at present,' Fox told them. 'We have to be sure.' He looked thoughtful. What was needed was for one of the smallest creatures, and one who could swim well, to get as close as was necessary without being noticed. But how could he ask for a volunteer? As it turned out, he did not have to. Toad had come forward himself.

'I'll soon find out if he's in there,' he offered boldly.

'Are you sure, Toad?' Fox asked his friend dubiously. 'You see, it would mean going some way into the hole itself to be certain. I don't want to send you to – '

'Don't be concerned,' Toad interrupted. He had not bargained for doing any more than having a little swim, but he thought it would look cowardly now to withdraw. 'Is the Beast,' he continued, 'going to take any notice of a tiny inedible mouthful such as me?' He tried to sound humorous.

'Perhaps you're right,' Fox answered. 'But I'm still not very happy about it. Please, Toad, do use the utmost care!'

'Of course I will,' said Toad as he moved to the edge of the bank. Then, with a little kick from his hind legs, he jumped into the water. His small body hardly disturbed the surface. He swam in short spurts to the lair entrance and pulled himself out on to the muddy strand. Then, a few centimetres at a time, he crawled into the darkness.

Toad was probably the most suited of all the animals for the job. He was small and therefore light-footed, unexcitable, and naturally unhurried and quiet in his movements. Once he had left the stream he was hidden from view, and all the animals waited with bated breath in an unaccustomed stillness. Fox, above all, longed for Toad to reappear.

Time crept by. There was no sign of Toad. Fox began to fear the worst. Then, as if he had been engaged on nothing more serious than a pleasurable splash around, he was seen slowly swimming upstream, against the current, to where the others were assembled.

'Took rather longer – than I thought,' said Toad, arriving a bit short of breath. 'I had to – go in a long way. It's very dark; not much light gets in to see by. I could hear breathing – deep and steady, typical of a mammal when it's asleep. That gave me the confidence to go closer. The breathing got louder so I knew I was getting near. Then I saw a shape, curled up. I could make no more of it – too dark, you see. I wondered whether to leave then. But I thought – what's the good of that? I still don't know what's here.'

Toad paused for a rest. He was enjoying being the focus of attention and wanted to make the most of his story. Then he went on.

'I decided the only thing I could do was to go right up to the sleeper. So I did and I hopped all round, and it took me quite a while just to do that. I can tell you, the thing is enormous! It has silky fur, like a cat's – some of the hairs brushed me as I made my inspection. By then I was sure enough. No other creature of its size lives in *this* Park, except for the deer, and I know it wasn't one of them. So I left – slowly and cautiously. The breathing sounded the same. I heard nothing else. So I don't think I could have woken it. Now I don't know what you plan to do, Fox, but we should do something soon. The animal is there. We can seal off its exit and – we have it at bay!'

Toad's courageous deed was obscured by the urgency of taking action together. But it was not quite so simple, as Fox told him.

'We can't all stand or swim around in the water, Toad, waiting for it to come out. That's one escape route we can't deny it.'

'What about the strand?' Toad asked.

'How big is it?'

'Big enough for a few of the largest animals such as yourself to station yourselves there.'

'That's no use, then,' Fox commented. 'A few would just be tossed aside.'

'What shall we do then?'

'We must find out if there's another entrance to this lair. I think it unlikely the Cat would always get in from the water.'

Fox went off along the bank. He wanted to try and get in under the vegetation to see if there was an opening on the land side. The animals watched him go. They were keyed up, and some of the more highly-strung amongst them were no longer able to keep still. Rabbits and various groups of mice began to jump about nervously, wishing they had not come. It was quite apparent that the stranger would only have to show itself for them to turn tail and bolt.

Fox had set himself the most difficult of tasks. He did not want to rouse the sleeper. Yet it was quite impossible for him to avoid making a noise as he pushed himself into the clumps of growth. He thrust about with his muzzle, pausing tensely after each rustle and swish. Finally he managed to nose his way into the heart of the greenery. If there *was* another entrance he knew he might suddenly come face to face with the Beast, for every slight noise he made was magnified by his own fear. But he found nothing, though he made as thorough a search as he could.

As Fox was withdrawing from this screen he heard a noise break out; a noise of many voices. Animal and bird cries swelled in pitch and he knew something was astir. Above it all he could hear Vixen calling him and he hastily pulled himself clear. He imagined all sorts of horrors, but what he actually saw was so unexpected that it brought him to a halt. The collection of animals had pulled back, even the foxes. It seemed their confidence en masse had been a short-lived thing. Some of the rabbits had begun to run away, and were now paused at some distance, trying to gauge the situation. The smallest creatures – the mice and frogs – had already disappeared. And there, calmly seated by the waterside, was the Cat, watching them all with an expression of total disinterest. As Fox went by, the creature stretched each of its limbs luxuriously and then began to wash itself. It paid them less attention then if they had been a swarm of flies.

Fox joined Vixen at the head of the throng. He looked back at the stranger. It was a magnificent animal. Its body was clothed in glossy golden brown fur with darker blotches. It had long legs, a small compact head with rounded ears, and a long thick banded tail with a blunt end. It was easy to detect the power and grace of the creature even as it went through its cleaning performance. The muscles of the neck and shoulders rippled beneath its skin as it used its paws, feline fashion, to wipe its face; then it licked its coat, patch by patch, with loose, easy motions of the head. The animal's confidence in its own supremacy amounted to arrogance as it turned a disdainful glance on its audience. The motley collection of onlookers was, quite simply, overwhelmed. They had never seen such a beast before. They were overwhelmed by its size, by its majestic ease, and by a consciousness that it could scatter the whole pack of them if it should choose to do so. But they did not disperse. They were held by a fascination for the creature's beauty. To them it was perfection – a being from a strange world they did not know. They were lost in their admiration for it.

None of these lesser creatures could break the spell. That was left to the great Cat itself. When it was satisfied its coat was clean, it bent to take a few laps from the stream. Then, with a final glance in their direction that seemed to imply a sort of challenge, the Cat leapt into the water, dashing spray everywhere. In a few moments it had reached the opposite bank and, with a series of effortless bounds, it was away and lost from sight before the animals could draw breath.

But the spell was broken and all of the onlookers began to cry out to each other. Only then did they remember their purpose.

Whisper said to Fox, 'The Beast is huge – I think as big as a great mastiff dog that befriended Bold and myself. But this Cat is no friend. It's an enemy and an enemy we are powerless to stop.'

—12—

Thralldom

It was not long before the smaller and weaker animals disbanded. They did not even wait for their leader, Fox, to give them new directions. They had seen all they wanted to see. As far as they could tell, Fox was helpless, and they themselves were keen to get out of the unnaturally vulnerable position in which they were situated. Predators were on all sides.

The larger animals and the hunters among the group began to complain that they had come to do something and now the opportunity had been missed. They spoke from the safe knowledge that the Cat was no longer near.

The birds flew away. Their limited interest in the venture had soon been dissipated. Only Tawny Owl had the presence of mind to follow the Cat as far as he could.

Fox was silent. He knew his plan was a failure and he thought that probably it had been doomed from the outset. But he had felt a need to be doing *something* and so the expedition had been mounted. Now the Park's inhabitants would no longer believe he had any right to expect them to follow him. He had shown that he was as inadequate in dealing with the Cat as any of them.

Vixen watched him. She could guess much of what was in his heart. 'At least you tried,' she murmured to him.

'Tried!' he growled. 'The Beast showed its contempt for all of us. The entire Reserve is in thralldom.'

She tried to comfort him. 'We mustn't forget the skilfulness of Man,' she reminded him. 'There's always a chance the Warden will catch up with it.'

'Perhaps,' Fox said morosely. 'Anyway, that's our only hope now.'

The larger animals were gradually drifting away. Most of them were relieved that they had not actually had to prove themselves in a confrontation. As it was, they were not unduly pessimistic about the situation. They felt that, now the deer herd was in the open again, the rest of them would only be secondary targets. In the end only the Farthing Wood contingent remained.

'Did you find another entrance to the lair?' Toad asked Fox lamely.

'No. But there could be other bolt-holes all over the park, and what difference would it make?' Fox sounded bitter.

'We – we seemed to be hypnotized,' stammered Mossy. He was so purblind that he had not seen the Cat himself, but he understood the reaction.

'Exactly,' Badger corroborated. 'I found myself marvelling at the creature. I've lived a long time and seen all sorts of things, but never anything quite like that.'

The vixens were eager to get back to their dens and their cubs. It was only Fox the elder's call for solidarity that had induced them to leave them. So the numbers of animals dwindled bit by bit until only a handful were left, staring disconsolately across the water to where the Cat had vanished from sight.

'We don't seem to be achieving much by staying here,' Adder drawled, 'so I think I'll just slip away.'

None of the others attempted to stop him. Mossy was heartily glad to see the back of the snake. He was not sure that Adder was party to the conspiracy about 'Mole'. Toad alone called a farewell.

'I don't expect Tawny Owl will have achieved much either,' Weasel remarked. But his observation was not quite accurate.

There was a stretch of open land on the far side of the stream and Tawny Owl was able to keep the Cat in view quite well, though he could not match its pace. It moved very swiftly, with a bounding movement of its long legs. Owl realized it was heading directly for the Park's boundary but, surprisingly, on the side where it bordered a lane leading to human habitations. Eventually the Cat was lost among the first belt of trees. Tawny Owl flew on faithfully in its wake.

A ditch ran along the edge of the Park, just beyond the perimeter fence. Hazel bushes and young trees hung over it from the Park side. At one point under the fence animals had dug the soil away and there was a gap. The Cat knew about this, and it knew about the ditch. It had crossed a large chunk of the Reserve in broad daylight and now arrived at the boundary. It flattened its back and scrambled under the fence, then jumped down into the ditch. This channel was for drainage but it had not been cleared since the previous summer. Leaves and twigs had accumulated in it from the overhanging boughs, so much of it was reasonably dry. The Cat squatted in the bottom. Sunlight pierced the greenery irregularly, dappling the ground all about. The Cat's markings blended in perfectly with its surroundings. From the road it was hidden. No human stroller passing by would have noticed, nor suspected, the existence of a large beast skulking in the ditch. The Cat made sure its head was well out of sight. It had discovered that this spot was a good place to lie in wait for any prey that might wander in the trees. It had caught squirrels and rabbits here and once, in the evening, a deer had stepped almost close enough for a pounce. The Cat could see animals walking along the road too. It was not averse to the possibility of leaping out at an unaccompanied dog.

Tawny Owl reached this edge of the Reserve a minute or so after the Cat had hidden itself. He flew along the Park's perimeter, always searching for a sign of that tawny coat. He actually perched in a branch that overlooked the ditch, but the Cat's splendid camouflage fooled him for a while. Then the slightest of movements caught his roving eye. His head swivelled round and he stared long and hard. All was still. Was he imagining things? No, there it was again. Just a twitch of the back fur. A midge or spider had caused a moment's irritation. Now Owl could make out the long powerful body. What was it doing in the ditch? It certainly could not know it was being observed. Owl decided to move even closer.

He looked round and selected a stout sycamore sapling that grew right on the edge of the drainage channel. He fluttered over to it and alighted. It was not the best of landings. The sapling bent under his weight and he grappled for a firmer hold. The sycamore's leaves shook noticeably. The Cat turned sharply and looked directly at Tawny Owl. Its lips curled back in a soundless snarl, annoyed that it had been detected. This time Owl maintained his position, aware that he was out of reach, and stared back full in the Beast's face. The Cat's eyes did not waver and in the end it was Tawny Owl who looked away. But there was a magnetism about the Cat and it drew the bird's head round again. The Beast opened its mouth.

'I am of interest to you?' Its voice was strange, like a combination of a roar and a howl. It was a very strong voice and quite an alarming one. But although it spoke loudly and slowly, Tawny Owl had difficulty in understanding. This was partly due to his fright at the sound and partly due to the unexpectedness of it. He had never heard an animal cry of this kind before. He slipped a little on the sapling but quickly strengthened his grip.

'I – I'm afraid I didn't – er – follow that,' he fluted nervously.

In a grating sort of growl the Cat said, 'You have pursued me. You have much interest in me.'

Tawny Owl strained his ears and was able to catch the gist of the remarks.

'I'm certainly interested,' he replied. 'You're of interest to all of us.' He was very aware of his role as the mouthpiece of White Deer Park. 'Yes, I followed you. We need to know where you are.'

The Cat appeared to have no difficulty in understanding Owl and it snarled softly as he finished speaking. It did not like the idea of its movements being noted. 'You do not need to know,' it growled threateningly. 'Owls do not tempt my appetite. But you should not mistake. Trees are my playthings. I can stalk you.'

Tawny Owl marked the warning. Yet he realized the creature assumed he was speaking only for his own kind.

'The inhabitants of this Park,' he went on, 'are terrified of you. You arrived from we know not where with great suddenness – a frightening alien. Our humble little world has been rent apart. If we don't know where you are or when you might pounce, how can the animals guard their own safety?'

It was a foolish thing to say to a hunter and Tawny Owl soon perceived this when he saw a wicked feline grin spread slowly across the Cat's face.

'The secret of my success,' it acknowledged with a harsh sort of purr.

'No doubt,' remarked Tawny Owl. He had lost his unease and was beginning to enjoy himself. He anticipated what a celebrity he was to become – the first to hold a conversation with the great hunter! 'Your stealth,' he continued, 'is legendary amongst us. We respect your expertise and the way you even manage to evade the humans. But – '

The Cat interrupted him with a mocking roar. 'Humans!' it scoffed, growling. 'What do they know of my kind; our ancient lineage? They know nothing of our existence. We have roamed the land for longer than they. Never have they captured us, nor even seen enough to know what we are. We are survivors of the Old Animal Lore. How can they hope to comprehend? They think they are Masters. We know *no* Masters.'

Tawny Owl was rather taken aback by this mysterious speech, and did not himself understand much of it. In his familiar limited world Man was always evident. How could humans not know about the Cat and the rest of its kind? He was so puzzled he had to ask about it.

'Do you mean you have never been detected by Man at all?' he blurted out incredulously.

'Never,' roared the Cat with a sort of defiance. 'And so it will be. There are more creatures prowling their domains than *he* knows of.'

Tawny Owl was silent as he tried to digest the facts, which seemed to him almost unbelievable. He had to remind himself that none of the Park's animal population had ever seen such a Beast before. But humans were quite different – they were so clever, so wise, so all-knowing . . . . He tried to bring himself back to the subject in hand, but first he could not resist risking a gibe.

'I shouldn't roar quite so much,' he hooted with mock innocence, 'if you want to retain your history of secrecy.'

The Beast gave him such a withering look of contempt that Tawny Owl at once regretted the remark. He said hastily, 'Will you stay here long? Er – couldn't you perhaps hunt somewhere else?'

'Where I hunt is no concern of an owl,' the Cat rasped.

'But – but – you see,' Tawny Owl stuttered, 'we're all together in this. Er – I mean, we're all afraid and we feel while you remain in the Reserve we – er – we remain at risk. Er – all of us.'

The Cat flattened itself in the ditch bottom as a car approached along the road. When this had passed and its noise entirely disappeared, the animal said gruffly, 'I have told you. I do not prey on owls.' Then it added menacingly, 'Unless they try to meddle . . . .'

Tawny Owl knew it was hopeless. It was no use his endeavouring to explain that he was speaking for the whole community. The Cat would never understand they had a common interest in ridding their home of its threat. Nor could it ever appreciate how Owl and his closest friends were bound by the Farthing Wood Oath to help and act for each other. It belonged to a separate sort of existence altogether.

The Cat half pulled itself out of the ditch. Tawny Owl flew quickly to a higher point.

'You have been lucky,' the Cat told him. 'I made no special effort to avoid you. But I give you my word. You will go now and, after your departure, you will not see me again; not you nor any creature that ranges this area. *Though I shall still be here*. If I am wrong about this you shall have your wish. I shall leave for fresh terrain and never return, if any one of you, beast or bird, sets eyes on me and tells me so. Now go.'

With dumb obedience Tawny Owl took a last look at the strange beast and then flew away. He did not stop until he had arrived at one of his home perches. He pondered over the Cat's peculiar offer. Was it a challenge? Did it intend some amusement for itself, by giving such an exhibition of cunning and stealth to them all that it would exceed even that which had impressed them already? There was no telling what was in its mind. But Tawny Owl believed its word. To his way of thinking, they all had an incentive now. It only needed one sighting, by perhaps the lowliest of the Park's population, for the Cat's sway to end. So let the whole of White deer Park become like a thousand eyes looking inward, in a perpetual examination of every leaf, every twig, every blade of grass. Soon, surely, in this way the state of siege would be lifted.

—13—
The Pledge

Tawny Owl hastened to the side of the stream. When he had left it earlier, most of the population of the Reserve had been gathered there. Now it was deserted. Every bird, every beast, every reptile and amphibian had disappeared, just as if the assemblage had never existed. They had retreated like a defeated army. Tawny Owl saw it as the greatest demonstration of the Cat's power. It had won a complete victory without needing to deliver a blow.

Upstream a lone heron was fishing. Whistler had returned to his normal activities, almost as if he had never been interrupted. As Owl spotted him the tall bird bent his long neck and then stabbed down with his beak into the water. When he raised it again it contained a wriggling silver fish which was swallowed at a gulp. The entire sequence lasted but a few seconds.

'*He's* busy,' said Tawny Owl to himself. He was full of his conversation with the Cat and wanted to tell everyone. But he was also very weary and decided he would only do his tale full justice by relating it when he was more alert. He must get across to his friends the significance of the strange pledge the Cat had made. So he avoided the heron and returned to his roost. Daylight, he reflected, was definitely not the time when owls were at their best.

Dusk passed Tawny Owl by. The evening wore on and still he slept. So the warning that might have been carried sooner to the deer herd to be extra vigilant was too late to save another fawn. While Tawny Owl slumbered on, the Cat had ample time to select its victim, trail it and strike, first at the mother, then at her baby. Neither had an inkling that the predator was around. The hind was left where it had been killed. The young and tender fawn was carried off, limp and lifeless. The Cat was hidden again long before the deaths were discovered. But not in the ditch. That was abandoned. The owl would be the only creature to see the Beast there.

During the night Tawny Owl awoke. He rustled his wings sleepily without at first remembering any more than that the was in his own comfortable roost in the hollow tree. Then he remembered he was hungry. He was surprised to find he had left a couple of mice uneaten. He soon remedied that.

Whilst he was eating he thought he heard a voice calling him from somewhere in the tree. Owl was still dozy and could not at first make out where it was coming from. Then he saw Squirrel skipping down towards him from a high branch.

'We've all been wondering if you found out anything,' said the quicksilver creature, flicking his bushy tail restlessly.

Now Tawny Owl recalled his message and tried to hoot through the middle of a mouthful, nearly choking himself in the process. He swallowed elaborately.

'Yes, yes,' he spluttered. 'Most urgent. Glad you came, Squirrel. I've *spoken* to the Cat. It made a kind of bargain.'

Squirrel was showing his amazement by flicking his tail harder than ever. He sat on his hind legs one moment and then ran up a branch and back again the next moment, unable to keep still. 'The Beast *spoke*?' he chattered.

'More of a roar, really. A horrible sound,' Tawny Owl told him. 'But come with me, Squirrel. I must tell Fox and the rest.' He flew noiselessly away and Squirrel followed him, racing and leaping through the tree-tops.

It was some time before Tawny Owl managed to bring together Fox, Vixen, Weasel and Badger. He recounted his story with the exaggerations and embellishments that, by now, were expected of him. But his message was clear.

'We have a real chance this time,' he asserted. 'The whole Park was on watch before. But we must try harder this time. Our lives depend on it.'

'I'll talk to the Great Stag,' said Fox at once. 'The herd must be involved this time. They have to be especially wakeful. If the Beast wants a sort of contest of skills we'll give it one. Our eyes against his stealth.'

'That's what it will mean,' Tawny Owl averred.

'You did well to follow him,' Weasel congratulated the bird unexpectedly. 'Toad got close, but you alone have conversed with the Cat.'

Tawny Owl swelled visibly with pride. However there was no time for self-congratulation.

'We have a cause again,' Vixen remarked. 'Our future safety depends on us now – not just on our little band, but on every other one of the Park's inhabitants too. Even the smallest newt or fledgling has a stake in this, if it only needs one sighting for our home to return to its natural state.'

'Proof of a sighting,' Tawny Owl corrected her. 'And I'm afraid, as far as I understand, newts are dumb.'

'All right, Owl, I extended the list too far. But you told us – any creature, big or small, would serve the same purpose.'

'As far as I'm concerned,' said Fox, 'if I thought I could bring about our salvation I'd stay awake day and night till I found the brute.'

'And I too,' Badger wheezed. 'It would be one last useful achievement before I – '

'Now, Badger,' Weasel cut in. 'Don't start talking in that vein again. There's no question of it being a last anything, we hope. Think of Mo – er – Mole.'

'Oh yes. Poor Mole. How empty my tunnels would seem for him if I weren't around.'

'Well, then,' said Fox, 'shall we begin? We have to pass the word again. If we thought we searched and watched hard before, now we have a real test before us. I shall go straight to the deer herd.' He left and the group hurriedly broke up.

On his way across the Reserve towards the open area where the bulk of the white deer herd was usually found,

Fox fell in with Friendly. The younger animal confessed to his father that he had feelings of guilt about Husky's death.

'You weren't entirely to blame,' Fox told him. 'It was a rash adventure, but the reasons for which it was undertaken are commendable.'

'I feel I led him on – and the other youngsters,' Friendly went on. 'I shouldn't have pressed them into it.'

'I think none of us have really understood what we are up against,' Fox remarked generously. 'Now I think we're closer to it, after what we all saw by the stream. What were my empty words worth, about protecting and avenging our own? Dreams, Friendly, no more. We're out of our depth. I've felt myself to be weak and helpless as never before.'

Friendly looked at his father – the greying coat, the stiffer gait, the duller eye. Age was the great enemy, he thought. But Fox knew what was in his mind and denied it.

'Were I your age again,' he said, 'it would make no difference. I'd have no challenge to make to monsters.'

'Let's be thankful, then,' said Friendly, 'that we have some skills.'

'Yes,' conceded his father. 'At least we have our eyes.'

They went on together, feeling that they had helped to raise each other's spirits.

The Great White Stag saw them approaching, shoulder to shoulder, through the swift-growing grasses. He had the news of the killings ready for them.

'I am indeed sorry,' Fox responded afterwards. 'You have lost quite a few of this season's young?'

'Too many,' the Stag boomed in his deep voice. 'Fox, we appeal to you. You have been our friend since you came to our home. We deer have lived here, mostly at peace, for generations. But we cannot sustain these losses indefinitely. How do we fight back?'

'By the summer your antlers will have grown again,' Fox said. 'They are potent weapons. But it may not be necessary to wait for that. There is another weapon we all possess, Man and ourselves. Vision. And the hunter himself has told us how we can use it.' He went on to explain the Beast's pledge. 'Watchfulness,' he finished, 'from dawn to dusk and through the night. That's the only hope for any of us.'

'We have watched,' replied the leader of the herd. 'And when we were enclosed, the men watched for us. But still it was of no use.'

'We *must* have a chance,' Fox declared, 'and we must believe that we have it. The Cat is not invisible. We have to remember that.'

'We shall try,' the Stag said unhappily. 'What else can we do?' He began to walk away in his sedate manner. Then he turned back. 'Last time it killed my favourite hind,' he bemoaned. 'She had borne many young.' He looked away and murmured, 'It has such contempt for us all.'

His words were uncannily accurate. Even as they spoke, the Cat returned to drag away the hind's carcass. It meant to ensure that its larder was well stocked.

So word travelled round the Park again. Tawny Owl and Whistler spread it amongst the birds who were the best carriers of messages, and the beasts played their part too. Soon all were aware that they now had a real hope of banishing the threat from their lives by their own efforts.

Meanwhile the Warden was taking stock too. The morning after the kill he went to take count of the deer herd as he did every morning. He was pariculary concerned about the survival of the young, and he quickly noticed another was missing. He knew the hinds too; each one that had given birth that season. So he realized the mother had been taken as well.

The next day Vixen's words were borne out. A party of men began a systematic search of White Deer Park. Some were on horseback, some on foot. Many were armed. Others had brought apparatus for capturing the Beast. The search lasted throughout the day. The whole of the Reserve was combed. No trace of the hunter was found.

The other animals in the Park kept themselves out of sight, too, whilst the men roamed around. The more intelligent ones guessed what was going on, and hoped fervently that the Cat would be discovered and removed by human hand. But they heard no report of guns and the birds noted that the men went away empty-handed. Tawny Owl recalled the Cat's words and was not surprised. However, the men had not finished. They were about to use new tactics.

The day after the search they returned. Under the leadership of the Warden traps were laid at various points throughout the Reserve and baited with fresh raw meat. The Warden had taken the utmost care to ensure that these traps could only be sprung by a large and very powerful animal – the huge chunks of meat were set in such a way that no fox or smaller carnivore would have the strength to dislodge them. The men retired again and then the waiting began. The Warden reckoned that the hunter probably had sufficient food for itself for quite some time.

The days went by. The Cat went nowhere near any of the traps. Each day the Warden went to inspect them, sometimes by himself, and sometimes with a helper. The meat was renewed at intervals. At night many of the smaller animals had investigated these unusual food sources. The foxes had been suspicious and only sniffed at them. Some of the smaller meat-eaters had tried to pull the lumps away, failed, and then contended themselves with nibbling at them where they were.

After some time both the Warden and his charges began to think that the Beast had decided it had nothing to gain by staying around that part of the world any longer. For not only had the traps been avoided, but no further deer had been taken. Indeed no smaller prey had been attacked either.

'I'm beginning to wonder about this "pledge" of the Cat's,' Weasel commented one day to Fox. 'How do we know it isn't a final trick on us – you know, to put us all on our guard for nothing, while he himself is as far away as – as – '

'Farthing Wood?' suggested Fox wryly.

'Precisely!'

'Yes, I've thought of that too,' Fox admitted. 'But don't tell Owl. He'll think you're doubting his word.'

'I know, I know,' said Weasel. 'But what would that matter by comparison with the benefit to us all? To be sure that White Deer Park is ours again!'

' "To be sure",' Fox echoed. 'That's the crux of it, Weasel. How can we ever be sure again?'

Weasel looked crestfallen. 'I hadn't thought of it like that,' he muttered. 'I suppose it would be preferable for one of us to see the great hunter again.'

But nobody did. And, understandably, the animals' wariness began to slacken and their watchfulness to be relaxed. They no longer believed they were watching for any purpose. As for the Warden, he did not bother to replace the bait in his traps any more. Replenishing the meat was costly and it was all to no avail. Besides which, he had still a lingering doubt about the risks involved – perhaps one of the traps might catch an animal that actually had a perfect right to be in the Reserve. After a few more days and much cogitation, the Warden at last decided to remove the traps altogether. So the guard was down of animal and human alike. And that was exactly what the Cat had been waiting for.

It had eaten well at the beginning. The fawn and its mother provided plenty of meat. Eventually every scrap of the carcasses was gone, leaving only skeletons. The Cat even crunched some of the bones. It had managed to lap at the dew and take rainwater from the plentiful showers, so that thirst had been no problem for it. As time passed, hunger returned, but it knew it would not have long to wait, and it was content. It had found itself an underground home which served its need for secrecy and stealth perfectly. It waited with patience for its great cunning to work its effect.

Then one dusk the Beast knew that the time was right. It waited for the true darkness that came late at that period of the year. Then it crept forth from its den and embarked on a small orgy of slaughter, prompted by its long fast. It killed rabbits and hares and any small creatures it could find on the ground. Voles and frogs were snapped up at a gulp. Then it climbed into the trees and caught birds on their nests and squirrels in their dreys. Those creatures that were not eaten at once were carried back to the den for future use. But it did not approach the deer herd. It was too clever for that.

Leveret missed being taken by a whisker. The instinctive leap that took him to safety exposed his mate and she was taken instead. Leveret ran at full tilt through the grass. His electrifying pace could outdistance almost any creature. He did not stop to see if he was pursued. So he did not see the Cat. He kept right on running until he ran into Badger, nearly bowling him over.

'Leveret!' Badger gasped, badly winded. 'What's the alarm?'

The hare explained at once about the attack. Neither of them could be sure whether it was the Cat at work again, but they both jumped to conclusions.

'And we thought it had gone,' Badger murmured. 'It's been playing with us.'

'Well, it's not playing now,' Leveret said harshly.

Their suspicions were justified. Knowledge soon spread of the killings. There seemed to be a new savagery about these, as if the Cat had a lust to kill for the sake of it, to demonstrate its mastery over the rest of them.

No animal, no bird had seen it. But all of the Park soon knew the stranger was still around. There was only one clue that impressed itself on the more intelligent of the population. The slaughter had been confined to one corner of the Reserve. And that was the corner where the animals from Farthing Wood had established their homes.

'Can it be deliberate?' they asked each other.

'Is it hiding nearby?'

Squirrel was terrified and planned to move his home. Leveret discovered the loss of his mate and no longer cared if the hunter should return. Fox and Vixen racked their brains as to the whereabouts of the Beast. After such killings, how could it just vanish again? Tawny Owl perched in his tree and hoped no one would come near him. He had the awful feeling that in some way he was to blame for this: that the Cat meant to prove something to him. He was to be punished for his previous presumption, not personally perhaps, but through the deaths of his friends.

—14—
Hearts and Minds

The animal friends waited for the next strike with a fear that had become all-consuming. They scarcely dared to go about their necessary activities. The collection of food was now a hurried, furtive business – something to be done as quickly as possible before scurrying back to cower at home. Only the birds, Adder and Toad felt comparatively secure. Adder had not been seen for a while, but the others worried daily about the safety of their companions. Tawny Owl, in particular, was in a state of unending misery. He could not bring himself to talk to anyone. He had started to think that, if he did, that animal would be the next one singled out for the Cat's attention.

Friendly wanted to make one last attempt to go on the offensive. His mate, Russet, was terrified for her growing cubs, who had now reached the stage of wanting to explore farther than around their parent's earth. Other vixens, Charmer and Whisper, were in the same situation. Friendly thought they could not continue to live their lives under threat. He suggested to his father that the only way to break the dreadful monotony was to sniff out the blood trail once more, and follow it to the Cat's hideout.

'There would be no fighting,' he assured his father. 'It would just need one of us to go close enough to *see*.'

'I understand how you feel,' said Fox. 'But it's far too dangerous. Probably the Beast is waiting for just such a foolhardy creature as you to come along. What would another death achieve?'

'There will be deaths anyway,' said Friendly. 'Why skulk here where the hunter can pounce as it chooses? *I'm* willing to take the risk. I ask for no supporters.'

Fox admired his courage, not for the first time. 'Wait a while yet, Friendly,' he pleaded. 'I have a feeling the Cat might make a slip, and it only needs one.'

'What if it decides not to honour this wonderful pledge Owl talks about?' Friendly growled. 'There would be nothing any of us could do about it.'

'Then why do you wish to track it?' Fox asked at once.

Friendly had tripped himself up and knew it. He looked glum. 'All right,' he conceded. 'I'll do as you say. But I hope it won't result in suffering for my cubs.'

Since the gathering by the stream, Adder had had something else on his mind besides the Cat – something very private. It was a she-viper that occupied his mind, a female adder with a bold disposition and a coolness of temperament that matched his own. Whilst he wondered why she was in his thoughts, he constantly asked himself whether he was in hers. There was no doubt that, if Adder had been more familiar with such things, he would have realized that he wanted her company.

Of course, he would never have deliberately sought her out. But it was strange how he found himself, without intention, returning to the places where he had seen her before. She was not in any of them. It was hardly likely she would have been, he told himself. Why should she stay around there? So it must have been coincidence that prompted their next meeting.

Adder had caught and eaten two wood mice amongst the grasses. He was no longer hungry now, but his hunting instincts had not subsided and he was still very much alert. He caught the soft rustling of a creature moving through the stems close to the ground. He prepared himself to ambush another mouse. But, as the mouse came into view, with its nose quivering incessantly, another snake shot from hiding and seized it. Adder watched with feigned indifference as the plump little morsel went down another throat. The she-viper, in the ecstatic throes of a series of swallows, had not yet noticed him. However, when the last muscular ripple had passed along her body, she became aware of his presence.

'The solitude-lover,' she remarked, as if to herself. 'I'd better not stay here too long and risk complaint.'

'It's not necessary for you to move just yet,' Adder answered quickly. (He thought this sounded like someone else talking.) 'Er – have you caught many mice?'

'Very many,' she quipped. 'One gets through quite a lot in a season.'

'You know I didn't mean that,' he lisped with a mild sense of irritation. 'Are you always so clever?'

'Only when I have the opportunity,' she told him coolly. Her face was as expressionless as ever. 'Are you still looking for the Cat?' she asked next.

'I? *I'm* not looking,' Adder declared, as if the idea of his putting himself out was quite absurd.

'But I thought the plan was for every creature to keep its eyes open?'

'Oh, my eyes are open,' he responded, 'but I'm not – er – looking . . . .' (How silly that sounded.)

The she-viper refrained from comment but she stared at him. So Adder stared back. At last she said: 'You're looking fatter than when I saw you before.'

'Frogs, insects and mice,' he explained succinctly.

'I though the adder that came here from a distant place wasn't supposed to eat mammals?' she went on.

'I didn't know you knew who I was,' he answered.

'The shortness of your tail gives you away.'

'I see. Well, if you're referring to that ridiculous Oath I was made to swear before I was allowed to travel here with the others, it only forbade *certain* mice and voles from my diet. Those being, of course, the ones from my old home.'

'How do you tell them apart?'

'Oh, they're all dead now. They live lives of extra-ordinary brevity. Of course I left them alone while they did live. But they've produced so many generations since we arrived here that I can't tell the difference any more.'

'So what do you do?'

'Eat whenever I feel like it,' he declared. 'As far as I'm concerned that Oath doesn't stretch into infinity.'

'Very wise of you,' the she-viper remarked. 'The whole thing is difficult to understand – how you consort with mammals at all.'

Adder was in a quandary. He never liked to admit he

owed obligations to any creature. Yet there still remained a select few for whom, and with whom, he felt bound. Fox and Vixen, Badger, Toad and – yes, he supposed Tawny Owl and Weasel. All of them were bound irrevocably and for ever. But he was not going to tell the she-viper.

'I don't seek them out,' he said truthfully. 'But, you see, there is an old association.' That was as far as he would go.

The she-viper's next words startled him with their implication. 'How would you feel about a new association?'

How was he to take this? Was she suggesting . . . ?

'I'm not entirely sure . . . .' he began guardedly.

'Oh yes, Adder. You're quite sure,' she drawled with a certain amount of ironic humour. 'You're the lover of solitude.'

Now that he was being branded with this description, Adder was not completely happy to own it. There had been moments, he recalled, when he . . . . When he what? he asked himself. He did not know if he could bring himself to admit that he had hoped for company at times. And then again, *whose* company? Oh, he was in a rare old muddle.

'I do like solitude,' he hissed uncertainly. 'But I suppose how much I like it is governed by how much of it I get.' (What did that convey? he wondered. Had he given something away?)

'And that depends on how much of it you seek,' she returned. She was determined to put him on the spot and was relishing every moment.

'Well, yes, that would appear to be the case,' Adder said. (Wherever would all of this end? He was almost beginning to feel uncomfortable.)

'You can call me Sinuous,' she offered.

'Can I? Is that how you're known?'

'It's how I'd like to be known by you.'

Adder wanted to get away. He was not competent to deal with situations of this kind. But he could not put his body into motion.

'It's very warm,' said Sinuous. 'If you've eaten enough it would be a good time to bask.'

The invitation was obvious. Adder felt he was powerless to resist. He made no answer. Sinuous took this as a sign of agreement and began to slither away through the grass stalks. Adder followed her mechanically.

The she-viper led him to a small depression in the ground where the grass had been flattened by a larger animal. It felt dry and hot. Adder wondered fleetingly what creature had been lying there before.

'I like this spot,' commented Sinuous. 'It's well hidden.'

'It seems that another has found it favourable too,' Adder remarked.

'Yes, I saw him once or twice before I started using it,' she answered.

'Saw him? Whom?'

'The Cat.'

'The Cat! Does he still come here?' Adder hissed urgently.

'Oh no. He's disappeared, hasn't he?' Sinuous sounded uninterested. She was coiling herself up.

Adder was irritated. 'You're very secretive,' he told her. 'If we'd known this earlier, it might have saved – '

'It wouldn't have saved anything,' she interrupted. 'I know the terms of the Beast's so-called pledge and, since then, I've naturally kept a look-out here. But, of course, I don't expect to see anything now.'

'I see,' said Adder. 'No, it's not likely to return to any of its old haunts. It must know this whole Reserve better than any of us. Yet I still don't understand how it can remain in the Park and stay concealed.'

'Supposing it is not *in* the Park but under it?' Sinuous suggested nonchalantly. 'Perhaps that's the answer.' She seemed to want to finish with the subject and enjoy her sunbath. But the remark had the very opposite effect on Adder.

'Underground,' he hissed. 'Yesss.' All thought of repose left him. 'That's where it must be.'

Sinuous paid no attention. Adder could only think of those of his old companions who made their homes underground, and who might be able to make use of this theory. Fox and Vixen, Badger and Weasel sprang immediately to mind. It was a pity Mole, that champion tunneller, was no longer with them. But then Adder recalled something about one of Mole's kin who had come into the picture recently. The relationship escaped him.

'My basking will have to be postponed,' he informed Sinuous. 'This idea can't be kept to ourselves.'

'Ah – the old association,' Sinuous murmured. 'Well, you must go to your warm-blooded friends.'

'I must. But – er – well, I shall remember this place,' said Adder. He was unable to make more of a commitment than that. He slid away.

'Only the place?' Sinuous asked him. But Adder's hearing was not good.

He went first of all to Badger.

It was broad daylight and the old animal's snoring seemed to reverberate through his network of tunnels as Adder entered the set. The snake was glad of this, for the pitch darkness engulfed him almost at once, but he was able to guide himself to Badger's sleeping chamber by the sound. Badger was not easily woken. He slept deeply and Adder's lisping voice was not the most resonant.

The snake became more and more aggravated as his efforts to rouse the sleeper continued to fail. He considered whether he should risk a nip at the thickest part of Badger's coat, where his dangerous fangs would be very unlikely to penetrate the skin. Luckily such a gamble did not prove necessary. Badger stirred.

'At last!' Adder hissed. 'I've been here for an eternity.'

Badger quickly roused himself. 'Adder? Whatever are you – '

'No time for that,' the snake answered shortly. 'I need your advice. Listen.' He explained the theory of the she-viper without mentioning her.

'Oh no. That's not likely. I've already rejected the idea,' Badger informed him. 'There's no set or earth around here big enough to take that huge beast.'

'Who said anything about around here?' Adder queried impatiently. 'In the length and breadth of the Reserve there might be many holes it could hide itself in.'

'No,' Badger insisted. 'I would know about it. And if *I* didn't, it would be known by the foxes or the rabbits or the weasels or – or – the moles. Besides which, Adder, we know the Cat *is* in our neck of the woods.'

'Just because it hunted around here doesn't mean it hides around here,' Adder argued. 'Not all the time.'

'Well, Squirrel is convinced of it. He's taken his family and set up home in another quarter.'

'Squirrel is not the most knowledgeable of the community,' Adder drawled. 'I feel it would be worthwhile for all the foxes and animals like yourself, and maybe the rabbits, to be consulted. They may know of a likely den.'

'I'll ask Mole when I see him,' Badger said. 'He's the greatest digger of us all.'

'Don't be absurd, Badger,' Adder rasped. 'Your memory is playing you tricks again.'

'Oh no,' Badger contradicted him. 'You're mistaken. I often talk to him.'

Adder thought it was futile to continue this line of conversation, so he told Badger he was going to pay a visit on Fox and then leave everything to him. The cold and dark of Badger's set made him wish he had not left the warm sunny spot where Sinuous was now lying.

'Wait,' said Badger. 'I'll come with you.'

'No need,' the snake told him. Then he added unkindly, 'You'd better stay here in case Mole decides to make one of his miraculous returns.'

Fox responded in the same way to the underground theory. But he agreed to talk to all his relatives to see if they might know of a large hideout under the Park.

'It's more than possible,' Adder pointed out. 'You didn't know of the existence of the lair by the stream until I told you of it.'

'You're right, Adder,' Fox said. 'But where did *you* learn of it? You never did say definitely. Perhaps from the same source as this latest idea?'

Adder never had any difficulty in retaining his equanimity. His natural expression was one of immobility. His ceaselessly flickering tongue was the only sign of movement from his face.

'The source isn't important,' he replied enigmatically.

Fox knew he would not be permitted to pry any further. So he said, 'Have you spoken to Mossy?'

Adder searched his memory. 'Mossy?' he muttered.

Fox reminded him.

'A descendant of Mole? Well, it's likely that Badger will see him first then. Who knows – perhaps this Mossy will be in the company of his forefather!'

'I'm glad Badger's not around to hear that,' said Fox. 'Poor old creature, he's never been able to accept the loss of Mole. This game he plays is the only way he can come to terms with it.'

'I wish you'd explain, Fox. Badger was rambling on about Mole when I spoke to him just now. I think he must have been still half-asleep.'

'On no, it's quite deliberate. I thought you knew about it. The rest of us take part.' He told Adder about Mossy's role.

'Now I comprehend,' said the snake. 'But I certainly don't approve. I'm surprised at you all, making such fools of yourselves.'

'You sound just like Owl,' Fox remarked. 'Think of Badger. Haven't you any heart?'

'I shouldn't be talking to you now if I hadn't. But perhaps the reptilian variety hasn't the same capacity as a mammal's for spreading warmth.'

'Perhaps.'

'Don't worry, I shan't upset anything of your "game". And now I'll leave you to your subterranean explorations. I'm for a warmer place. Who knows' – and now Adder was talking to himself as much as to Fox – 'perhaps my heart will benefit from it.'

—15—
Mossy's Mission

Fox and Vixen discussed the underground theory with their kindred. Friendly and Russet, Charmer and Ranger, Whisper, Pace and Rusty had no knowledge that was of any use. Ranger volunteered to consult Trip and the other foxes in the Park. Meanwhile Weasel talked to his own kind whilst Leveret spoke to his cousins the rabbits. All of the inquiries drew a blank. Then the other badgers in the Reserve were brought in. All of them were of the opinion that none of the sets they knew about had entrances or tunnels wide enough to admit a creature the size of the Cat.

The Cat itself, since its last hunting spree, was lying low

in more than one sense. But it was about to replenish its stores of food. At the time when its hunger dictated, it emerged from its new lair. The night was dark. There was no moon, and clouds completely obscured the heavens. The Cat was well aware the animals expected another strike in the same neighbourhood. So it avoided that and slunk through the shadows on its noiseless way towards the stream. But not to where the stream ran past its old lair in the bank. Another lower reach of the water was its objective.

The Cat was a good swimmer and it decided now to explore the food potential not only of the banks, but of the water itself. It caught a couple of unsuspecting water-voles, hooked out some small fish, and completely obliterated a family of coots on their midstream nest. But it was not satisfied. It was disappointed in this aquatic hunt, and a few frogs made very little difference to its appetite. As the sky began to lighten, the Cat loped back towards its den, determined to snatch itself something more substantial on the way.

The Reserve seemed deserted. The animals were still spending most of their time out of sight. The Cat stopped dead, thinking of the taste of deer flesh. Its mouth watered. But it was too late now. The first signs of dawn were in the sky. It padded back, angry and frustrated, to its den. The next night it meant to eat deer again. At the entrace to its lair it roared its anger to the cowering inhabitants of the Park. The roar rose in pitch and finished in an unearthly scream that carried far beyond the boundaries of the Reserve. The Warden of White Deer Park woke in his bed, dressed hurriedly, snatched his gun and a torch and ran from the house. He stayed near the deer herd until broad day, but he saw nothing.

That night Mossy had decided to travel one of his tunnels that led into Badger's set. It was a passage that had been often trodden by his father. He began to call to Badger in between snacks of earthworms which he collected as he went along. Badger did not reply, so Mossy settled down for a proper feast. Eating was such an absorbing pastime for a mole that, by the time he dropped into the set, Mossy had no idea it was nearly daybreak.

Badger had returnd from a half-hearted foraging trip and was preparing himself for a snooze. But when Mossy appeared, he was delighted to postpone it.

'Mole! Just the fellow I've been thinking about,' was the greeting. 'Adder came to see me and – you won't guess! – he has the idea that the Cat is living underground like us.'

Mossy gave a cry of alarm but Badger soon reassured him.

'It's all nonsense,' he said. 'How could it do so? There's no hole big enough. I told Adder that, but you know Adder.'

Mossy did not. He had never associated with the snake in a personal way, nor did he want to. He did not like snakes at all and could not understand how Badger had made a friend of one. However, he was about to make a remark on the existence of a very large hole he had heard about, when there was a deafening roar. Both Mossy and Badger froze. Mossy's blood nearly curdled in his veins as the scream rent the outside air. The vibrations of the terrible sound seemed to echo through the maze of passages surrounding them. They turned to each other.

'The Beast!' they whispered together.

'That must be its h-hunting c-call,' Mossy stammered.

'I hope all our friends are safely at home,' said Badger. 'What a horrible cry.'

When Mossy had recovered himself he remembered what he had been going to say. 'The hole,' he said, and then had to stop again. He was still quivering.

'The hole?'

'Yes. My mother – ' Poor Mossy broke off again. He had started to explain that his mother Mirthful had told him of a great hole. Then he recalled that Mirthful could not be his mother, as far as Badger was concerned. Mirthful had been his father's mate. He hesitated. Now what could he say? It was *so* awkward.

'Your mother,' Badger prompted him. 'I've never known you to mention your mother before, Mole.'

'Er – no. What I mean is, the – er – female you called Mirthful – she – er – she told me that there *is* a great chamber underground in the Reserve. She came across it by accident once. She thought it was something the humans must have made.'

Badger drew his breath in sharply. 'Is this true?' he almost snapped at Mossy. All other considerations were forgotten now.

'Yes, quite true. I assure you, Badger.'

'Where? Where is this chamber?'

'I don't know. I've never been there. But – but – it can't be far from here. My – er – that is, Mirthful – she lived around here before she – er – mated.'

'Then we must find it,' said Badger. 'And when we've found it . . . ' he stopped and pondered, then he finished lamely, 'we'll know if the Cat uses it.'

'Oh dear. What if the Cat is there when we find it?' Mossy asked tremulously.

'We only have to *see* it,' Badger growled. 'I'll do the seeing. You only have to find the chamber.'

'But – but – '

'No "buts", Mole. This is our very last chance. You're the greatest tunneller of us all. If anybody can find it, you can. Then you can come back to me, tell me where it's situated and I'll go overland. I'll go by day. The Cat will be asleep perhaps. I make a noise' – Badger was enacting the scene in his mind – 'it wakes up. It sees me. I see the Cat. I tell it so – and the threat is removed. The Cat leaves White Deer Park.' He looked at Mossy triumphantly.

'You make it sound very simple,' said the little animal. 'Are you sure there's no more of a risk than that?'

'Only to me,' said Badger, 'and what does that matter? My days are numbered.'

'Oh, Badger,' Mossy pleaded, 'don't start on that again.'

'Very well. I'll say no more,' he answered. 'But I'm relying on you. You're the one now that the whole population of the Reserve depends on, whether they realize it or not.'

Mossy gulped. He did not know if he was equal to such a tremendous responsibility. 'I – I'll do my best,' he said, not very happily. 'I can't do more than that.'

'Of course you can't,' Badger assured him. 'But I know what "best" means for the most efficient of all tunnel travellers. Off with you now. There's no time to lose,'

Mossy scurried away. How was he to begin this impossible task?

He headed first of all for his own comfortable nest where, he was pretty sure, he had left some immobilized worms uneaten. He was glad to find that indeed this was the case. Whilst he was chewing on these, he tried very hard to think of all that Mirthful had told him about the great chamber. The network of underground passages used by his parents was all around him. Many of them he still used himself. In addition to these were some others that his mother had used before she had become mate to his father. Somewhere the two systems connected, because it had been at that point where his parents had first encountered each other. Mossy knew roughly in what direction this place would be, and so that must be the first stage of his exploration. Afterwards he would have to reconnoitre the old tunnels used by Mirthful, in the hope that one of them would bring him to the chamber he sought. He ate a last worm in a pensive sort of way and set off.

He found the connecting point without trouble and ran along the first passage. This led into another and that one into a further passage and it was remarkable, he thought, how free of debris they had remained in all this time. One passage came to a dead end and there, at the end of it, was the remains of an old nest. The materials – dry grass and leaves – had not yet disintegrated entirely. Mossy paused. A feeling of sweet but distant sadness stole over him. He had stumbled across one of his mother's old resting-places.

But there was no time for sentimentality. Underneath the nest was a bolt-hole. Mossy pulled himself into it and simply followed his nose. And it was his nose that was starting to cause problems. Along the passages the scent of earthworms pervaded the damp, close air. Their little burrows were everywhere and often they dropped unsuspectingly into a mole's tunnel. Mossy was having the utmost difficulty in ignoring the sensations picked up by his nose. Although he had eaten recently, he already felt hungry again. He tried to remember the importance of his mission, but the worms intruded more and more into his awareness and, eventually he was unable to resist any longer. He snapped at one and ate it hurriedly. Then he moved on, collecting one here, one there, and stopping each time to devour it. Without realizing it, his journey of exploration had become a worm hunt. He was so intent on satisfying his voracious appetite that he lost all idea of time, where he was going, and what he was meant to be doing. In the midst of grabbing a particularly plump worm from the earth walls, he suddenly seemed to lose his footing. The loose soil gave way beneath him and he found himself plunging down as if into a void. Then there was a bump as he landed abruptly at the bottom.

Luckily he had fallen on to more earth and he was more shaken by the surprise than the severity of the fall. Mossy pulled himself together. A dim light enabled him to see a little. He soon noticed a patch of daylight, like a round piece of whiteness against the mass of black. He knew it was from there that the feeble light filtered through, and he guessed it was a large entrance hole. Then, with a start, he realized where he was. He was in a sort of cavern. Out there, beyond the patch of daylight, lay the Park. Mossy had found the great chamber!

Now he was very frightened. The passage he had fallen from was high up the cavern wall and there was no way by which he could climb back up to it. The only way out was through the main entrance hole. But how could he get to it and out of it safely when the Cat might arrive at any moment? Then his heart turned over. The Cat might even now be inside the cavern, only a few steps away. He did not know – yet. Mossy held himself very still. His heart hammered wildly at the thought. He tried to test the dank air for animal scents, wrinkling his snout all around. There *was* a smell – a warm, sharp sort of smell, which was almost certainly given off by the animal's body. Mossy began to tremble uncontrollably. He could scarcely prevent his teeth from chattering with fright. How he wished someone else were there – Badger preferably – to suggest what he should do. Then he recalled that *he* had to report to Badger. He had to get out into the Park – somehow – so that he could describe the location of the chamber.

Mossy tried to calm himself. Even if an animal *was* present somewhere near him in that cavern, it might be something smaller and less ferocious than the Cat. So he argued to himself. But it was no use. He *knew*, without actually seeing it, that it was the Cat. Now he had two options. One was to try and creep to the exit without being noticed. He did not know if he had the courage to do that. The other was to wait, still and noiseless, until darkness fell again, and hope that the Beast would itself leave on a hunting trip. What an ordeal that would be. It was a good thing he had eaten well. But supposing he waited – how many more lives, perhaps of those whom he knew, would be lost if the Cat rampaged around again? If he could get out now he could prevent this happening.

There was no sound. Was the Cat sleeping or wakeful? At any rate, his – Mossy's – abrupt entry into the chamber did not seem to have been detected. So if his presence was not suspected already, a small animal like himself could have a fair chance of remaining unseen. Keeping close to the side of the chamber, Mossy moved a few centimetres. Then he froze, waiting for a reaction. There was none. He moved a little farther; then farther still in the direction of the disc of daylight. Oh, it seemed so far away. This cavern was really enormous.

Mossy reached a point along the wall where he got, as it were, behind the shaft of faint light that shone into the murky interior. Now he could see part of the chamber quite well where the light fell. And there he saw four huge tawny legs, belonging to a body the rest of which remained in shadow. It was obvious, from the position of the legs, that the body was lying on its side. Evidently the Cat slept. Mossy was encouraged. But he could not resist pausing to peer for a long time, through his weak eyes, at the impressive sight. He compared the huge paws with his own diminutive ones and this set him scuttling on his way again. The exit was closer now and the daylight seemed to be dimming. He could see foliage beyond – thick encompassing foliage that hid the entrance to the chamber from those abroad in the Park. Mossy moved on, nearer and nearer, still keeping as quiet and slow as he could. When he was about two metres from regaining the Park, he heard a stir behind him. The Cat had woken and was stretching its limbs where it lay. There was a muffled growl and Mossy thought he was discovered. He waited, almost dead with fright. But nothing happened. After a while, he started on again. He was nearly there. A breeze blew from ouside and wafted into the chamber, ruffling the Cat's fur. Some dust must have blown into its nostrils, too. Mossy heard a tremendous sneeze. Then the Cat was up and padding towards him. He tried to hurry but it was no use. The Cat, on its long legs, was there before him.

He was seen. The Cat growled softly. Mossy could think of only one thing to do. 'You're seen!' he cried. 'I see you!'

It might have been that the shrill squeaks of the little mole were more or less inaudible to the Cat, or it might have been that the great beast saw Mossy as a welcome extra morsel after the previous night's bad hunting. Either way it paid no attention to his feeble challenge, except to extend one vast paw to pull him close.

Somehow Mossy managed to circumvent the paw and he scurried out of the chamber and began to dig frantically at the soil outside. He was a lightning fast digger and, with three heaves, his head and front paws and half his body had disappeared to safety. He tore at the earth in fury, pulling his body after him, down, down and down into the familiar territory of darkness that enveloped him like a caress.

The Cat was not to be outdone, however. It saw where the tiny animal had gone and set about digging after him. It ripped up clods of the soft soil, scrabbling with both front paws in an angry fit of exasperaton. Mossy could hear the thunder above him and dug down deeper. But the Cat's paws were gaining.

A witness of the struggle flew desparately to help. The miserable and sleepless Tawny Owl was now brave Mossy's only hope.

Tawny Owl had been perched on a branch, away from his friends, unhappily contemplating the prospect of further deaths in the community. He had tried in vain to doze in the sunlight, although for a time he kept his eyes firmly shut. At last he gave up and when he opened his eyes he saw, at a distance, the Cat emerge from the midst of a thick bush and begin digging determinedly. Owl was too far away to have seen the small body of Mossy but he knew, better than any creature, that it was now time for the Cat to honour its pledge.

He launched himself into the air and flew swiftly to a nearby tree. Then, at the top of his voice, he cried, 'I CAN SEE YOU, CAT!'

The animal stopped its digging momentarily and looked around. When it spied Tawny Owl it snarled angrily. Owl quivered but held on. The respite allowed Mossy to tunnel deeper and get farther away.

Tawny Owl noted the Cat made no move. There was a look of fury on its face at being discovered. Owl said, 'You said I'd never see you again. You were wrong. I think you – er – must yield now.'

'YIELD?' the Cat roared terrifyingly. 'To an owl?'

'You gave your word,' Tawny Owl whispered, barely

able to speak. He guessed the pledge was worthless and that now there was no hope for any of them.

The Cat roared again, making the ground vibrate with the din. Badger had heard the first roar and had run to his set entrance in alarm. He had regretted sending the tiny mole on such a dangerous exploration and now he looked around for him in desperation. When the second roar rang out he could stand still no longer. He started to run towards the sound.

By the time he could see the Cat, the animal was digging again and Badger surmised immediately what it was digging for.

'Oh Mole,' he cried to himself in anguish and he increased his pace. Now he noticed Tawny Owl. 'Owl, Owl,' he called breathlessly. 'Do something!'

'It's no use,' the bird wailed. 'We're helpless. The Beast has broken its promise.'

Badger lumbered up, panting but filled with resolution.

'Leave that worthless morsel,' he gasped, putting himself in front of the Cat. 'What good is that mouthful to you? *I'm* more fitted to your appetite. Let me take his place.'

The Cat paused. It turned round and, with a malicious glare, stared at Badger in the fading daylight with undisguised contempt.

'Feeble, powerless weaklings,' it spat at him. 'I could slay *all* of you!'

Badger quailed, despite his determination. Tawny Owl watched in agony on his branch. What *could* he do?

The Cat's eyes blazed with the intensity of living fire. Suddenly a roar, like a distant echo of the Cat's, could be heard far away. The Beast's majestic head snapped round, its ears pricking up erect as sentinels. The sound was repeated on a higher note. In an instant the Cat forgot about Badger, Tawny Owl and the hidden Mossy and, in the failing light, lifted up its head and roared deafeningly. The call was answered, now not so distant. The Cat leapt up gracefully, clearing all the surrounding obstacles with ease, and bounded away through the trees.

Badger and Tawny Owl, the two old friends, looked at each other hesitantly. Was there *another* of the Beasts? As they held their silence, more roars could be heard, the one answering the other. Now more Park animals began to make themselves seen, asking each other what these awful sounds portended.

Badger said quietly to Tawny Owl, 'Let's go back and mix with the others. Mole will make his own way home.'

Now Tawny Owl understood about the digging. He made no comment on Badger's use of the name 'Mole'.

They found Fox and Vixen and Weasel in a cheerful mood that contrasted strangely with their own.

'Why such long faces?' Weasel chided them. 'This is cause for celebration.'

'Celebration?' Badger muttered. 'How can you – ' He broke off. A light seemed to penetrate his thoughts. 'Can it be?' he asked himself. And then he heard it. The cries of hundreds of birds, chirping and singing joyfully.

'Oh tell me, Weasel – Fox – someone – tell me what you think,' begged Badger.

'Those roars can mean only one thing,' said Weasel. 'The Cat has been called away. It's still spring. That could only be the call of a female crying for a mate!'

The roars were becoming fainter and, as they listened, dusk began to descend.

'Yes,' said Fox. 'It seems that what we've striven for so

hopelessly all along, has now been achieved by an outside influence.'

The birds were still singing. The animals thrilled at the sound. They were crying, 'It's left the Park! It's left the Park!'

Epilogue

During the last few days of spring the animals could not quite believe their Park had been returned to them. The Farthing Wood community had listened to Mossy's description of the cavern, and they had gone to the spot to look at the entrance behind the thick bushes that concealed it. Fox and Vixen had even scrambled inside to look. But the grisly remains of the Beast's last meals had soon prompted their return to fresher air. They told none of the others what they had seen.

Some of the birds who had so gladly broadcast the Cat's departure had not been satisfied with that alone. They had flown into open country to follow the route it took. They saw the other Cat that had called it away – a slightly smaller beast, but equally powerful in their eyes. And this one's power did not extend merely to strength. With some surprise, the birds watched the excited meeting of the two Cats. For the smaller animal appeared to dominate the great creature that had terrorized the Park. Wherever she led, the male followed. She called to him frequently as they went and, almost with a sort of meekness, he was content to do her bidding. He ambled in her wake quite happily, and such was their stride that they were soon a long way from the Reserve. It was apparent that the female's territory was in quite another area. Eventually the birds returned home with the news.

One of them remarked that 'it was as if the Beast had been tamed'.

So the roars and screams of the great Cat were heard no more in White Deer Park. The animals' lives resumed an ordinariness that at times seemed almost dull by its comparison with the frights and fears they had endured for so long.

'It almost seems now,' Friendly remarked to his father, 'that the danger we faced day after day added a sort of zest to our existence.'

Fox disagreed. 'When you reach my time of life,' he replied, 'what you call "zest" is something you only want to recall in your memories. And Vixen and I have plenty of those.'

Soon Squirrel came back to the fold and the group of old friends was more or less complete again.

The opinions of the older creatures – Badger, Tawny Owl, Weasel, Toad and Whistler – tallied with those of Fox. They looked forward to nothing more than a period of peace to enjoy for as long as they were able to gather together. But the opinion of one old friend was not known, and that was Adder's. He had not put in an appearance since the siege of the Nature Reserve had been lifted. Only Leveret had seen him since that time, and the snake's excuse had been, as usual, a cryptic one. His remark had puzzled Leveret who had passed it on to the others, hoping for some enlightenment. There was none offered. They were as mystified as he. For Adder had merely referred to the fact that he had recently become interested 'in a new association'.

The summer waxed and waned and the chill of autumn crackled with the clash of antlers of the stags in the white deer herd. The Great Stag had many rivals now and had more difficulty than ever before in holding his place. The fawns who had survived the ravages of the stranger's raids had grown too, and eventually the leadership would be passed on, perhaps many seasons hence, to one of these. Whatever happened, the herd that had given the Park its name would still be there, stepping gracefully through the woods and grassland of the Nature Reserve.

Another winter beckoned. Deep in his set, with a thick pile of bedding around him, Badger wondered if it would be his last. His old bones were beginning to ache with age and the cold, and he found himself thinking again about his ancient system of tunnels in Farthing Wood. In a soft, rather feeble but warm voice he said to Mossy, who was visiting, 'It was a wonderful set, Mole. Do you remember the Assembly, when the whole Wood gathered in my home to talk?'

'Oh yes,' said Mossy. 'I remember. I wonder what Farthing Wood is like now?'

In the Path of the Storm

Colin Dann

Illustrations by Trevor Newton

Contents

In Memory of Frederick C. Brown,
friend and naturalist

Prologue

Whistler the heron stood in the shallows of the stream in White Deer Park one early morning in March. It was late winter. Or was it early spring? It was difficult to tell, as there isn't much difference between a mild winter and a cold spring. And the weather seemed to have stayed in the same pattern for months. There had been no snow; no ice. But there had been many gales and a great deal of rain. It was raining now. Whistler was supposed to be fishing, but the disturbance caused by the raindrops on the surface of the water made his prey harder to detect. He had fallen into a semi-doze, his slate-grey back hunched in its usual attitude. He was motionless.

From the fringe of woodland near the stream bank a towering figure emerged, his white coat ghostlike in the murk of the slanting rain. The Great Stag stepped sedately forward to drink. He noticed the heron but

didn't disturb him. He was an old, wise animal who
respected all other creatures in the Nature Reserve and
he knew when to leave well alone. He knew Whistler
was catching fish and he paused to drink with caution,
making sure any ripples caused by his lowered muzzle
didn't interfere with the bird's occupation. He drank
and slowly raised his head.

Whistler came out of his reverie as he saw movement. He turned his head to the stag. As he looked the
deer's body was seized by a sort of spasm and, quite
suddenly, the legs collapsed and the great beast
crashed on to his side. The stag seemed to tremble; then
all was still except that, almost imperceptibly, the body
began to slide down the muddy bank towards the
stream where it became lodged, half in and half out of
the water. Whistler launched himself into the air and,
with a few flaps of his wings, reached the deer's side.
The glassy look of the Great Stag's eyes and the beast's
utter stillness confirmed the heron's fears. The leader of
the White Deer Park herd was dead.

Whistler was so distressed he did not, at first, know
what to do. The Great Stag had been so much a part of
life in the Nature Reserve for the heron and for all his
friends who had travelled there to seek sanctuary from
their ruined birthplace, Farthing Wood, that he had
epitomised the very name of their new home, White
Deer Park. Not that it was such a new home to them
now, for they would soon be entering their fourth
season there. And now here was the lordly animal who
had welcomed them into the Park on the first day of
their arrival all that time ago, and whom all of them
revered, lying lifeless at the heron's feet. It was just too

much for Whistler to contemplate alone. He needed to share the burden. He took a last look at the sad sight of the great deer's carcass and flew hurriedly away.

His powerful wings took him quickly to that corner of the Park where his old friends had settled. The first creature he saw was Badger who was busy collecting fresh bedding for his set. Badger looked up as he heard the familiar whistle of the heron's damaged wing. The old animal's sight was very bad now but he knew Whistler so well by his sound that he didn't need to wait until he could see him properly. He called out a greeting in his gruff voice.

'Hallo, Whistler! More rain, more rain. Everything's sopping. My set's waterlogged and –' He broke off as the heron landed beside him and now even Badger could see the look of anguish in the great bird's eyes. 'Why, whatever's the matter, my friend?' he asked kindly. 'You look as if you've seen a ghost.'

'I – I have – almost,' Whistler stammered. He hadn't yet recovered from his shock. 'An awful thing, Badger. The Great Stag. . . .' His voice petered out.

'Well?' Badger prompted him.

'He – he's dead.'

'Dead?' cried Badger. 'Are you sure? I saw him only recently and –'

'He's dead, Badger,' Whistler repeated. His voice was hushed. 'I saw him die. Just a moment ago. It was horribly sudden. He was drinking at the stream and then – he – he just keeled over and lay still.'

Badger was stunned. He could scarcely believe it. 'How dreadful,' he murmured.

For a while neither spoke, lost in their own thoughts.

At last Whistler said, 'I suppose he was a great age.'

Badger said, 'Aren't we all, Whistler?' He was reminded of his own longevity. 'I don't know how I've survived when. . . .' He didn't finish. The rain still beat down relentlessly. 'I suppose I should get this bedding underground,' he mumbled.

'I'll tell the others,' Whistler informed him.

But Badger didn't hear. His thoughts were full of the momentousness of the heron's discovery. How would the Great Stag's death change things? Would the Park become a different place? He dragged the damp bracken and leaves he had gathered backwards into his set entrance. 'Never dry, never dry,' he muttered as he reached his sleeping-chamber. 'My old bones won't stand this for ever. I'm not immortal either.'

Later the rain ceased for a while. The animals from Farthing Wood, together with their friends and relations, had collected to bid farewell to the Great Stag as a mark of respect to an old acquaintance.

'It's the end of the old order,' said Fox. He looked about him. Vixen, his beloved partner, Weasel, Whistler, Tawny Owl and Badger met his eyes. They were all thinking the same thing. How long before they too would succumb? The stag's death seemed to bring their own a little closer.

'It's so sad,' said Vixen. There was a catch in her voice. 'He was a good friend to us all.'

'Who'll take his place?' Leveret asked. The young hare's question dispelled the older animals' gloomy thoughts. 'There will be a new leader, won't there?'

'There'll be a battle first,' Tawny Owl asserted. 'There's no obvious successor.'

'Someone will win through,' Weasel remarked. 'One of the younger stags.'

'Of *course* he'll be younger,' Tawny Owl said impatiently. 'That goes without saying, doesn't it?'

'I wonder who it'll be?' Mossy said anxiously. He didn't like change.

'We won't know that, Mole,' Badger said to him, 'until their breeding season. And that's a long way off.'

The body of the aged leader of the deer herd rocked gently in the rush of the swollen stream.

Owl is Discomfited

The weather continued very wet. Toad and Adder emerged from hibernation to see the Park wreathed in damp mists and the low-lying ground turned marshy. Toad was in his element. He loved such conditions and his warty skin glistened in harmony. But Adder grumbled. He craved warmth.

'We've come out too soon,' he moaned to his companion.

'Nonsense,' returned Toad, jumping up and down in his glee. 'Things couldn't be better.' Adder turned his back on him with a contemptuous hiss.

Toad leapt away to White Deer Pond and found it brimming over. The Edible Frogs were calling lustily to each other. One of them spied Toad and soon told him of the sad demise of the Great Stag. Like his friends from Farthing Wood, Toad was shocked. He remembered how the leader of the herd had befriended them all and Toad felt he wanted to be amongst his close companions now to share his sadness. He left the Pond without a word and travelled to the corner of the Reserve where he knew he would find his old friends. On the way he overtook Adder who was slithering through the mire with an expression of the utmost distaste on his face.

Toad broke the news to him. Adder halted. Never one to give vent to his emotions, the snake was nonetheless unable to prevent his expression wavering. And there was an unusually long pause before he replied simply, 'I see.' Toad knew Adder better than anyone and he guessed the news had had the same impact on the snake as on all the community. They continued their journey in silence.

They reached the area where their animal friends had settled, near the Hollow. It was a while before any of them put in an appearance. Tawny Owl was the first to see them from his perch in an oak tree where he was alternately dozing and watching. He flew down to greet them after their winter absence.

'Another season,' he remarked.

'Yes, and a sad start to it,' Toad replied.

Tawny Owl blinked sleepily. It was a while since the Great Stag had died. The deer carcass had been removed by the Warden and Owl had almost forgotten about it.

'He means the deceased beast,' Adder lisped.

Tawny Owl stared. Then, 'Ah! Yes,' he nodded. 'The Stag. It was by the stream, you know.'

Toad said with concern: 'There have been no other deaths? I mean –'

'No, no,' Owl cut in. 'None of us old 'uns. Badger's still around And – well, so am I.'

'Evidently,' Adder drawled.

'And Fox?' prompted Toad.

'Oh yes. Fox and Vixen. And Weasel. And Whistler. It was Whistler who saw the Stag die.'

'He was a noble beast,' Toad said.

'Yes.' Even Adder concurred with that.

'There's another thing about the stream,' Tawny Owl resumed. 'There appears to be a dearth of food in it at present, according to Whistler. He has to go outside the Park to fish.'

The three creatures contemplated this but could come to no conclusions. Tawny Owl decided to return to his roost. He always slept a lot during the day.

'I'm going to find myself a dry spot – if there is such a thing,' Adder said. His red eyes glinted. 'But that won't do for you,' he addressed Toad. 'So I'll leave you to your own devices.'

'All right. I understand,' Toad answered. 'I'll stay around for a bit until I've seen some of the others. I'll give them your good wishes, shall I?'

'Do as you please,' Adder hissed under his breath as he slid away. He headed for Badger's set. '*That'll* be dry,' he told himself.

There were many births that spring amongst the Farthing Wood community and their descendants. The Farthing Wood Fox and his mate Vixen had lived to see their lineage reach the fourth generation. A grandson of Bold (their cub who had left the Park and not survived) was born whom Vixen swore was the image of his grandfather at that age. She and Fox watched his progress with great interest. He was named Plucky.

Spring turned into summer and everywhere there were rabbits, hedgehogs, squirrels, mice and voles who were White Deer Park animals through and through, but who owed their existence to their doughty fore-fathers who had travelled across countryside and Man's terrain to reach the Reserve. There were moles and weasels and hares. And toads, kestrels and herons. Soon there would be adders. Only Badger and Tawny Owl remained solitary. Badger was ancient now and didn't always know what he was about. He had become very forgetful. The younger animals loved and respected him.

But sometimes they teased Tawny Owl who had not yet entered real old age. Weasel, too, could not resist a gibe now and then.

'Well, Owl,' he said, 'when will you muster up the courage to go a-courting?'

'When I choose to,' replied the bird loftily.

'It seems to me you don't choose to,' Weasel continued. 'At least, not on the evidence of three seasons in the Park.'

'How would you know? Can you fly?' Tawny Owl retorted.

'I don't need to,' answered Weasel. 'Everyone knows you've never been seen in the company of a female.'

Tawny Owl didn't remain to hear any more insults. He flew away in a huff. But there was no relief for him. Pace and Rusty, two of the younger foxes now parents themselves, found his shelter and goaded him cheekily.

'Here's the only old bachelor left of the originals,' Pace remarked to his cousin.

'Poor old Owl – he can't find a mate,' Rusty added provocatively.

Tawny Owl tried to maintain his calm, moving to a higher perch.

'Have all the females been snapped up, Owl?' Pace persisted, raising his voice.

'Stop chaffing me,' Tawny Owl called down irritably. He was becoming ruffled. 'Haven't you got anything better to do?'

'Haven't you?' Rusty gibed.

'Perhaps not.'

'But think of all those lady owls dying for a word from you, the famous Owl from Farthing Wood,' Pace taunted him.

'They'll have to wait then, won't they?' Tawny Owl answered. He knew he was foolish to take any notice but their raillery was impossible to ignore.

'Wait for what?'

'For me to choose to visit them,' Owl said superciliously.

'Oh – oh. Hark at that, Rusty. Don't you think it might be *they* who haven't chosen Tawny Owl?'

'Must be,' agreed Rusty. 'After all, he *is* the only bachelor.'

'I'm NOT the only bachelor,' Tawny Owl screeched furiously. 'What about Badger?'

'Poor old Badger? He's almost senile,' declared Rusty. 'You can't count –' He broke off as he saw his mother, Charmer, approaching.

'What's going on?' she enquired. She sensed the young foxes were up to some mischief.

'They're baiting me,' Tawny Owl complained querulously.

'Why – whatever for?'

'It's only about his bachelorhood,' Pace explained.

'Whatever business is that of yours?' Charmer demanded angrily. 'Haven't you got responsibilities of your own now that are more important than being disrespectful to your elders? You leave Tawny Owl in peace. He deserves all the quiet he can get.' She lowered her voice. 'And why should you want to scoff at another's misfortune?'

The young foxes looked contrite. They hadn't really meant any harm. Unfortunately Tawny Owl had heard Charmer's last remark and was mortified. Misfortune? What did they take him for? He – Tawny Owl, one of the most revered inhabitants of the Reserve? *He'd* show them! He was seething. He flapped up from his perch so impulsively he almost banged his head on the branch above. But he extricated himself and, trying hard to recover his usual dignity, sailed away across the treetops. When he finally perched again he was a long way from where any of his unkind persecutors could get at him. His anger eventually subsided. But, though he could never have owned up to it, he had been well and truly hurt. And now he knew he had to do something to prove them wrong.

The trouble was, he knew most, if not all, of the female owls would already have paired off. However, he needed to find out for sure. So, in rather a half-hearted way, he began to make a tour of the Park and its nesting sites. He soon discovered that the other male owls were very jealous of their territory and would drive him off if he attempted to approach too close. It was a demoralizing experience for him. At night he concentrated on catching his prey and, while he ate, pondered on his next move.

'Nothing else for it,' he told himself. 'I'll have to extend my search outside the Park.' In a way he was quite relieved at this state of affairs. There would be a wider area to roam, with the likelihood of better opportunities of finding what he sought. And, best of all, none of his old companions – or new ones – would have any way of following his progress.

One night he flew out, over the downland, skimming effortlessly through the air on his silent wings. He looked back at the boundary fence of White Deer Park and the dark silhouettes of its trees. Although he often flew beyond the bounds of the Park, the significance of his flight this time made him feel just a mite apprehensive, since he didn't know for sure how long it might be before he would return there. But he turned his head resolutely and set a course for the nearest patch of woodland.

2

A Rendezvous

In May and June that season's White Deer Park fawns
were born. The young deer were born with the usual
dappled coats. It was only as they matured that the
animals took on the white colouring that gave the
Nature Reserve its name.

The Farthing Wood animals knew that amongst
these newborns there was a future dominant male in
whose veins the blood of the Great Stag was coursing.
But the older creatures knew they would never know
him. What they were interested in was which of the
present mature stags would assume the role of the
Great Stag's successor. At this time of the year the stags
separated themselves from the hinds and wandered,
sometimes together, sometimes alone. To the watching
animals there already seemed to be one obvious
contender for the leadership. He was the largest and
sturdiest of the beasts and was certainly aware of his

strength. He was cool and self-possessed in the other males' company and had a superior air. His antlers were still growing but he already had a greater head than his companions. He was known as Trey. The animals were impressed by him and began to wonder how they would fare in relationship to him.

'He's a proud creature,' Fox remarked when he and Vixen stopped one evening to watch. 'Look at the way he carries himself.'

'Yes,' Vixen agreed. 'He seems to realize even now he has no real rivals. It's in his bearing.'

'There will be some challengers,' Fox answered her. 'It's in the nature of things.'

'My only concern is that he won't interfere with our way of life or our friends',' Vixen said, voicing Fox's own fears. 'It's been so peaceful since the departure of the huge hunting Cat.'

'We'll keep ourselves to ourselves,' Fox vowed. 'No creature can take exception to that.'

So the Farthing Wood community went about their business as usual without upsetting anybody.

Badger had had a tenant for much of the spring in his set, and an unlooked-for one at that. Because of the long period of wet weather Adder had set up home in a dry spot near the mouth of one of Badger's tunnels. He had not asked permission and Badger was too old and polite a friend to object. But when a drier patch of weather set in and Adder showed no sign of wanting to leave, Badger began to make some pointed comments. It wasn't that Adder was there all the time. He couldn't be. He had to go out to catch his food. Yet the way he used the set as his base, constantly returning to it as if he had some kind of right, really got under Badger's hide.

One bright morning when the snake didn't seem at all disposed to stir Badger said: 'Why don't you go for a sunbathe? I thought you didn't like temperatures too cool?'

Adder grinned enigmatically. 'There's quite enough warmth to suit me here, thank you, Badger,' he replied.

'Isn't it time you ate?' Badger hinted. 'I don't think you've moved for days.'

'I don't need to hunt every day,' was the reply and Adder coiled himself up even more comfortably. 'I suppose you couldn't spare a few more of those dry leaves for this corner?' His tongue flickered in and out as he savoured the smell of the bedding.

'No, I couldn't,' Badger said shortly. 'I'm not your housekeeper. I didn't mind sheltering you during the constant downpours. I like company. But there are times when I also like solitude.'

Adder ignored him. He merely stared straight back at Badger with a blissful expression on his face. Badger lumbered away, growling to himself.

Later Mossy visited his ancient friend via one of the mole's connecting tunnels that led straight into the set. Badger immediately began talking about Adder as if Mossy had been there all day. 'He's taken up permanent residence here,' he complained. 'Snakes should find their own burrows. What am I to do, Mole?'

Mossy didn't consider he was in a position to advise. 'You've known Adder much longer than I,' he replied. 'I wouldn't dream of –'

'And then, what do you think?' Badger continued

without listening. 'He wants his bedding provided. He always had the cheek of all his kind but this time – well!' He lapsed into peevish mutterings.

Mossy thought it best to change the subject. 'Have you seen Tawny Owl recently?' he enquired.

'What? What? Owl? No, I haven't. What of it?' Badger answered irritably.

'I met Weasel earlier. He says he thinks Owl's disappeared. No-one's seen him since – um – well, since. . . .'

'Since what?' Badger snapped.

'Since the young foxes badgered him,' Mossy finished and tittered nervously.

'Very amusing, Mole,' Badger commented humourlessly. But he was interested. 'What's this all about?' he asked.

Mossy explained. 'Weasel told me the tale. He was involved too. He admitted it. They've been goading Tawny Owl because of his solitariness.'

'Nothing wrong with solitariness,' Badger replied at once. '*I'd* relish it.'

'That wasn't quite what I meant.' Mossy went on to describe the circumstances.

'Oh,' said Badger. 'I see. Poor old Owl. Why treat him like that? And he's disappeared, you say? Disappeared where? To another quarter of the Park?'

'Weasel says not. It seems Whistler hasn't seen Owl flying over any part of the Park for ages.'

'Well, we can't let this rest. Perhaps he's keeping to his roost. He could be ill.'

'None of his favourite haunts are occupied. Whistler's been to look. Weasel is convinced Owl's left the Park.'

Badger was really concerned. 'Oh no. That would be awful. Driven out like that! I hope the young foxes have been –'

'They're very upset about it,' Mossy interrupted. 'Weasel told me.'

Adder had heard the voices coming from Badger's far chamber. He put two and two together. 'The bird's gone searching for a mate,' he hissed under his breath. 'How absurd at his age.'

Badger trundled up the tunnel to give Adder the news.

'I heard,' Adder said abruptly. 'Well, Badger, I think we can look forward to a long absence from our friend Tawny Owl.'

'How can you be so unfeeling?' Badger demanded.

'Not unfeeling; just realistic,' Adder answered, quite unperturbed. 'Old Owl's not exactly a glossy-plumed youngster, just out of the nest.'

'I shall speak to Fox,' Badger said determinedly. 'We must do something. Bring Owl back.' He lumbered away.

'And how do you propose to do that? Sprout wings?' Adder called after him sarcastically.

Mossy followed faithfully in Badger's footsteps for a while. Adder watched them go. 'I suppose they'll mount a search,' he muttered. But the topic of Tawny Owl had reminded him of a search he had been contemplating making himself now that there was dry summer weather. He had expected – perhaps had even hoped – to come across Sinuous in his wanderings. But he hadn't done so. Adder had a feeling, though, that he knew one place where he could find her. It was a favourite spot of the she-viper's, near the stream. So, despite his comfortable surroundings, he issued forth from the set into the sunshine.

Since the death of the Great Stag the stream had generally been avoided by the Farthing Wood animals. Without actually giving voice to their feelings, the stream had become for them a place of portent. That the stag had died on its banks was like an omen. It gave the site an air of mystery. Whistler was unable to fish there. And the long wet spell had made it unnecessary for use as a drinking place. However, all this was immaterial to Adder as he slithered over the ground, bent on his rendezvous.

Sinuous detected his approach before he saw her. She was sunning herself on a mossy patch amongst the new young ferns. She lay on slightly rising ground. She observed Adder a few metres distant, his tongue darting incessantly as he sought for her scent. Sinuous allowed her face to take on the typical grin of the snake; a sort of leer. She was pleased and a little flattered Adder had come looking for her.

When Adder was close by, she said: 'Our trails cross at last. I've been wondering why it hasn't happened before?'

Adder slid to an abrupt halt at the sound. He didn't wish it to be too obvious that he was on a search. He looked up and saw Sinuous on her couch of moss. 'I haven't been in these parts for a while,' he told her.

'I'm well aware of that,' Sinuous answered. 'What brings you here now?'

'Oh well, one has to go somewhere,' Adder said dismissively.

The she-adder's grin broadened. Her tongue picked up Adder's scent. 'Have you been travelling in a hurry?' she asked archly.

'Um – well, not particularly,' Adder fibbed. 'But my movements are always more lively on a warm, sunny day.' He moved closer. 'The wet weather kept me rather under wraps, as it were,' he joked.

'And in all that time, didn't you spare a thought for me, Adder-of-the-blunt-tail?'

The snake pondered his reply. He *had* thought about her, though only intermittently. 'Oh yes,' he said. 'I think about everyone and everything from time to time.'

'Non-committal as ever,' Sinuous summarized. Her tone changed. 'It's been so quiet here. Almost lonely. Ever since the stream. . . .' She did not complete the sentence.

'Since the stream what?' Adder prompted.

'Became out of bounds.'

Adder considered. 'You were going to say something else at first, I think?'

'No – o,' Sinuous said slowly. 'No, not really. Only that it's as though the animals have become afraid of it.'

'Because of the Stag's death?'

'There may be more to it,' she suggested.

Adder held her gaze. Was she giving him a warning? 'I don't plan to swim there,' he informed her.

'No. Nor I. But there are creatures who are more partial to watery pursuits than we snakes. Toads, for instance . . .'

3

Familiar Terrain

By the time Badger was discussing the bird's where-abouts with Fox and Vixen, Tawny Owl was far away. He had met with no luck in any nearby woods or copses and so had flown on further. Prey was easy to find and so were places to roost during the daylight hours. But his quest for a partner proved elusive.

It wasn't long before certain features of the land-scape began to strike chords in Tawny Owl's memory. This was because he had travelled over it before, from the opposite direction, on the epic journey to the Nature Reserve – oh! so long ago. He began to recall events that had occurred at certain places which he now recognized, or what had been said by one of his friends at a particular spot. It was uncanny. Many of those friends he remembered were now gone. Yet they seemed to live on in this countryside. He perched in an oak and looked up at the gleaming sky. He seemed to

see Kestrel, hovering, keen-eyed, a speck in the blue,
spying out the land ahead. What a flier he had been! An
aerial acrobat.

Tawny Owl shook the memories away. He must
concentrate on the present and on his new purpose. He
rested and as he dozed he dreamed. He dreamed of his
old home and his birthplace in Farthing Wood. And at
dusk he awoke with a jolt and with a new idea. Why
shouldn't he fly back there? Retrace the animals'
historic journey? Back to their beginnings, to the place
of their forefathers. Of course it would be changed,
massively changed. He knew that. But whatever was
left, whatever was there now, still enshrined the old
home they had all shared all those seasons ago. And
perhaps there was still a corner with a few trees where
he could stay awhile and survey the new landscape.
What a story he would have to tell on his return to
White Deer Park! And somewhere on his journey, over
all that wide expanse, he would be bound to find that
special companion to fly with him. . . .

The more he thought, the more excited Tawny Owl
became. He felt younger in spirit than he would ever
have dreamed possible again. But he needed to be
cautious. For he wasn't young. He must fly within his
capabilities; not take risks nor indulge in any foolishness. There was plenty of time. He was very pleased
with himself and he flew a little loop around the oak
tree to celebrate. His stomach, however, soon reminded him of the necessity of keeping his strength up
and he set himself without further ado to obey its
commands.

His hunting techniques were born of long experience. He knew where to look and listen for shrews and wood mice. Soon he had caught and eaten enough to sustain himself. Then he flew well above the tree tops towards a much higher landmark that loomed on the horizon, a shape blacker than the dark sky that surrounded it. Tawny Owl had recognized it and now flew unerringly towards it. It was a church tower.

Flying high as he was he naturally headed straight for the open belfry. He landed on a stone sill and glanced around. 'I've been here before,' he murmured. It all seemed so familiar. This church had been the Farthing Wood party's last sheltering place before reaching White Deer Park. Owl's head swivelled round and he looked out at the sky. The stars glittered.

'I'll shelter here again,' he decided. 'It's an ideal spot. No-one to disturb me here.'

He watched the night sky pensively, his thoughts turning once again to those long-ago events inside the church during the animals' previous visit. Presently dawn glimmered in the east. Tawny Owl's head drooped. He shifted his talons, then closed his eyes. He was soon asleep.

But he wasn't allowed to sleep for long. Because there were other occupants of the church belfry who, in the gathering dawn, began to return there from their nocturnal hunting flights. And they objected to the presence of a large bird at their roost.

Tawny Owl half awoke as something zipped past his ear. He opened one eye but saw nothing. Then the little snap! of noise came again. Now he was quite awake. He was curious. He opened both eyes fully and looked around. Against the pale backdrop of the lightening sky he saw a number of small darting creatures criss-crossing on their different swooping flights. Occasionally one would dart directly at the church tower, then veer away at the last second. More and more swelled these numbers. Some came close enough to Tawny Owl to glance at him but none of them dared do more than chatter at the intruder, before they flitted away again. The big bird of prey unsettled them. They were angry, but wary of him. Tawny Owl realized he had usurped the resting place of a colony of bats.

The tiny animals fascinated yet irritated him. He admired, as only a bird could, their flying dexterity. But he wanted to sleep and the bats made this impossible. Evidently they wished to sleep, too, during the coming daylight, yet none of them was sufficiently bold to enter the belfry. They chivvied and chided him, but Tawny Owl refused to be dislodged. They buzzed around and past him in a miniature aerial bombardment.

'Will you stop this annoyance?' he cried at them. 'I'm staying put.'

The bats paid no heed but continued their dive-bombing.

'I just want to sleep,' Tawny Owl hooted. 'Can't you leave me alone? You'll get no rest either!'

'Fly away, begone.' 'Move away, leave our roost.' The bats shrieked at him in their tiny high-pitched voices.

Tawny Owl lost his temper. He launched himself from the stonework and swooped into their midst, scattering the animals briefly before they resumed their skimming, skipping flights all around him. Wherever he flew they followed him. But he could never catch any. They could turn and bank in a fraction of a second and reappear a moment later in a different spot. All around the sky the bats darted in varying patterns and directions, never colliding and never settling.

Aggravated as he was, Tawny Owl watched their effortless skill with wonder. He felt himself to be clumsy and cumbersome by comparison. He didn't relish being outshone in the field of flying. Disgruntled, he returned to his perch on the stone sill. The bats resumed their skirmishes. Tawny Owl moved further inside the belfry and perched on a rafter. He put his head under his wing and tried to ignore the animals' squeals and squeaks. It was in vain. His patience was now entirely exhausted.

'How dare you keep this up!' he thundered. 'Do you know who I am? Tawny Owl from Farthing Wood!' He waited for the expected result of this piece of information.

The bats, however, had either never heard of him or treated the news with disdain. Their behaviour changed not at all.

'This is intolerable,' Tawny Owl moaned to himself. 'First I'm driven away from the Park by insults and goading. Now I'm starved of sleep by puny little creatures no bigger than a vole. What have I done to deserve this? I won't be driven out!' he declared finally. 'I want to rest!' he screeched. 'I don't want to eat you. I want nothing to do with you! If I can ignore you, can't you all just do likewise?'

For a brief period the bats stayed outside the belfry, their movements less frantic and antagonistic. They seemed to be communing with one another. Then, chattering and muttering together, they flew into the belfry and began to hang themselves upside down, one by one, from their favoured roosting spots. Their little long-eared heads turned all in one direction as they gazed at Tawny Owl.

At last one piped up: 'How do we know you won't eat us while we sleep?'

Tawny Owl fixed the tiny furry creature with his enormous eyes. He realized the bat's face was up the wrong way so he tried to accommodate him by twisting his own head as far as he could in order to meet his eyes. In doing so he very nearly toppled from his perch. The sudden movement startled the bats and they began to leave their places and dart about again.

Tawny Owl was beside himself. 'Stop it! Stop it!' he begged. 'Calm yourselves, please. I can't hang upside down like you so we'll just have to talk to each other the – er – wrong way up, if you see what I mean.' He waited until they were more or less settled again. 'Look,' he said, 'I don't eat bats. I couldn't catch you if I wanted to. And as for eating you while you're asleep, how could I do that if I'm asleep myself?'

He looked around at the little bodies, each of which seemed to be swaying gently from one leg. 'I've already eaten,' he rejoined to doubly reassure them. 'I'm not hungry. Only weary. I sleep through the daylight hours just like you. When it's dusk I'll depart. Is that a bargain?'

There was a barrage of squeaky voices. Then one rose above all the others. 'We won't bargain with you,' the bat said, 'because we can't trust you. We don't know who you are. So one of us will stay awake all day in case you mean to take advantage. That's our answer.'

'You're silly little creatures, all of you,' Tawny Owl said derogatorily. 'I always keep my word. Haven't you ever heard of the Oath of the Animals of Farthing Wood?'

There was silence. Owl took this as assent. 'Well, the Oath can be extended to any other animals we choose,' he informed them grandiosely. 'So if I extend the Oath of Mutual Protection to you, your safety is assured, isn't it?'

None of the bats chose to respond. Most of them hadn't the faintest idea what the bird was talking about. Some of the older animals did have an inkling of the legendary Oath that Owl was referring to, though they didn't understand enough to realize how it could be applied to the bat community. So silence reigned as they tried to puzzle it all out.

Silence was the one thing that Tawny Owl craved. In a trice he had fallen asleep while the diminutive animals kept themselves awake by their perplexity.

The sun rose steadily in the sky. Tawny Owl slept. Many of the bats still fidgeted. The sun reached its zenith. Tawny Owl slept on peacefully. Some bats shifted their skinny wings as they watched him. The sun slipped slowly down to the horizon. In the afterglow Owl awoke refreshed, stretched his wings and awaited dusk. When it was quite dark he prepared to fly on. All around the belfry tower the suspended bats were fast asleep. Tawny Owl left the church behind with a chuckle.

The lights of a nearby town drew him onwards. He flew well above its buildings and when he had crossed it he looked for another landmark to guide him. The distant but steady hum of heavy traffic reminded him of his direction. He flew over some farmland and alighted in a tall ash whose late-opened leaves were still a fresh new green. From here he could see the dazzling lights of the motorway traffic streaking across the foreground like miniature shooting stars. But the terrifying dangers of such a man-made obstacle as this great highway were no barrier to a bird. Tawny Owl looked on almost scornfully. All at once his reverie was interrupted. An owl had hooted from another tree. Or was he mistaken? He strained his ears to catch a repetition above the roar of the machines. Sure enough the call was repeated.

Tawny Owl replied with the answering call. 'Kee-wick.'

The stranger owl's next call was nearer at hand. Tawny Owl located it amongst a stand of poplars planted as a windbreak at the border of a field. He was confident the calling bird was a female and that she had noticed him and wanted him to come closer. So he obliged.

He alighted on the neighbouring tree to where the other owl was perched.

'I've been watching you,' said the bird who was indeed a female.

'Watching me?'

'Yes, for quite a while. I saw you roosting at the church building and your battle with the bats.'

'Battle!' Tawny Owl exclaimed contemptuously. 'There was no battle. Only a minor irritation.'

'Your flight is very purposeful,' was the next observation.

Tawny Owl took this as a compliment. 'I'm on a journey,' he explained.

'A journey? To where?'

'To an old territory of mine.'

'What for?' the female owl enquired. She sounded intrigued.

'Oh, it's a long story,' Tawny Owl replied. 'I'm flying to an old hunting ground I used to frequent.'

'Is the hunting good?'

'I don't know any more. It used to be when I lived there. But there have been changes.'

'Then why go back there? Can't you find what you want round here?'

Tawny Owl was struck by the aptness of her question, innocent though it was. 'That depends,' he answered with a sideways look at her that was intended to be full of meaning.

The female owl didn't notice the significance of his expression. 'Depends on what?' she fluted.

'Well – you know.' Owl ruffled his wings impatiently. 'Certain things. How much of the terrain is occupied and – er – by whom. . . .'

'What difference does that make? Can't you defend yourself?'

'Of course I can!' he answered huffily. 'I meant, is the area fully marked out and – er – claimed?'

The female owl looked at him for a long time before

answering. 'Now I see why you're returning to your old area,' she surmised. 'You haven't paired.'

This was a sore point with Tawny Owl. He shifted his stance and the slender poplar branch rippled elastically. 'No, no, I haven't paired,' he admitted grumpily.

'Small chance round here for you then,' the female informed him. 'You'd better press on.'

Tawny Owl glared. 'But you – you were calling. Where is your mate then?'

'Collecting food, I hope,' she answered. 'He's been gone a long time. My babies are almost fully fledged. They're always hungry. They never stop nagging for food so I've been trying to hasten his return. They've eaten all we've brought them.'

The last thing Tawny Owl wanted to hear about was the details of other owls' family life, especially in his present predicament. He hastened to be gone.

'I must be on my way,' he muttered and leapt from his branch.

'Where do you head now?' she called after him.

'Farthing Wood,' he hooted, 'if it's still there.' He tarried no longer but sped straight for the motorway. The female owl watched with beak agape. Abruptly she concluded just whom she had been addressing. The Farthing Wood Owl!

4

Trey

Badger's concern about his old friend Tawny Owl's disappearance was shared by Fox and Vixen.

'To think of one of the elders of the Farthing Wood community feeling himself forced to quit the Park!' Fox bemoaned. 'It's outrageous and Pace and Rusty must be reprimanded. They may think they're grown-up foxes but their behaviour shows otherwise. I shan't take them to task myself. Their own parents have that duty to perform.'

'But in the meantime, Fox, what can we do to get Owl back?' Badger wailed. 'I think he's too old to go off scouring the countryside on some fool's errand such as this.'

'Don't worry, my dear friend,' Fox answered. 'We'll think of something.'

'Does Owl actually plan to stay outside the Reserve?' Vixen queried.

'As far as I can tell he intends not to return until he has someone to accompany him,' Badger replied. 'I think Weasel could tell you more about how all this arose.'

'Weasel? Yes,' Fox mused. 'He and Owl always had their differences, didn't they? Seemed to have a penchant for needling each other unnecessarily. But Weasel ought to know better than to joke about vital things like pairing off. You say he's partly to blame, Badger?'

'Yes, I'm sure of it. He couldn't have foreseen the result, of course,' he added, trying as ever to smooth things over.

'I think we should have a word with Weasel,' Fox asserted. 'The onus is on him to help in this matter. Come on; he's bound to be around close by.'

There was no difficulty in finding Weasel but he didn't prove to be very disposed to help.

'What can I do?' he asked them coolly. 'Tawny Owl's simply gone off in a huff. He'll be back soon enough when he's recovered himself.'

'Really, Weasel, I don't know what you were thinking of, talking to him the way you did. You know how touchy he is,' said Fox.

'I wasn't to know he would go to such lengths,' was Weasel's answer. 'Do you think I'd have said a word if I'd known he'd be so nonsensical?'

'You always have enjoyed teasing him,' Fox recalled.

'Yes, but . . . well, he's never reacted so extremely before, has he? It's no use worrying yourself, Fox. Nor you, Badger. We're past the age when we could mount missions of rescue.'

Fox looked at Weasel's grizzled fur with a wry expression. 'Yes,' he said. 'Our colouring complements each other.' He was only too aware of his own greying coat. As for Badger, he hadn't even regained his breath.

'But we can't desert Tawny Owl, can we?' Vixen pleaded.

'We haven't done so, Vixen,' declared Weasel. 'He's deserted *us*, hasn't he? Purely in a fit of pique. There's just nothing to be done – except wait. Even if we were still our young adventurous selves it would be quite impracticable for mammals to go searching for a bird.'

'Oh dear, he could be far away by now,' Badger wailed. 'And I don't think he's any better equipped than we are to deal with the perils outside the Park.'

'Of course he is,' Weasel said kindly, trying to comfort. 'He has wings to carry him above any danger. Now don't fret. I'm certain we shall soon see –' Weasel stopped suddenly. He was looking away over their heads at something in the background. The others followed his glance.

It was Trey the large white stag that Weasel was looking at. And Trey was looking at them. He was on his own. He stood stock still and stared haughtily. Then, with a proud toss of his head, he began to step sedately towards them. He was a fine powerful-looking beast.

'You're some of the old travellers who came here long ago from another place, if I'm not mistaken,' he said without preamble. He had a harsh voice.

'Yes,' said Fox. 'We are.'

'You realize, I suppose, we only tolerate your presence here, we don't invite it?'

'Tolerate? Presence? What are you talking about?' demanded Fox. 'And who's "we"?'

'The herd, naturally.'

'Oh, you've been elected to speak for all of them, have you?' Weasel interjected sardonically.

The stag gave the tiny animal a contemptuous look as if such a midget wasn't even worthy of an answer. 'I am now the natural leader of the herd,' he said, addressing the two foxes and Badger, 'and therefore I wish you to understand your position.'

Fox ignored the last remark. 'I should have thought some of the other stags might have something to say about whether you're the natural leader?' he suggested. 'That's if I have learnt anything about the pattern of a deer herd's behaviour during my time in the Park.'

'Who is there to challenge *me*, *Trey*?' he asked boastfully. 'I am a royal stag. Have you ever seen antlers as splendid as these?'

'Yes,' Vixen replied coolly. 'The Great Stag, your precursor, had finer ones in his heyday.'

Trey glowered. But he was honest enough to admit, 'He was a superb specimen, it's true. But,' he added, 'his heyday was over long before he died. Now he's gone things will change – and not just in the herd.'

'We'd like to know about these changes,' Badger spoke for all of his friends, 'since we live here too.'

'Exactly,' Trey said. 'You live here too. We deer have allowed all you smaller animals to do just that, whereas in reality this Nature Reserve was set aside for us alone. We gave the Reserve its name. The Park belongs to us. Do you think for one moment, if it hadn't been for such a rare and valuable white deer herd, that this area of land would have been reserved for paltry common or garden creatures such as yourselves?'

The animals were open-mouthed.

'You don't answer me,' prompted Trey.

'We are dumbfounded by your arrogance,' Fox answered the stag. He drew himself up. 'I'm old now,' he said. 'But I also have authority and am respected in this Park. Your ancestor would never have spoken to me – or any of us – like that. I'd like to see you brought down to earth. You'll have rivals, sure enough, in due season. Then perhaps you'll find brute strength is more than a match for conceit.'

'The only thing I shall find,' said Trey, 'is every foolhardy rival running from my lowered antlers, one by one. And I mean to be not only the leader of the deer herd but Lord of the Reserve. So you must stay in your corner of the Park, all of you. I want no interference with my herd's grazing. The most succulent shoots, the sweetest grasses, the tenderest leaves are ours alone. Smaller creatures must make do with our leavings. Otherwise you'll be permitted here no longer. So tell your friends the rabbits and hares and suchlike to keep clear. You've all had the run of our Reserve for too long. And what have you brought us in return? Nothing but mayhem: a succession of dangers in what was once a place of tranquillity. You Farthing Wood animals are our Bad Luck.' With that he turned on his heel and walked away with a distinct swagger.

The friends were speechless. They could find no answer to Trey's accusation. At last Vixen murmured, somewhat defensively, 'I'm sure the rest of the herd don't see us that way.'

'Of course they don't!' Weasel exclaimed vehemently. ' "Bad Luck" indeed.'

Fox said: 'We're going to have trouble with that animal. I know it. "Lord of the Reserve",' he quoted. 'A rather premature claim, I feel, but it gives us all an indication of his intentions. I don't know what he meant about dangers and mayhem, do you?' He appealed to his companions.

Badger surprised them. 'I have an inkling,' he admitted. 'It's something that's been in my mind from time to time.'

'What, trouble that we've brought to the Park?' Weasel demanded angrily.

'No, no, Weasel, of course not,' Badger pacified him. 'It'd be more true to say that trouble seems to have followed us.'

Fox looked serious. 'Go on, old friend,' he urged. 'Let's hear your thoughts.'

'Well, I've often considered the irony of our lives here,' Badger resumed. 'Maybe you have too. After all, we journeyed here over hostile terrain, at great risk to ourselves the whole way, believing we were coming to a safe haven in the Nature Reserve. All along, during that arduous journey, it was that thought that buoyed us up. Yet it's been far from a safe haven. The first winter after we arrived we nearly starved to death. Then there were the poachers shooting at all and sundry, but particularly the deer. So Trey was right about *that* danger. Somehow we struggled through that winter to find ourselves the following spring involved in a war with other inhabitants of the Park led by Scarface. To cap it all, last summer a huge hunting animal prowls the Park, picking off its victims at will without any of us being able to mount any resistance to it. If we'd wanted a life of constant adventure and hardship we couldn't have chosen a better site! Quite honestly, I sometimes wonder if it wasn't more peaceful in Farthing Wood.'

'There's a lot of truth in what you say,' Fox avowed. 'The important thing though, surely, is that we've survived all of it. And the reason for that is that we've pulled together; helped one another. It wasn't like that in Farthing Wood. We were all following our own paths. The Farthing Wood animals were brought together by our journey in a unique way. We had one common aim. And that spirit has continued ever since. For that alone we should rejoice we came to White Deer Park. And I think some of our beliefs have been passed on to our descendants. The dangers that have occurred here would have occurred anywhere else. There's no such thing as a sanctuary entirely free of danger for wild creatures. Not anywhere.'

'The stag Trey seems to think otherwise,' Weasel observed.

'He's blaming us for a set of coincidences,' Fox answered. 'We weren't responsible for inviting danger here. The poaching men with their guns came because this is a Deer Park, not because the animals of Farthing Wood chose to take up residence here.'

'The thing is: what do we do about his threat?' Weasel asked. '*I* don't intend to be intimidated. I'll go on roaming the whole area of the Reserve. Why should we be holed up here? It'd be like the Great Cat's thraldom all over again.'

'It won't make any difference to me,' Badger said. 'I hardly venture further from my set than the nearest meal. Unless I need to see you dear friends. But even that I find taxing these days. My sight's so bad. . . .'

'Yes, we know,' Weasel cut in before Badger developed the theme. 'But I really don't think the threat was aimed at an old creature such as yourself.'

'We'll continue to live our lives as we choose to,' Fox said resolutely. 'Trey's a powerful beast and could be a formidable adversary. But his words may all be bluster. His apparent dominance of the herd may have gone to his head.'

'What of the smaller animals?' Vixen prompted. 'He mentioned the rabbits and hares.'

'We'll warn Leveret to be cautious and to spread the word,' Fox answered. 'But we'll call Trey's bluff.'

'We've been diverted, haven't we?' Vixen reminded them. 'We never did decide what to do about Tawny Owl.'

'Yes, we did,' Weasel contradicted. 'Wait for him to return. *That's* what we'll do. I bet he'd love to think he's put us all in a pet by his absence.'

'Perhaps Whistler will sight him somewhere,' Fox said. 'He's such a silly old owl sometimes.' He sighed. 'But Friendly *must* reprimand the youngsters. They look up to him.'

There was nothing more to discuss and the friends parted.

Over on the other side of the Park, Leveret, the young hare, was munching the juiciest stalks he could find, oblivious of the altercation with Trey. Every so often he raised himself on his hind legs amongst the tall grasses to scan his surroundings. His prominent eyes and sensitive ears were invaluable in detecting the slightest hint of an alarm. His speed, like that of his father, the Farthing Wood Hare, was legendary. Nothing in the Park could catch him, not even the deer. Not that they tried to do so. Prior to the old White Stag's death, the deer herd had lived equably with its neighbours. And it might have been because of this that Leveret was not quite so alert all of the time as he would have been outside the Reserve.

The grasses and vegetation, generally, were particularly lush that year in the Park, thanks to the long rainy spell. So there was more than enough for everyone. The insect population thrived and there was a glut of caterpillars and grubs. The birds found food easily for their nestlings and the Park's inhabitants enjoyed a period of plenty. Trey, however, was not content with this. He wanted to be acknowledged by all as the paramount being of the Reserve's animal kingdom. He therefore lost no opportunity to enforce this idea. Whenever he could make his presence felt he did so in some way, sometimes bullying, sometimes threatening. The animals resented this but there was nothing they could do about it except long for the stags' rutting season.

There came a day when, because of his familiarity with the deer and his belief in their inoffensiveness, Leveret was, quite literally, caught napping. He had made his couch in the softest, greenest area of grassland and, since he hadn't sought out his Farthing Wood comrades recently, he was quite unaware of the risks he was running as he lay amongst that choice verdure.

The sun was warm on his back, the air balmy; he slumbered peacefully. But a movement, a rustle of the grass and Leveret was instinctively awake. He opened his eyes. A huge white head bearing massive antlers confronted him. Leveret at first wasn't disturbed. Just another member of the deer herd, he thought. Then he noticed the stag's expression. It was not a friendly one.

Trey lowered his head and he scraped the ground with a front hoof as he looked at the hare. He looked like a bull about to charge. Leveret didn't wait to find out. He leapt up and bounded through the grasses. Trey galloped after him. He was in an ugly mood. This animal had ignored his ruling. He meant to punish him. The hare must be made an example to deter others. The stag crashed through the grassland area, flattening the succulent stalks he was so determined to save for the herd's sole enjoyment. Fleet of foot as Trey was, Leveret's elastic bounds left the deer farther and farther behind. The hare's constantly veering course was impossible to follow for long. At last, Trey pulled up. He tossed his head, half in frustration, half in bewilderment at Leveret's pace. But he was content that he had driven home his lesson. He didn't think Leveret would be back.

Trey was correct in his assumption. Leveret had been alarmed and frightened. He kept running and leaping long after the grassland was well behind him. He was a highly strung animal and so intent on flight that he almost collided with Friendly, Fox and Vixen's son, who was lapping listlessly from a puddle.

'Hey! Slow down! What's the hurry?' Friendly called out, cheerfully. 'It's too hot for racing.'

The well-known tones of the affectionate animal's voice halted Leveret's career. He turned, relieved to find a companion.

'Whatever's the matter?' Friendly asked. 'You look badly scared.'

Leveret brought his breath and racing heart under control before he attempted to answer. 'There's a mad creature amongst the deer herd,' he explained. He was still distressed. 'He *attacked* me. Charged at me, the great brute, while I was sleeping. A small animal like me! Without a word of warning. If it's some sort of stupid game. . . .'

Friendly recognized the culprit at once. 'Oh, you've encountered Trey, have you? The mighty new Lord of the Reserve!' He sounded contemptuous. 'No, Leveret, this is no game. Haven't you heard? This stag has set himself up as the successor to his great ancestor. Only he's not satisfied with dominating the deer herd. He wants all of us to pay him homage.'

'But – but – a deer?' Leveret spluttered. 'I thought we had nothing to fear from any of them. They've been our friends – allies even – in the old days.'

'Well, these are new days, Leveret. The old order, you see, has passed. And it seems we're to accept it – or go.'

5

Owl's Progress

Tawny Owl skimmed over the motorway to the open countryside again. Quietness enveloped him. Soon he felt hungry once more. He caught what he needed and ate, comfortably lodged in the fork of a tree. He was quite alone and he was beginning to enjoy it. He thought for a moment about his companions in White Deer Park but then quickly dismissed them from his mind. He was relishing his solitude, away from Weasel's carping comments and the young foxes' teasing that he had endured for too long. He looked forward to reaching his destination, to re-visiting the old haunts and, above all, to the awe in which he would be held as the only Farthing Wood creature to have dared to journey back. Just let those young foxes hear his story! They'd soon change their tune, especially when he arrived on the scene with the missing female they had loved to joke about.

Tawny Owl rested only briefly after eating. He was eager to press on. He felt fresh and full of energy. He flitted noiselessly through the moonlit summer night over the fox-hunting terrain where Vixen had so nearly lost her life. By dawn he was within sight of the river. An ancient hollow oak beckoned him to roost. He fluttered down and settled himself inside.

A short distance outside White Deer Park, Whistler was dutifully beginning his search for the errant Owl.

The next evening Tawny Owl crossed the river. Memories flooded back once again of Fox's accident in the water when he had been carried away downstream, away from his friends. But all that was ancient history. With the river behind him Owl travelled more circumspectly. He wasn't so sure of recognizing the route. Until he reached Farthing Wood itself, there would be no more prominent landmarks. However he *felt* his direction was correct. His instincts seemed to guide him. What didn't ring quite true was the ease with which he was travelling. Of course the journey of the animals from Farthing Wood to the Nature Reserve had been infinitely more difficult for land-travelling creatures, especially when the whole party had agreed to adapt its pace to accommodate the smallest representatives such as Toad, who had actively been demonstrating the route part of the time, and voles and fieldmice: tiny creatures who could only go in short stages. Up in the air, problems and barriers to progress that had seemed almost insurmountable on that journey, were as nothing.

The speed with which Tawny Owl covered the

distance surprised him more than anything. The long odyssey which he and his companions had undergone before had seemed at times as if it would never end. Now, alone, and flying at his own pace, it appeared that his journey would be completed in a matter of days. When he picked out from the air a certain copse whose shape was remarkably familiar, Tawny Owl felt he was indeed getting close. The copse was chiefly memorable for its rookery.

Tawny Owl glided in under cover of darkness and holed up in a dead elm. He meant to surprise the rooks by his presence when they awoke in the morning. Some of them would be bound to recognize him. As he had eaten on the way he allowed himself a semi-doze as he watched, fitfully, the gleaming stars begin to pale. But his doze was rudely interrupted.

The rooks began to call harshly and urgently at the first glimmer of daylight. They were not calls proclaiming territory or ownership but calls of alarm and warning. Still perched on their untidy nests of twigs they passed angry calls from one to another that echoed back and forth in the tree tops. Tawny Owl had been spied and he was not welcome. There were young still in the nests.

Owl clung uncertainly to the grey barkless branch of the stricken tree. He wasn't sure what to do. He supposed, in this murky light, he must seem to the rooks to be just another threatening predator. He decided to wait until the full light of day would reveal to them who it was who had come amongst them. The light grew but there was no lessening of the clamour. Indeed the calls became more raucous, more strident.

Eventually some of the angry birds left their nests and flew close to Owl in a mobbing action. They jeered at him, calling him offensive names such as murderer, robber and vandal. Owl was most put out. He tried to recognize amongst these rooks one who would have known him in the past. He and the Farthing Wood animals had spent a while in their copse and had been warmly welcomed by their hosts as heroes. But as he searched the faces with their long pointed beaks and glittering eyes he could see no hint of dawning friendliness in any of them. And they all looked the same. He couldn't have told them apart. Purple-black plumage with an iridescent sheen that reflected the early rays of the sun. Sharp, malevolent features. They span around him, deliberately malicious, hoping to rid their copse of his presence by their unremitting pressure.

'What, isn't there one of you who knows me?' Tawny Owl called out in bewilderment. 'Not one of you who knows the name of Farthing Wood?'

'Never heard of it.'

'No such place.'

'Farthing Wood? This is Rookery Copse. No other stand of woodland round here.'

Their voices screeched at him. They knew nothing of his past.

'Fox, Badger, Toad, Kestrel, Tawny Owl,' the besieged bird cried, desperately attempting to call himself to mind. 'We travelled here. Before. You made us welcome.'

'Welcome? Welcome? *They'd* be welcome, I don't think,' one screeched back.

'No friends of ours.'

'None of them!'

'But you must remember,' Tawny Owl almost pleaded. 'If not you, then your elders. Where are they?'

'What do you want with them? Leave them alone.'

'Get away from our copse!'

'Don't you see?' Tawny Owl wheedled. 'The older birds will recognize me. I was here before.'

They didn't want to hear. An owl was an enemy when young were in the nests. That's all they knew. They flew at him, buffeting him with their wings. They hoped to topple him from his perch. When that didn't work, the braver among them began aiming their beaks at him, stabbing downwards as they fluttered close. Tawny Owl gave ground. It was futile to resist any longer. Times were changed. There was no camaraderie to be looked for here. He flapped away from his branch and even then the rooks chased him, egged on by their success. They screamed their delight at his defeat, trying to make his retreat as humiliating as they could. The disappointed owl found himself putting on speed to rid himself of their deafening cries. At last they fell back, satisfied they had defended their nest sites with great daring.

Tawny Owl flew on dispiritedly. Now solitude didn't seem so attractive. He longed for some creature, animal or bird, to show him a jot of fellow feeling. He had lived for so long among friends he had forgotten what life was like in the usually hostile environment of nature. He thought of Bold, Fox's and Vixen's cub, who must have encountered just the same suspicion and enmity during his bid for independence away from the influence of his father. And what a hard time *he* had had of it. Owl put the thought behind him. The rooks' unpleasantness had tired him out, even frightened him a little. He needed to sleep and, first of all, to compose himself.

Without realizing it, Tawny Owl was flying back on himself, back in the direction from which he'd come to the copse. His one thought was to find a suitable perch. He didn't enjoy daylight very much except as a time to rest. He found a solitary hawthorn whose branches were almost impenetrable. Inside the thick canopy of greenery he could at last relax. The day passed him by and the few small songbirds who alighted on the thorn soon left again when they saw an owl hiding in its midst.

As usual Tawny Owl roused at dusk. He got himself airborne and immediately felt that he had been thrown off course. But he wanted to avoid the rookery at all costs, so he could not use the copse as a guide again. What he could do, however, was to use the noise of the rooks themselves as a clue. He knew that at dusk there was always a sort of concert of cawing as the birds settled themselves for the night. So he circled for a while until he picked up their sound. Congratulating himself on this brainwave, Tawny Owl flew towards the sound without ever getting too close to give himself trouble. The noise reached a crescendo and then gradually faded behind him and so Owl knew he had passed Rookery Copse and should soon be on the right track again. But it didn't prove as simple as that. He couldn't seem to get his bearings. In his mind he pictured an orchard, a marsh, a road and rows of houses. That was the way back if things were still as they had been before, but he found he couldn't locate any of these features. Then Tawny Owl berated himself for his stupidity. Of course things weren't the same as before. How could they be? All that time ago. . . .

He broke off his efforts at navigation to hunt. He decided he must then seek guidance. He caught himself a rat that was trying to raid a squirrels' drey. As he disposed of his prey it occurred to him that the squirrels might be able to help. He finished his meal. Then he flew back to the birch tree where the drey was sited. The tree grew alongside a couple of young oaks in a patch of undergrowth.

The squirrels at first scolded Tawny Owl for coming too close, just as they tried to warn off any predator from the youngsters they had to protect. But when the bird pointed out the good turn he had done them they quietened down and listened.

'Do you know a place called Farthing Wood?' Owl asked. 'It's not far from here.'

'Wood? There's no wood anywhere around here,' the mother squirrel replied. '*We'd* be living there if there were. . . .'

Tawny Owl sighed. The same reaction as from the rooks. 'But you must have heard of it, at least,' he suggested. 'There was woodland around here once. I used to live in it.'

'Doubtless there was,' the male squirrel conceded. 'But what's the use of asking us about a place that doesn't exist?'

'I only wanted to know if you'd heard the name,' Tawny Owl said. He decided he wouldn't tell them he was attempting to travel to a wood that they believed was non-existent.

The squirrels looked at each other. 'I've heard the name,' said the female. 'But not for a long time. I seem to recall there was some sort of tale attached to it.'

Tawny Owl perked up considerably. 'Yes, there was,' he said eagerly. 'I – I mean,' he added quickly, 'that I believe the tale would have been about how the inhabitants of the Wood had to leave it. Isn't that so?'

'Yes. Yes, that's it,' the squirrel answered. 'The wildlife all around here used to talk about them. Many of the older ones saw them pass. But they never knew for sure what happened to them.'

Tawny Owl was burning to tell the squirrels. But he fought the inclination down in order to pursue his main objective. With bated breath he asked: 'In which direction would Farthing Wood have been?'

The squirrels flicked their bushy tails as they pondered. 'It must have been,' the father squirrel said slowly, 'where the human dwellings have spread.'

'Yes, yes!' cried Tawny Owl. 'The men built over it, didn't they?' He was becoming excited.

'Well, if you know that, you must know where it was,' the squirrel rejoined in a puzzled way.

'But I haven't seen any human dwellings,' Tawny Owl spluttered. This was so exasperating!

'You can't have been over the hill then,' the female squirrel told him. 'They're all around there. Now then, if you have nothing further to bother us with, we'll go back to our rest.'

'Nothing more, nothing more,' Tawny Owl called. He was already in the air.

'Thank you again for the rat-killing,' the father squirrel cried generously. 'We really are –'

But Tawny Owl was away. He saw where the land began to rise and followed it directly. At the top of the little hill he looked over and there, below, were the bright lights of human habitations and streets.

'So!' he breathed to himself. 'I'm home.'

But he wasn't. Not quite.

6

Water Rights

Whistler the heron abandoned his search when it was obvious that Tawny Owl had left the immediate environs of White Deer Park. 'I'll keep a look-out for him from time to time,' he told himself. 'But I can't go combing the entire countryside.' On his return he flew along the length of the stream and was distressed at what he found there. At intervals there were dead bodies of small creatures, mainly watervoles, lying either on the banks or at the edge of the water, bobbing on the ripples. There was a pair of coots who had suffered the same fate. Their deserted nest amongst some reeds had two fairly well-grown, but lifeless, youngsters in it.

'This is terrible,' Whistler said. 'I wonder what's caused this?'

He flew up and down, peering at the water for any sign that would give an explanation. But he could see nothing unusual. Later he noticed Adder and Sinuous sunning themselves in their favourite spot. These days they were always together. Whistler wasn't sure if he should disturb them but he guessed Adder had seen him so he decided in the end to fly over.

'Have you found anything?' Adder enquired without much interest. He knew Whistler had been looking for Tawny Owl.

Whistler mistook him. 'Have you seen them too?' he asked, referring to the dead creatures.

Adder looked at him curiously. 'Them?' he repeated. 'You don't mean to say. . . .' He was picturing Tawny Owl flying back in triumph with his consort.

'Bodies,' Whistler said. 'By the stream. A number of them.'

'I told you so,' Sinuous remarked to her companion.

Whistler waited politely for an explanation.

'She thinks the place has become one of menace,' the snake said. 'Ever since the Great Stag pegged out there.' He was never one to show overmuch respect.

'I'm not the only one who thinks so. Most of you are steering well clear of the area,' Sinuous said to the heron.

'Yes. Except those who live on its fringes,' he said. 'But now it seems they're at risk. I don't know how long those bodies have been there. *I* haven't been near the stream for a long while.'

Adder ventured a quip. 'When Whistler the heron ceases to patrol the stream's banks there's something fishy going on.'

Whistler chuckled. 'That's just it, Adder. There *are* no fish.'

Now Adder was serious. He had remembered Toad. 'Best to leave the place well alone,' he said. 'I wish I'd seen Toad. He sometimes swims there.'

Whistler was surprised at his words. The snake didn't often commit himself to pangs of anxiety. 'The land is damp and humid enough for him at present, I hope,' said the heron. 'And he does spend a lot of time with his friends the frogs in the Pond, I believe?'

'He's a great traveller, our Toad,' said Adder. 'Nobody knows that better than I. There's no knowing where he might turn up.'

'He must look out for himself then, mustn't he?' Sinuous observed primly. She was well aware of the little clique of Farthing Wood animals who continued to concern themselves about each other. The idea bored her as she wasn't party to it.

'I think I'll look out for him as well,' Adder lisped, 'if you've no objection?'

Toad was actually nowhere in the vicinity of the stream. He was enjoying the bonanza of grubs, worms and insects that was all around him. He was a very plump Toad indeed. Swimming wasn't on his mind very much and, in common with his friends, he hadn't much desire at present to visit the stream. The Edible Frogs around the Pond didn't see much of him either. However, they did see a lot of other creatures. Many of the Park's inhabitants were using the Pond as their chief drinking place now. Amongst these were the Deer themselves as well as those members of the g Wood community who ranged most widely, such as the younger foxes. So it was only a matter of time before one of them was confronted by Trey.

The young fox Plucky, still barely more than a cub, had his grandfather Bold's liking for roaming far afield. As soon as he was big enough he began to acquaint himself with every corner of the Nature Reserve. It happened one day he was drinking at the Pond when Trey arrived. Trey was suspicious. He knew there were no fox-holes anywhere near the Pond.

'What quarter of the Park do you come from?' Trey demanded.

'None in particular,' Plucky answered him coolly.

'This Pond is the deer herd's drinking place,' Trey announced.

'Yes, it's very convenient, isn't it?' Plucky remarked. 'I believe a lot of animals use it.'

'Do they indeed? We'll see about that,' the stag responded. 'The deer herd needs to have a constant supply of the freshest water. This Pond was always intended as our water-hole. So I'm reserving it for our exclusive use.'

Plucky looked at him in amazement. 'But, surely, it's big enough for every creature to use who wants to?' he questioned.

'Maybe not if we should have a long dry spell,' Trey replied. 'Anyway, you smaller animals can make do with any odd puddle. You don't need the quantity of water a fully-grown deer needs. And there are many of us.'

Plucky knew about the Great Stag. 'If what you say is true, why did your father drink at the stream?'

'He was a creature of habit,' Trey answered. 'He

preferred to drink from running water. And he wasn't my father. Our relationship was very distant.'

'Grandfather perhaps? You resemble him a good deal.'

'No. I'm nothing like him – as you'll find out.' Trey sounded angry and threatening. 'He was always too tolerant of lesser creatures,' he added scornfully.

Plucky was in no way abashed. He simply stared back at the beast, then finished quenching his thirst. As he ambled away the stag called after him: 'Remember what I've said.'

Plucky did. And he remembered to tell all his relatives, too. The seniors, Fox and Vixen, were already incensed by the incident with Leveret. This was the last straw.

'We won't take this lying down,' Fox said grimly. 'Who does this creature think he is, dictating to us?'

'He'll put himself in a false position,' Vixen commented. 'He doesn't speak for the rest of the herd. The hinds are as friendly as ever.'

'He's talking poppycock,' Fox declared. 'He must have a small mind if he thinks he can push ideas like this on to us. We must all meet and work out our course of action. Plucky, I want you to take the word round. The Hollow. Dusk tomorrow.'

The next night the Farthing Wood elders assembled in their traditional meeting place. Plucky had gathered them all. He knew just where to find each one. Badger, Weasel, Whistler, Adder and Toad had obeyed the summons. Leveret and Mossy were there, as were Fox and Vixen's offspring Friendly and Charmer together with others of their relatives. Plucky was the youngest animal present. The fox clan was the most numerous. They were also the most daring and skilful of the animals. But of the original band of travellers, only Tawny Owl was absent.

'We all know the situation,' Fox began. 'The question is, what are we going to do about it?'

'Just as you said before, Fox,' Weasel replied. 'Call Trey's bluff. What can he do? He can't deal with all of us. We're too many and too scattered.'

'I've seen what he can do,' Leveret spoke up. 'He'll wreak his will on the more vulnerable of us.'

'We can't allow that,' said Friendly. 'He'll find he's got too many enemies to handle.'

'What could you do, Friendly?' asked his mate Russet. 'Attack him?'

'No, he's too powerful,' Friendly admitted. 'But we can outwit him. My father is the shrewdest, wiliest animal in the Park. He's more than a match for the wits of Trey.'

'Thank you, Friendly,' said Fox. 'One plan has occurred to me and it's one that wouldn't actually involve any of us. Not directly, anyhow.' Every eye was on him expectantly. 'We need a champion,' he announced.

'A – champion?' Toad echoed. 'A champion what?'

'A champion fool, I should think,' drawled Adder, 'if he tries to meddle with that creature.'

'You don't understand, Adder,' said Fox. 'I'm not talking about one of us.'

'Do I perceive, Fox, that your thoughts lie amongst

the other stags in the herd?' Whistler asked in his old-fashioned way.

'Exactly that. You've guessed it, old friend. We need to find someone who'll challenge him.'

'How do we do that?' Badger wanted to know. 'Trey already seems to have cowed them all into submission.'

'No, no, Badger, not really,' Fox answered. 'He only assumes he has. They're content to leave him well alone at the moment. But it won't be like that at the rut. Don't you remember how the Great Stag himself had to fight to keep command at those times?'

'Do you have anyone in mind as our ch-champion?' Mossy stammered. He was a little overawed by all the bigger animals present.

'Not yet,' Fox replied. 'But I mean to do a bit of scouting around.'

'Sort of – look over the material?' joked Toad.

'Sort of.' Fox grinned. 'It may be I can drop a hint here and there.' He put his head on one side. 'Perhaps,' he considered, 'we can all help. Stir a few of them up. You know, set them on. We might have quite a few champions at the end of it all.'

'I still think he could defeat all comers,' Leveret said pessimistically. He laid his long ears flat against his back. 'He's a mighty figure.'

'I think you're right,' agreed Fox, 'if it were to be one by one. But what if they should take him on together?'

'Deer never fight like that,' Vixen reasoned. 'We can't change their nature, my dearest.'

There was a long silence. Then Fox said: 'I obviously need to do some more thinking. But in the meantime a word in an ear here and there. . . .'

'They may listen to you foxes,' said Adder, 'but what message is so important that these stags are likely to give attention to a toad or a snake or a mole?' He looked at Mossy so disdainfully that the little animal quailed, not because he was a coward – he was far from that – but because he felt so insignificant.

'Well, that's straightforward enough,' Fox answered. 'You simply tell them that Trey intends to drive all rivals from the Park.'

7

Farthinghurst

Tawny Owl was bewildered. There were just so many buildings! They were all big and frightening and their myriad lights dazzled him. It was a long time since he had come so close to a mass of human dwellings and now he began to ask himself why he had come here. His original reason for leaving White Deer Park was quite different to the one that had spurred him on to re-visit his old home and birthplace. He hadn't found that suitable companion during his flight across country. And now, as he viewed from the wing this man-built sprawl, he knew there was certainly no likelihood of any owl being found in its alien landscape.

'Can that really be where Farthing Wood once flourished?' he murmured to himself. 'Or have I, after all, taken the wrong direction?'

No, the squirrels had been quite specific. Well, there was no use his expecting to recognize any feature in that conglomeration. Certainly not by night when the artificial lights blazed so confusingly.

'I may take a close look in the daylight,' Tawny Owl said. 'It's just possible there's something down there that'll trigger a reaction in my poor old brain. I can't turn tail now without making sure.'

He needed to find somewhere to roost. But where? He didn't want to go back to the few trees where the squirrels had built their drey. He examined the nearest gardens below. There were trees in them – for ornamentation – but such puny, immature saplings could only provide cover and support for the smallest of birds. The buildings were mostly in tall blocks and these were flat-roofed so there was no chance of Owl tucking himself away in a sheltered corner or in the lee of a chimney-stack. The smaller buildings had sloping roofs. There was nothing to perch on amongst those. But he did notice one of them had a gaping and invitingly dark entrance hole, like an open mouth, high up on one side of its roof. There were no lights there. All the lights in that house were much lower down and well away from the hole which left it in undisturbed darkness and privacy. Tawny Owl was sorely tempted to hide himself in there until dawn. But could he be sure it was quite safe?

He flew down closer to the building. It certainly seemed quiet enough. Following the slope of the roof he fluttered awkwardly until he was able to perch at the opening itself. Although he didn't know it his talons were resting on the window-ledge of an open attic window. He shuffled along it and peered inside. His feet made scuffling noises but they didn't seem to have caused any disturbance. He waited awhile. The room was quiet and bare except for a long wall of shelving filled with books. Tawny Owl saw the racks as potential perching posts. After a few moments he entered the room and fluttered across to its far end. On the top shelf of the book racks there was a perfect gap between two rows of volumes which was just wide enough for Owl to wedge himself comfortably in. He settled himself but remained wakeful.

For some time noises were detectable underneath this converted loft – human noises. But to Tawny Owl they seemed distant enough to be overlooked. Eventually they ceased. The night sky grew darker as he watched. All over the estate lights were being switched off as the human community retired to rest. The bird waited patiently for dawn.

As the night wore on a breeze began to blow into the room. Half-awake, half-asleep, Tawny Owl shifted his feet and ruffled his feathers. The breeze stiffened. The open window began to swing gently to and fro. Tawny Owl couldn't foresee the danger. The wind strengthened steadily and, now blowing directly against the window, pushed it gradually back, closing the gap and thus the owl's escape route a fraction at a time. Tawny Owl recognized his danger all too late. As he hurled himself from the shelf in a frantic bid to squeeze through the narrowing outlet, a particularly strong gust finally slammed the window shut. Tawny Owl's head and wings were battered against the glass and he dropped to the floor stunned.

It was broad day when he recovered. He struggled to his feet and fluttered up to the inside sill. The window was fast closed. He looked out on a scene of alarming activity; alarming because it was human. Cars and other vehicles moved along the network of roads. People seemed to be everywhere – walking, standing, working in their gardens. Children and dogs were running about. Cats sunned themselves in patches of warmth, oblivious of everything including the watching owl, trapped in a garret.

What was he to do? He began to inspect the room. The first thing he noticed which had not been apparent in the pitch dark was that the loft door stood ajar. Was there some other way out for him? Noises in the lower part of the building reminded him that this door was also the way in to the roost he had so foolishly chosen, for any creature, human or otherwise, who lived underneath. He gulped nervously and sought his night perch, feeling more secure between the tightly-stacked books as if in some way they might protect him.

Time drifted past to the accompaniment of human sounds, inside and outside, which deterred the poor bird from making any rash movement. He was both hungry and thirsty. There was dust everywhere and Tawny Owl felt as if a quantity of it had lodged in his throat. Well, he couldn't stay there indefinitely. The window wasn't going to open of its own accord so he must try the other way. He needed to muster up some of that old Farthing Wood spirit: the spirit of adventure. Tawny Owl stretched himself and preened his feathers. He looked towards the door. He was trying to steel himself for action. The noise from beneath increased in volume. He sank back. After all, he told himself, there was no point in taking unnecessary risks. He would wait until the house grew quiet.

But it didn't grow quiet. In fact the bird soon became aware of something approaching his secret hidey-hole. There were footfalls – soft, cautious footfalls like those of a creature who might be exploring new territory. Tawny Owl kept his great eyes trained on the door. It was difficult for him to keep still as the regular pad – pad – pad of feet approached ever nearer. He tensed, ready for flight.

A black cat came into the room and paused, just inside the door. It raised one paw uncertainly and sniffed the air. Its head turned slowly to Tawny Owl's end of the room. It wasn't a large cat and the bird tried to tell himself it could pose no threat to an owl. But his efforts were unavailing. He was well and truly alarmed for the consequences if he should be discovered. He remained as still as he could, hoping he blended in with his incongruous surroundings. It was an absurd hope. The cat had sensed something was in the room and was systematically searching for it.

'Ah – there you are,' she said as her eyes alighted on the forlorn owl. 'I knew you were here somewhere.'

'I – I'm just leaving,' Tawny Owl hooted ineptly.

'I don't think you can,' the cat, who had noticed the window was closed, replied. 'How did you get in here?'

'Flew in – how do you think?' the bird blustered.

The cat sat down and regarded him coolly. 'You're not making much sense,' she said at length. 'How long have you been here?'

'Since the night. I meant to leave at dawn but –'

'You can't fly through glass,' the cat finished for him.

Tawny Owl was silent. Was the cat playing with him?

'You won't be able to stay here, you know,' the cat resumed. 'This isn't an aviary.'

'I don't want to stay here,' Tawny Owl declared. 'But how do I get out? Can you show me?'

The cat considered. 'I don't know about that,' she answered. 'You see, I'm supposed to be responsible for vermin. There was a problem with mice here. Up until recently. It took me quite a time to round them all up. But they're all gone now. I don't know if you'd be classed as vermin?'

Tawny Owl gaped at the implied insult and now he was angry. 'How dare you!' he screeched. 'Vermin indeed! I am an owl. I *hunt* vermin. I *eat* vermin. I – I –'

'All right,' the cat said smoothly. 'I get the message. You're not vermin. But I may still have to come after you.'

Tawny Owl's anger saved him. His temper was up. 'Try me!' he cried. He flexed his talons. His huge eyes glared at the cat's presumption. He was exasperated that he couldn't open his wings to their full span. That would have shaken the animal.

The black cat stared at the bird, in particular at his talons. She was weighing up her chances. She began to see that this was no ordinary bird.

'Sooty! Sooty!' a child's voice called from below. The cat's attention wavered. 'Sooty! Are you there?' The cat turned away. The child was mounting the stairs.

Tawny Owl heard these new footsteps in great alarm. He wanted nothing to do with humans. They were unpredictable and beyond a wild creature's understanding. He didn't know whether to stay put or make a dash for the open doorway. The cat had temporarily forgotten his existence as she waited for the child to appear.

'Soo – ty, Soo – ty,' the shrill voice chanted, ever louder as its owner neared the top stair. The cat miaowed, raising her black tail as she saw her seeker.

'There you are!' cried the child triumphantly. A little red-haired boy of about six years came into the room, stooping to give his pet a cuddle. The cat pushed herself against his legs affectionately and nuzzled his eager hands.

Tawny Owl guessed there was no threat to him here and decided it was his best opportunity for escape. He fluttered off the bookshelf, causing the startled boy to scream, and swooped over his head through the doorway, banking sharply to make the tight turn down the staircase. The bird had no idea where he was heading, but was intent on finding the first available opening to the outside world.

The boy's scream had already stirred the rest of the household. Now he was calling out in the utmost excitement from upstairs. 'Daddy, a bird! A bird in the loft!'

The father came running from below. Tawny Owl had skimmed down the first flight of stairs and reached the landing of the first storey. Bedroom doors were open here and Owl lunged for the first entrance he saw and flew straight for the window. A girl shrieked as his wings clipped her face as she sat at her dressing-table. Fooled by the gleamingly clean picture window which appeared to the bird to be open air, Tawny Owl almost crashed against the glass but managed to swerve at the last moment. The confined space of the bedroom was difficult to negotiate. The girl was adding her cries to the small boy's. It was enough to terrify any wild animal and now the father arrived on the scene, believing his children were being attacked. He saw the great bird and, instinctively protective, tried to knock it to the floor. Tawny Owl veered from right to left and back again to avoid the man's flailing arms. Surprisingly the girl came to his aid.

'Don't hit him, Dad, please,' she begged. 'He just wants to get out. Open the window!'

The man ran to the window. Now Tawny Owl had more room. He flapped through the door and continued along the landing. He ignored the other open doorways, having learnt his lesson. He came to another staircase and followed it down. Now he was in the hall. The front door was closed. He fluttered to the floor and tried to gain breath. His head was in a whirl. But the man and his children, together with the cat, were in hot pursuit. Tawny Owl didn't understand their intentions. He struggled on again into a room leading off to the right. It was full of furniture – fearsome obstacles for Owl. But what he saw ahead of him made his heart leap. An open window!

It was a small window – a fanlight – left on the latch. But he was determined to squeeze through it even if it should mean leaving some of his feathers. He reached the latch and perched on it. He saw the opening was even tighter than he had feared. As the family came into the room, all talking at the tops of their voices and pointing at him, Tawny Owl pushed his head outside.

The feel of the wind on his face, added to the din behind him, encouraged him onwards. His talons grappled the latch. He pushed and thrust his body through the gap. He felt the hard edges of the window gripping his sides, pinching him like a sort of vice. But he refused to give up. A little more discomfort and, with a final heave, he popped out of the window like a cork out of a bottle.

Instantly he soared upwards despite his throbbing sides, enjoying the supreme luxury of spreading his wings in the free fresh air; in unobstructed and limitless space. He looked around him as he rose higher in the air. Human faces pressed against the glass, watching his progress in admiration, almost in envy. Envy of the supreme freedom of the flight of a bird.

The man said: 'That's the first time an owl has been seen in Farthinghurst. You must remember this, children.'

'And he chose us to visit,' said the girl. 'Look, here are some of his feathers.'

Tawny Owl flew on. Hunger and thirst were forgotten as he flew over the houses, the blocks of flats, the shops. For he knew now that beneath him was what was once Farthing Wood. Its soil, its plants, its roots lay under this man-made wilderness of concrete and brick and metal. And he knew it was Farthing Wood because there was just one remnant of it still existing. The remnant was a tree: a solitary, isolated but massive beech. Tawny Owl had recognized it at once as its great sweeping branches beckoned to him like welcoming arms which longed to draw him into their lonely embrace. This great beech, which now straddled the boundaries of two identical plots on the estate and therefore belonged to nobody, was the very same beech which had served as a meeting-point for the animals of Farthing Wood as they had embarked on their hazardous journey. It was from beneath this very tree, that now enfolded Tawny Owl in its rich greenery, that their long trek had begun. And this was all that the industrious humans and their machines had allowed to stand of Farthing Wood.

8

Holly

The beech's generous cover hid Tawny Owl for the rest of the day. He didn't dare to venture forth again even to moisten his parched mouth. He waited. And he thought.

He thought of his carefree days in Farthing Wood before the humans had come, when he had been so much younger. He thought of the other creatures who had lived there who had become his travelling companions first and then his trusted friends. What feelings would they experience were they to join him at the Great Beech now? How their world had changed! Yet, oddly enough, Owl didn't feel sentimental about his old home. That life was too far back in the past. He found himself thinking more about White Deer Park. He was surprised at himself. And what surprised him most of all was that he actually felt homesick for it.

By twilight Tawny Owl had come to the conclusion

that he had made a mistake coming to this place. It was barren. Barren of hunting opportunities and barren of company. When he felt ready for it he would begin the flight back. In the meantime his ordeal in the house had exhausted him and he needed to get his strength back.

Under cover of darkness he sought water. A garden pond soon provided him with that. Food, however, would be a problem. Then he remembered what the black cat had said about mice. So there must be prey to be caught somewhere in the area. Of course, mice inside a house were no use to an owl. But mice got into human dwellings from outside and so in that case, thought Owl, there would be others to find.

'And if anyone can find mice,' he told himself again, '*I* can.' So he began to search the gardens; along the fence bottoms, around the sheds, under the hedges. And pretty soon he found them all right. And he also found he wasn't the only one hunting them. From time to time he caught a glimpse of another bird swooping in the darkness, never very close, always keeping its distance. And he heard the squeals of mice *he* hadn't caught, just a few garden plots away from where he was intent on his own quest.

Each time Tawny Owl made a kill he took it back to the beech and ate in seclusion on one of the broad grey branches. He wondered where the other hunter perched to eat. He didn't know that in between his visits to the tree the second bird was using it as well. Finally their trips coincided. Each was aware there was another occupant in a separate part of the tree. Tawny Owl wondered what sort of bird was sharing his roosting site. As it was a nocturnal hunter like himself he had every reason to suppose it was another owl. He was curious. But the other bird spoke first.

'How long have you been hunting this area?'

Tawny Owl swivelled round in excitement. The voice belonged to a female. 'That depends on how you look at it,' he answered.

'What do you mean?'

'It means that I know the area as well as any living creature and better than most,' he explained grandly. 'But I've been absent for a long while.'

'Then you can't know it as well as you think,' came the reply. 'The area has been steadily changing ever since I can remember.'

'You don't have to tell me,' Tawny Owl said, very much on his dignity. 'I know all about Farthing Wood, believe you me.'

'I believe you,' said the other owl. 'But do you know about Farthinghurst?'

'Farthinghurst?'

'Yes, that's the name of this area now. Farthing Wood is long gone.'

'I can see that!' Tawny Owl exclaimed irritably. 'But, did you know that we are now perching in a part of it?'

'Oh yes. I've known and used this tree for several seasons. I think it's always been here.'

'As long as the Wood itself. And now it's all that remains.'

The owl was intrigued. 'How do you know so much?'

'If you're a good listener, I've a long story to tell you. But for the moment, suffice to say that Farthing Wood was my home from the day I hatched. When its destruction was imminent I left. And now, as you see, I've returned.'

'I don't pretend to understand your reasons,' said the other owl, 'since your Wood has now disappeared.'

'Ah – that's another matter,' Tawny Owl told her. 'But what about you? Is this your permanent territory? Tell me about yourself.'

'Not much to tell.' The female owl fluttered to a closer branch. She was another Tawny. 'I was hatched on the fringes of the Wood amidst the roar of men's machinery. There was just a tiny patch of woodland then but, from what you say, I think it may once have been much larger. Most of my kin were killed or found other territories. I stayed around, though.'

'Why?'

'Simple. Abundant food. In my early days there was almost a plague of mice who came in from the countryside to raid the humans' buildings. They were attracted originally by a great barn where grain was stored. This was on the edge of the estate. From there they spread all over, getting into the humans' own dwelling-places. So there was never a shortage of prey for me. Of course, the humans got to work to eradicate my food supply. But they could never quite winkle out every last mouse. So I've hung on here. I compete with cats and others but I've never starved. I suppose I've been lazy in some ways.'

'Far from it,' Tawny Owl contended. 'It always makes sense to exploit a constant source of food. And where do you roost?'

'Well – right here, of course. Where else is there?'

'Here? But I was sheltering here myself during the day. I didn't realize. . . .'

'No reason why you should. I saw you, but you were, by all appearances, oblivious of everything.'

'I was exhausted,' Tawny Owl explained. Then he told her about his adventure in the loft.

'That was an error on your part, to go inside a man-dwelling,' the female owl asserted. 'I've learnt to steer well clear of them.'

'You're right, of course,' he agreed. 'But that was nothing compared to my previous adventures.'

'Oh? And when am I to have the privilege of hearing about them?'

'Any time you wish,' Tawny Owl promised. He was eager to impress. 'What do you call yourself?'

'I don't call myself anything,' she answered. 'And there's no-one else around to give me a name. At least,' she added, 'not until now. Perhaps you'd like to think of one for me?'

'Well, I – I don't know if I'm much good at that sort of thing,' he said awkwardly. 'But I'll try.'

'Do you have a name?'

'Yes. Tawny Owl,' he said.

'I can see that.' The female owl was amused. 'But what of your own individual name?'

'Well, that *is* it.' He rustled his wings. 'I've never needed another. My friends always called me that. I was the only owl in the party, you see.'

'Party?' she queried. 'No, I don't see.'

'I think I'd better tell you my story,' he said.

'I wish you would.'

So Tawny Owl related the story of the Animals of Farthing Wood and of their long journey to a new safe home. His companion was an avid listener. She was thrilled and awed by his descriptions of the adventures they had encountered on the way, so much so that she wasn't absolutely sure whether he might not be embellishing some of them. But he wasn't, of course. He didn't have any need of embellishments. She hardly spoke a word until he had finished. 'A thrilling tale indeed,' she said. 'And so you all made your homes in White Deer Park?'

'Yes, we did. And soon I shall return there.'

'Forgive me, but I don't understand why you ever left it?'

'Aha,' Tawny Owl returned. 'That's quite another story.'

The female owl didn't press him. She was beginning to feel drowsy. She said, 'It seems so strange for a bird to have mammals as his closest companions – and even a reptile, too. I never heard of such a thing.'

'They've been true comrades, all of them,' he said. He had got himself into quite an emotional state during the recounting of his story, even to the point of being prepared to forgive Weasel his teasing. 'Don't you ever get lonely?'

'I hadn't thought about it before,' she answered. 'But now I see the advantage of friends in times of difficulty.'

'I – er – could be a friend, you know,' Tawny Owl offered hopefully.

'Well, I think maybe you already are,' she replied. 'And so really I think you must give me a name.'

'Yes, yes, now let me think . . . I have it!' he cried suddenly. 'I shall call you Holly.'

'Holly! Why?'

'Because it's a good name for an owl,' he answered promptly. 'And besides – I can't think of anything else.'

She was not displeased. 'Holly, Holly,' she repeated, testing the name. 'Yes, I rather think I like it. It's nice to be called something.'

Tawny Owl was thoroughly pleased with himself. Now his thoughts took another turn and he felt glad he had come this far, after all. He hardly dared to hope that all his plans would be fulfilled. Yet Fate had brought him to this tree, the symbol of Farthing Wood, and here he had found Holly, its last survivor. There had to be some meaning to it all. His thoughts were interrupted.

'Where did you roost last?' she was asking.

'Here – on this very branch.'

'Then I shall join you there,' she said purposefully. And she flew over. 'We may as well start as we mean to go on, don't you think?' she added, perching by his side. 'Friends must stick together, mustn't they?'

9

A Rival in the Air

So the two birds roosted together in the beech tree during daylight. At night they hunted mice together. This became the pattern of Tawny Owl's new life and he had no complaints for the moment. He still intended to return to White Deer Park and, of course, he intended to take Holly along with him. But she seemed so content with her lot that he hesitated to broach the subject, fearing she might decline. In this he was quite wrong. Holly had of necessity lived a solitary life. Now she was enjoying the change and would not have wanted to be left alone again. She was a clever bird and also a little cunning. She knew Tawny Owl wanted her to stay with him; she guessed easily enough that he lacked a mate and she took this to be because of his age. From that it was simple enough to surmise that he would be keen to keep her and would therefore be willing to do her bidding. So she decided to make use of this situation. And, first of all, she would test his feelings towards her.

'I don't think you'll be going back to your Nature Reserve,' she remarked to him coyly one evening as they rested from hunting.

'I certainly shall,' he asserted.

'When will it be?'

Tawny Owl shuffled his feet. 'I – er – I'm not quite sure,' he answered.

'Why leave? Aren't you happy here?' Holly asked next.

'Up to a point, yes,' he had to say.

'We have an abundance of food, we have shelter, haven't we?'

'Yes, but you see, I don't feel this is my home any more. How could I? I belong in White Deer Park.'

'Then why did you come here?'

'I didn't plan to – at first,' he answered.

'What changed your mind?'

'Oh well, I'd already flown a considerable distance away from the Reserve and it occurred to me I might as well come a little further and see what the old place looked like. And, until recently, I wished I hadn't.'

Holly knew perfectly well what he was alluding to. But she pretended otherwise. 'I wonder why you changed your opinion?' she mused.

'Oh, you know,' he said gruffly.

'Do I?' she asked with feigned innocence.

'Well, I had hoped you understood,' Tawny Owl said. 'I mean, most creatures like company of a sort.'

'But weren't you telling me you had plenty of

company in the Park? Your friends the fox and the badger. . . .' She was making it difficult for him.

'Of course,' he said. He shifted up and down. Then he mumbled, 'But one always prefers company of one's own kind.'

'Ah. I see,' said Holly. 'How flattering,' she added softly. Then, 'How important is it to you?'

'Very,' he confessed.

'Then I ought to tell you something. You may lose my company.'

'How? Why?' Tawny Owl blustered.

'I think you may have a rival for it.'

'A rival? Oh, that's of no consequence. He'd soon quit the field when he saw I was around,' Tawny Owl told her self-importantly. He – the Farthing Wood Owl!

'You may be right, I can't tell,' Holly said. She wished to appear impartial. 'But – forgive me for saying it – he seems a much younger bird than yourself. I think I should warn you.'

Tawny Owl's self-esteem was rocked a little by this news. He wondered whether fame alone would be enough to ward off any challenge. And then, if the owl should be really young, would he have heard of the Owl from Farthing Wood? After all, Holly hadn't seemed aware of his status.

'Where have you seen this bird?' he asked cautiously.

Holly thought hard. The story was all invention. How could she make it seem convincing? 'Oh, I've seen him around for a long while,' she answered airily. 'He flits about in the distance, over the house-tops and along the hedge-plants. Sometimes he comes right by our roost and looks up inquisitively. He watches me, you know. I was aware of his presence before you arrived.'

'*I've* never seen him,' Tawny Owl declared. 'But I'll look out for him from now on!' He sounded determined. In fact he wasn't at all sure he believed her. Holly, however, was pleased with his reaction.

The next time they hunted together Tawny Owl really kept his eyes peeled for the slightest sign. He saw nothing large enough in the air to be an owl. When they were back on their perch he questioned his companion. Had she seen anything?

'Oh yes. He was around,' she told him with the greatest composure.

'But he couldn't have been!' Tawny Owl remonstrated. 'I looked everywhere.' He was becoming suspicious.

'You have to know where to look,' Holly pointed out. 'And besides, he's probably wary of you.'

This remark boosted Owl's ego. It was meant as a compliment and he took it as such. Holly's subtlety had dispelled his doubts for the time being. He didn't mention the other bird again but waited for her to do so. And she did.

Each night she pretended to have seen it, sometimes in one place, sometimes in another. And, according to her, this other male on occasion still flew close to the beech tree while they were resting.

'Not much of a rival, is he?' Tawny Owl remarked sarcastically. 'He never dares to show his face.'

Holly saw she might have miscalculated. She had to retrieve the situation. 'I'm so afraid he's just looking for his opportunity,' she said. 'When you're asleep, for instance. You always doze off long before I do.'

'Do I indeed?' Tawny Owl returned grumpily. He never liked to be reminded of his tendency to drowsiness. 'Well, I tell you what then. In future I'll stay awake and wait for him.'

For the next few days he did just that. He made a supreme effort to keep his eyes open although a full stomach always made him feel sleepy. He stared through the mass of branches until long after dawn when the beech gradually took on its colours of leaf green and silver grey.

'I saw nothing and nobody,' he kept telling her.

'I think he's waiting till your guard is down,' was Holly's answer. 'He's so clever.'

Tawny Owl was tiring of this game. He decided to bring it to a conclusion. 'Oh yes, he's clever all right,' he said. 'He's so clever at eluding me he's as good as invisible.'

'Oh, Tawny Owl,' responded Holly archly. 'Do you doubt me?'

Owl was sorely tempted to say so but refrained. 'No, no,' he lied. 'Why should I? But I mean to see off this interloper once and for all. So the next time you see him, you tell me straight away where he is and I'll get after him and drive him off.'

Holly was excited. 'Would you? Would you really?' she asked.

'Just see if I don't,' he answered grimly, but inwardly he smiled. He wondered how she would manage the affair.

That night Holly didn't see the elusive bird. Tawny

Owl's inward smile broadened. The next night and the night after that were the same. Owl was beside himself with glee. But Holly was deliberately lulling him into a state of unpreparedness. On the fourth night, as they skimmed together over the gardens searching for mice, he was on the point of remarking that his rival seemed to have given up when she suddenly startled him with cries of: 'There he is! There he is!'

Tawny Owl nearly plummeted to earth in his astonishment, but managed to correct his flight to save himself. 'Where?' he gasped breathlessly.

'There, look! Do you see where those new man-dwellings are being built?' She indicated by changing direction.

'Yes, I – I think I do.'

'He's skulking over there!' she screeched. Her cries were so convincingly raucous that for a moment Tawny Owl almost believed he could himself make out something in the distance. Did he see a fluttering figure?

'Quickly!' Holly urged him. 'He'll be gone.'

Now there was no choice for him. He had to fall in with her plan or appear cowardly. He flapped his wings hastily, increasing his speed, and zoomed towards his objective. Holly watched him with satisfaction.

Tawny Owl was really flying fast. He hoped that if a rival were around the bird would be frightened off by his purposefulness. But there was no rival around and Tawny Owl blundered straight into some almost invisible netting that flapped in the breeze, entangling himself and landing with a thump on a partially laid and unhardened concrete driveway that the netting had been erected to protect. As he struggled to free himself from the nylon mesh his talons and wings became daubed with gouts of thick wet cement mix. He got himself into the air. Now he knew very well there had been no other owl. He was furious with Holly for playing games with him. As yet he didn't realize the full extent of the plight he was in. He only knew his wing feathers were tacky and uncomfortable and that he couldn't move them as he wished. He felt strangely out of balance as if one side of his body was heavier than the other and it was most difficult for him to steer the course he wanted. He lumbered awkwardly back to Holly who had just pounced on a mouse.

'You can bring that back to the roost for *me*!' Tawny Owl cried imperiously. 'I've done your bidding and look at my reward.' He exhibited his cement-coated talons. 'I'll do no more hunting tonight – neither of mouse nor owl!' He bumbled his way to the beech in a sort of zigzag motion. He found it impossible to fly straight. He landed with extreme awkwardness, his plastered claws encumbering his ability to perch safely.

Holly obediently brought him her most recent kill. She thought he deserved it. She didn't understand his predicament yet and believed Tawny Owl was only grumpy because he had soiled his plumage when he fell.

'You and your stupid stories!' he berated her. 'There never was another owl, was there?'

Holly replied by meekly laying the dead mouse within his reach.

Tawny Owl was hungry and tore mouthfuls off the carcass so that he could continue his tirade in between swallowing. Usually he disposed of a mouse whole. 'I don't know what fun you've been having at my expense,' he snapped, 'but I can tell you it's over. No doubt you think there's no fool' – gulp – 'like an old fool but you'll find out that Tawny' – gulp – 'Owl from Farthing Wood is nobody's fool!'

'Oh, it's not a game,' said Holly. 'You've got me all wrong.' She looked at him with her huge round eyes. 'I only wanted to tell if you were in earnest about me and our keeping company.'

A shaft of brilliant moonlight penetrated the clouds and illuminated the entire tree. Now she saw the sorry state Tawny Owl was in. 'Oh, what a mess,' she commiserated with him. 'I'm so sorry you fell. I had no idea there was such a trap.'

'Neither had I,' Tawny Owl remarked ruefully. He was partially soothed by her words. 'I may as well admit it – I'm too old for such capers. For the time being you'll have to catch enough food for both of us. I feel as if I couldn't fly at present to save my life.'

'I'll go at once,' Holly said willingly. 'I owe you that much. You stay here and rest.'

Tawny Owl watched her disappear over the gardens. She was absent a long time. Once or twice he tried his wings but each time he nearly overbalanced because his encrusted talons prevented him from gripping the branch properly. When Holly finally did return, carrying three mice in her beak, Tawny Owl could hardly move at all. It was as though his wings were encased. He felt weighed down and almost rigid.

'I don't know what I've done to myself,' he blurted out. He sounded scared. 'I seem to have lost the use of my wings. I think I may never be able to fly again!'

10

The Tainted Stream

Since their meeting in the Hollow the Farthing Wood animals and their dependants had continued to visit the Pond when they needed to. However they were sensible about it and took pains to ensure first that Trey was not in the vicinity. Meanwhile they began seeking out some of the other stags. Fox's message was received with varying responses. Most of the stags were indignant at Trey's presumption.

'Drive me out of the Park? He wouldn't dare go that far,' said one.

'This Reserve is for all the deer, no matter whether one is stronger than another,' said a second.

Some of them were disbelieving. 'How do you know his intentions? He's made no such threat to me,' one questioned.

'Preposterous! The Warden would never allow it. He has to look after the entire herd,' remarked another.

Another saw the impossibility of it straight away. 'How could Trey do it with a fence all around the Park's perimeter?' he demanded.

There were others who were obviously intimidated already by Trey's commanding presence. 'I have no quarrel with him.' 'I'm no contender to be the Great Stag's heir. Trey won't bother with me.'

But all in all the animals succeeded in at least implanting the idea in the male deer's minds that one of their numbers had too low an opinion of his fellows. This naturally rankled and, slowly, a general resentment of Trey's air of superiority began to build up. Fox still hoped that when the time was ripe the haughty stag might find he had assumed too much.

The summer sun shone on the Park and dried out the puddles and pools that had lain so conveniently close to Badger's set since the rainy season earlier in the year. As the stream was still shunned by his friends, Badger realized that before long he too would have to make a trip to the Pond. It would be a laborious journey for the old creature. His sight was now very poor and his legs were stiff and often ached, especially when he tried to be too energetic. But he had to drink like everyone else and one evening he stood just inside his set entrance, sniffing the breezes and vainly attempting to detect a hint of approaching rain.

'It's no use,' he muttered to himself. 'I shall have to make a move. Everything around here's as dry as can be.' And he shuffled off in the direction of the Pond. He hadn't gone far when he halted abruptly. 'This is silly,' he said. 'The stream's much closer. How do we know there's anything wrong with it? I could go and look for myself anyway.' He didn't turn round at once. He was in two minds about it.

'Suppose I should find something wrong there?' he pondered. 'Then it would be even further for me to go across the Park to the Pond. It's a nuisance the stream's the opposite way. Oh dear, now what shall I do?'

In the end his own curiosity as well as comfort decided the issue. He headed for the stream. It was a close muggy evening and Badger was soon tired. He was glad when he could see the stream in the distance because by then he was very thirsty indeed. When he reached the nearest bank he stood and looked at the water for a long time. The stream was low and slow-moving but, apart from that, didn't appear to be any different from usual as far as Badger could make out.

'Of course my eyes aren't the best judges in the world,' he told himself. 'I'll just go down the bank and see if the water smells as it should.' He grunted as he stumbled down to the stream's edge. He sniffed carefully and methodically. His sensitive snout had lost none of its powers. He raised his striped head. He was still uncertain. There was nothing definite and yet. . . .

'I'll just go a little way along to see if anyone else is drinking,' he decided.

It wasn't long before he did indeed hear the sound of an animal drinking. It was a dainty quiet lapping, not at all like the noisy habit of a fox, for instance. He peered ahead but it was too dark for him to see what creature was there. He hurried on. He wanted to talk to any animal who might know something he didn't. But all at once the sounds of drinking ceased.

'Don't go!' Badger called. 'Whoever's there – please wait. I'd like to speak to you.'

There was silence. Badger didn't think the animal had moved off. He heard no noise of its departure. He guessed it was waiting to see him before deciding if it was safe to remain.

'It's only me – old Badger,' he reassured the animal. He shuffled on.

'All right, I'll wait,' the animal called back. It was obviously satisfied it was not in danger.

Badger could tell from the voice it was a rabbit's, but not one he knew well. The rabbit came into view. When it saw Badger it paused on the lip of the bank. Its body was taut, ready to spring away hastily if necessary. Badger came puffing up. 'You – you were drinking?' he enquired.

'Yes.'

'Notice anything strange about the water?'

'No.'

'No funny taste or – or – anything?'

'No.'

'Well that's a relief,' Badger sighed. 'It'll save me a lot of effort anyway.' He headed straight back to the water's edge and bent his head. He took a couple of laps.

'*He's* not around, is he?' the rabbit suddenly asked nervously.

Badger raised his head. 'Who's "he"?'

'The – the deer,' the rabbit answered. 'The massive one with antlers like oak branches.'

Badger was puzzled. 'No–o,' he said slowly. 'There's

no deer around here. Are you referring to the stag called Trey?'

'I don't know his name but – he's mean and aggressive. He drove me off.'

'Off what?' Badger asked.

'Off his territory, he would claim,' the rabbit replied. 'That's why I came here to drink. It's been so dry, hasn't it? I had to come here. I didn't want to. The others said it was a risk, but what was I to do? It's water, at least, even if it is . . . is. . . .' It didn't finish. Its voice died away.

Badger was alarmed. 'Is what?' he gasped.

'I don't know,' the rabbit said. 'There've been stories. Birds dying here and – and – I don't know what else.'

Badger guessed the situation now. 'You were prevented from drinking at the Pond. That's it, isn't it? So you came here?' His questions were urgent.

'Of course. I told you. I wouldn't have come here otherwise.'

'What about the others in your warren? They have to drink, don't they?'

'They were lucky. They got back from the Pond in time. I was the last. He – he was standing there like a sort of sentry as if he'd been waiting for me.' The rabbit coughed.

'What's the matter?' Badger snapped sharply. He was on edge.

'Nothing. I – I'm not sure,' said the rabbit. 'Just a sort of – tickle.'

'A tickle?'

'Yes. My – my throat feels sort of hot.'

'You'd better get back to your burrow,' Badger advised him.

'I will, but now I feel so dry again. I must have another drink.' The rabbit ran towards the stream.

'Don't!' Badger called. He was full of dread. But the rabbit was heedless in its desperation to get to the water. It drank deeply. Now Badger waited for something awful to happen. He was in a turmoil of expectation. The rabbit turned and ran up the bank, seemingly none the worse. It ran straight past Badger as if it had forgotten him entirely. Badger hastened after the animal. He wanted to keep it in sight.

The rabbit, of course, was far fleeter of foot. In no time at all it was lost from sight. Badger forced his aged body into a shambling run. He was desperate to see what would become of the rabbit. His weak eyes probed the darkness. For a while he saw no trace. He didn't even know if he had taken the right direction. But then, all at once, he knew he had. He glimpsed the rabbit ahead. The unfortunate creature had slowed almost to a halt and was staggering about uncertainly as if it had lost its sense of balance. Badger lumbered up, gasping hoarsely.

'What – what. . . .' he wheezed, but he was so short of breath he could manage no more.

The rabbit muttered: 'The burning, the burning . . . I – I'm –' It began to shake uncontrollably. It couldn't keep its feet. It toppled over and lay still. Its eyes stared up into Badger's face. It was dead.

Badger's sides heaved painfully. He stared back at the lifeless eyes in horror. Eventually he got his breathing under control. 'The stream's a killer,' he whispered to himself in the utmost dismay. 'I've drunk from it too. Oh, why was I so foolish? Better to have tired my legs out going to the Pond than this! What shall I do now?'

He tried to recall how much of the water he had drunk but he was in such a state of shock and anxiety he couldn't be sure. He only knew he was still extremely thirsty, as if he hadn't drunk at all. 'The rabbit had a raging thirst, too,' he wailed. He tried to calm himself but it was difficult. 'Pull yourself together. An old animal like me behaving so stupidly! I can't last for ever anyway. I was lucky to come through another winter,' he reasoned. Yet it was hard for him not to feel frightened.

'It may be too late,' he went on, 'but I must try to get to the Pond. If I drink some clean water it might . . . yes, yes, it might help.' He felt better now he had made the decision and he wasted no more time. With a last glance at the poor dead rabbit he trotted away. He could think only of filling himself up with untainted water. All thought of Trey, and why the rabbit had gone to the stream to begin with, had vanished from Badger's mind.

Several times on the way he stopped to regain his breath. He felt very alone and wished heartily for a friendly face to appear. But he saw no-one until he reached the Pond and then it wasn't someone who was friendly at all.

It was growing light by the time he got to the pondside. He pushed his way through the sedges and reeds and lowered his muzzle thankfully. He began to drink.

There was a sound of pounding hooves. 'Stop!' bellowed a deep voice.

Badger looked up. The stag Trey was galloping round the far side of the Pond towards him.

'You've no right to be here!' thundered Trey. 'This is not your area. I know where you come from.'

Badger was astounded. But his keen thirst overrode every other consideration and couldn't be denied. He bent again to lap.

Trey was infuriated. 'Do you defy me?' he boomed. He lowered his antlers threateningly.

'I'm an old animal. I have to drink where I can,' Badger reasoned.

'There are other places.'

'No. There aren't,' Badger answered. He was beginning to feel unwell. Why wouldn't the stag leave him alone?

'I know your area. The stream is closer for you,' Trey contended.

'The stream is tainted,' Badger growled. His discomfort made him bold.

Trey took in his words. 'What do you mean?' he asked more evenly.

'Didn't the Great Stag die there?' Badger cried irritably.

'He was old – like you,' Trey replied. 'His time had come.'

'A pity for us all,' Badger remarked. He was tired of bandying words with this domineering animal.

Unknown to the two of them a third animal had appeared on the scene and was watching them carefully. It was Plucky the young fox who was homeward bound for his earth. He crept closer without being noticed.

Trey bridled at Badger's remark. He thought he would teach this insolent old creature a lesson. As Badger tried once again to assuage his thirst, Trey cried: 'As you're so determined to have the water, perhaps I can help you reach it!' He directed his antlers at Badger's rump and prepared to butt him into the Pond.

Now Plucky guessed the stag's intention and, regardless of any danger to himself, ran up with fangs bared. As Trey ran forwards the young fox caught one of the deer's hind legs in his teeth and gave it a severe nip just above the ankle. Trey's headlong career towards Badger was obstructed but not altogether prevented. The full force behind his antlers was impaired, luckily for Badger. But the amiable old creature still received a considerable clout and he shot out towards the centre of the Pond. Now Trey pulled up and, as the startled Badger struggled to keep his head above water, the stag turned his attention to his attacker. His leg smarted painfully. He saw the youngster whose impudence was beyond belief.

'This time I'll make you pay!' roared Trey.

Plucky raced round the edge of the Pond with the stag on his tail. The fox feinted and changed direction like a hare, dashing this way and that. Trey's bulk was far less manoeuvrable. He couldn't catch the fox any more than he had Leveret and his anger was at boiling point. Plucky kept an eye on Badger in the water while he zipped this way and that. Badger was swimming gamely and was aiming for the opposite side. He had swum more than halfway across the Pond and the Edible Frogs who inhabited this spot most of the time were urging him on. Badger was so tired he was deaf to all their cries. Now Plucky began calling.

'Come on, Badger! Come over this way. There's a deserted set close by. He can't catch us!'

And Trey couldn't, try as he might. Plucky held him at bay, chasing this way and that and, eventually, the exhausted Badger, his bristly coat pouring water, pulled himself out of the Pond. He wanted only to collapse in a heap in a place of safety. His head was spinning, his throat irritated and his rump throbbed unmercifully but he kept going towards the hole in the ground. It was so close, so close. If only he could get inside it. But now Trey tried to head him off.

Plucky dashed up courageously and, dodging the stag's feet, jumped up to sink his teeth high up in Trey's thigh. Badger made his escape and bolted into the empty set. But even now he couldn't rest. He feared for the young fox. So he turned around in the tunnel and hauled himself back up to the entrance. Plucky was dancing about but now he had risked too much by coming in so close and Trey was aiming blows with his antlers to right and left. It seemed only a matter of time before one would catch him, with severe consequences to the young fox. Plucky's way to the entrance hole was barred by the stag and Badger could see that, despite his own fatigue, he must enter the fray. Trey's back was before Badger and the gallant old creature looked for a way to rescue the youngster whose bravery reminded him so much of his dear friend the Farthing Wood Fox. When the stag stepped back a pace Badger saw his chance and now he bit deeply into the leg that Plucky had already nipped earlier on. As Trey paused, registering this fresh outburst of pain, Plucky instantly made a dive for the hole and in the next second he and Badger were tumbling over each other in the safety of the tunnel.

Plucky scrambled to the nearest chamber inside the set and Badger crawled after him. He was entirely spent. Outside the set Trey bellowed his fury.

When he could muster up sufficient strength to speak, Badger said to Plucky: 'Once it's dark you must fetch the elders – the Farthing Wood Fox and Vixen.' He gasped agonizingly. 'Bring them here. And my other friends too. All you can find.' He gasped again. 'Tell them,' he panted, 'Badger's finished.'

11

The Animals Gather

For the whole of that day Plucky sheltered with Badger in the abandoned set. From time to time he went along the exit tunnel to see if Trey had gone. The stag hung around for a long while, hoping for revenge. In the end he realized he was achieving nothing and left with many threats of 'getting even' and 'teaching you not to try and thwart a royal stag' roared down the entrance hole.

Badger hardly uttered a word all day except in reply to Plucky's enquiries about his comfort. Every limb in Badger's body ached unbearably. His rump was sore from the blow of the stag's antlers. But, worst of all, his throat was hot and dry and he knew his drink at the stream might prove fatal. Indeed he expected to die. Every so often he was racked by a painful wheezing cough which was a constant reminder of the sufferings of the dead rabbit. Badger could think only of his need to survive through the hours of the coming night. It was imperative he give his warning to his friends. He willed himself to hold on.

At long last the late dusk began to descend. Plucky waited a little longer. He was frantic to leave, yet he could not afford the slightest risk. Under cover of darkness he bade farewell to Badger and went up to the entrance hole. He made a thorough check of the Pond's surroundings before actually setting off. There was no scent of deer on the air. He ran round the Pond and, keeping to the shadows as much as possible, made his way to Fox and Vixen's earth as swiftly as his young legs would carry him. There he related to them all that had happened. He knew nothing of the events at the stream.

'We must go to him at once,' Fox said. 'We won't wait for the others. Plucky, I leave it to you to tell them about Badger. Quickly now, explain to me where this set is.'

Plucky gave him the necessary directions.

'Come on, Vixen,' said Fox. 'I hope to goodness we'll be in time.'

The pair of foxes were silent as they picked their way across the Park. They were both deeply worried by Plucky's message. Fox himself, of all creatures, was closest to Badger. Their association and friendship went back such a long way that Fox simply couldn't bear to think what life would be like without him.

Vixen knew as well as if he had told her himself that these thoughts were passing through Fox's mind. Her sympathy for him was intense and, coupled with this, was her own grave concern. For Badger was her friend too. Next to Fox and her own offspring she had more affection for the kind-hearted old animal than any other creature. So it was a sad and sombre pair who arrived at the pond-side.

They were surprised to find Toad there waiting for them. 'I've been to see him,' Toad told them without preamble. 'The frogs told me what had happened when I arrived for a bathe. He really does look as if he's on his last legs.'

Fox and Vixen looked at each other unhappily.

'The set's this way,' Toad prompted and went on ahead, half-crawling and half-hopping until he reached the entrance hole.

'Is – is he badly injured?' Vixen asked with bated breath.

'I don't think so,' Toad answered. 'He's more concerned about something else. He begged me never to swim in the stream. It's the stream that's on his mind more than anything.'

Fox and Vixen hesitated no longer but followed the tunnel down to the chamber where Badger lay in agony.

'Fox! Vixen!' he croaked. 'Thank goodness you've come. I've managed to hang on for you.'

'Oh Badger, my dear, dear friend. You sound terrible,' Fox whispered. 'What's happened to you?'

'I'm done for, Fox,' Badger wheezed. 'It's all up with me. The stream has been poisoned somehow and I've drunk from it. None of you must ever go near it again. You must promise me!' he gasped insistently.

'Of course we promise,' Fox said. 'But how do you know all this?'

Badger told them about the rabbit and how he himself had unsuspectingly lapped the water before he had realized the danger. The foxes and Toad were unable to speak.

'Where are the others?' Badger asked. 'Where's Mole? And Weasel? They must promise too. I must know they're safe.'

'Plucky will find them. He'll find everybody,' Fox reassured him.

Badger relaxed. He was satisfied for the moment. He lapsed into silence but his friends listened to his harsh breathing with mounting alarm.

'Oh Badger, poor Badger,' Vixen wailed. 'Is there nothing we can do for you?'

'Nothing,' he answered. 'Don't fret yourself, dearest Vixen. There's nothing *to* be done. I've no complaints. I feel calm about it now. I've only myself to blame for what must come.'

Toad took Fox aside. 'Look here,' he said urgently, 'we can't just leave him like this. There's the Warden. D'you remember how he helped Badger before when he injured himself? Perhaps he could –'

'This is no injury, Toad,' Fox interrupted quietly. 'It's something much more serious. Even human help could do nothing. We all have to face this some time but – but –' his voice shook noticeably – 'it's difficult to bear, isn't it?'

'Then all we can do is to stay and comfort him,' Toad murmured sadly.

'Yes,' said Fox. 'We won't leave him now.'

Badger was extremely tired and he fell asleep. His wheezing breaths whistled in the dark underground chamber. Fox, Toad and Vixen remained nearby. They sat gloomily and scarcely dared to exchange a word. Later they were joined by a very subdued Weasel.

'Plucky is going to look for Whistler and Adder in the daylight,' he told them. 'Friendly and Charmer are coming but I told them to come unaccompanied. Badger could only cope with his oldest comrades, I think? The younger foxes will have to stay away. There wouldn't be room for them and the old fellow might be overwhelmed.'

'Too difficult a journey for Mossy, I suspect?' asked Fox.

'Yes. But Plucky said he's in a terrible state about this.'

'Mossy and Badger almost shared their homes, didn't they?' Vixen remarked.

'Just like dear old Mole in Farthing Wood,' Toad commented.

'I hope Badger won't start asking for him,' whispered Fox. 'I really don't think I could endure it.'

Daylight came but didn't penetrate the general gloom of the set. However Badger's breathing had eased a little. He awoke to find Friendly and Charmer had swelled the numbers. He made the newcomers swear never to visit the stream.

'Is everyone here now?' he murmured weakly. 'No – I don't smell Mole or Adder.'

'Adder's on his way,' Weasel told him, though he didn't know it for sure. 'It's a long crawl here for him and he'll have to be particularly careful now it's light.'

'Yes, yes,' said Badger. 'There mustn't be any

accidents on my account. That crazed stag has sworn to get even with us.' He was thoughtful. 'Perhaps it would be better for Mole to stay out of harm's way.'

'Thank goodness,' Fox whispered to Vixen. Then he spoke up. 'He's doing just that, Badger. No point in his coming, is there? He never visits the stream anyway.'

'Oh dear,' Badger sighed mournfully. 'I should have liked to see Tawny Owl just once before I –'

He broke off as he heard the sound of another animal arriving. Leveret had raced to the set and tumbled into it almost under the nose of Trey who had recommenced patrolling the area.

'He's got us bottled up here all right,' he announced as he joined the others. 'He's only waiting for one of us to make a false move.'

'He'll have a long wait then,' Friendly remarked grimly. 'He hasn't outwitted us yet.'

The animals listened to Trey's angry snorts outside the entrance hole. The stag stamped up and down, first one way, then another.

'He – he's standing guard over us,' Leveret murmured in awe.

They heard his regular hoof-beats. Sometimes Trey called out threateningly although he had no knowledge there was such a large gathering of creatures around Badger.

'This is sheer nonsense,' said Fox. 'Whatever can possess an animal to bear such a grudge?'

'His pride's offended,' Badger said. 'So far we've got the better of him. We've outrun him and outmanoeuvred him. And he's got the scars to prove it.'

'Scars?' Fox asked. 'What scars? I didn't know about this.'

'Plucky and myself left our teeth-marks on him,' Badger said.

'Did you though? My word, Badger, I don't think your days can be over after all. You attacked that huge stag!'

'Yes,' said Badger. 'It's not another animal that's put paid to me, you see, Fox. It's my own stupidity.'

'If Trey's been injured by his encounters with us it does put a different complexion on things,' Fox remarked. 'It's my opinion he'll be determined to redress the balance. He's a vain beast. How belittling for him that he's the dominant deer in the herd yet he's suffered humiliations from creatures far smaller than himself. We'll all have to be doubly cautious.'

It was late in the day when Adder, by subtle and hidden movements, arrived near the Pond. Several times during his journey he had been on the point of giving up. He wasn't known for demonstrations of deep affection or concern. He was, by his very nature, an unemotional animal. But each time he stopped some thought of Badger or some image of him in one of his acts of bravery or kindheartedness compelled the snake to continue. He saw Trey pacing up and down the length of the Pond and it took him an age to get to some cover close enough to the set so that he could get himself into it without trouble when the stag was most distant.

As Adder lay hidden amongst the sedges he saw Whistler fly in and begin a search of the terrain. He was looking for the position of the set where the animals were sheltering, although there was no possibility of his entering it himself. He seemed to Adder to be in a state of excitement. The whistle of his damaged wing sounded rhythmically over the water. Inside the set the animals detected the sound.

'Whistler's agitated,' Fox observed shrewdly. 'His wing's like a second voice. It's evident he can't settle.'

'The stag must still be around,' Friendly suggested.

'I think our heron friend wants to tell us something,' said Weasel.

Adder was thinking the same thing as he watched the great bird's flight. All at once the heron's sharp eyes picked out the snake's familiar patterned coils amongst the waterside vegetation. Taking careful note of Trey's position Whistler descended and, flapping briskly to steady himself, landed close to Adder's little nook.

'What are you doing?' hissed the snake. 'You couldn't make my presence more obvious if you were to pinpoint me with your bill!'

'Sorry,' croaked the heron. 'But I've made an important discovery about the stream. I can't get into Badger's shelter and I thought *you* could tell the others.'

'Tell them what?' Adder rasped crossly. 'The stag's turning this way!'

'It's the humans,' Whistler confided. 'They've poisoned it. They've dumped –' He interrupted himself and took awkwardly to flight as Trey began his approach. 'I'll be back!' he cried hurriedly.

'Irresponsible chump,' Adder muttered as he buried himself deeper inside some dead leaves. The deer was running to investigate.

Whistler was high in the air by this time and Trey

could find nothing on the ground, try as he might. Adder's camouflage was good enough to fool all but those with the keenest sight. Nevertheless he didn't choose to stay put and afford the heron a second chance of blowing his cover. As soon as Trey had wandered away again Adder emerged from his nest of leaves and slithered determinedly towards the set entrance.

Even then, when Whistler saw his movement, he endangered Adder's dash for safety. 'No, wait!' he called to the snake. 'I didn't finish. It's important!' he bawled at him thoughtlessly.

Adder cared nothing for its importance. Deaf to all entreaties he increased his effort and slid into the hole, cursing the heron roundly all the way.

'Bird-brained, bird-brained,' he hissed to himself over and over again until his anger was cooled by the mustiness of the earthen tunnels.

Weasel came to look. 'It's you!' he greeted him. 'Whatever's the fuss about? Badger needs quiet.'

'It's lucky that dolt of a heron can't get in here then,' Adder observed waspishly. 'He's worked himself into a lather about something and did his best to get me skewered on a pair of antlers!'

'Calm yourself,' said Weasel. 'This isn't the time for recriminations.'

Adder realized he had forgotten himself, though he didn't admit it. 'How is he?' he asked, referring to Badger, as he followed Weasel down the tunnel.

'Hanging on.'

'I'm afraid Badger's made himself an example for the rest of us,' Adder lisped. 'His suffering is our warning.'

'That's exactly why he's called us all here. We've all had to swear not to go near the stream. You'll be made to go through the ritual too.'

Badger was the last to hear Adder's voice though he was listening hard for each new arrival. In his old age he had become increasingly deaf but he was relieved when the others told him the snake had at last joined the throng. Adder dutifully went through the motions of promising never to enter the stream.

'I'm glad I've been able to make you the promise,' he said afterwards. 'I wondered if I'd ever talk to you again. Is the – er – pain very acute?'

'No worse and no better,' Badger answered cryptically. 'But I'm so parched, you see. I think I could drink the Pond dry. And I haven't eaten for an age, either.'

The animals began to murmur together questioningly.

'What?' Adder hissed. 'Are you saying you have an appetite?'

'Yes, I suppose I am,' Badger admitted. 'I don't think my stomach has a scrap of food in it.'

Adder's tongue flickered busily. 'Do you mean to tell me,' he demanded indignantly, 'that I've scraped my scales across the breadth of the Park merely to hear you complain that you're hungry?'

'Well, I – I can't help it, Adder,' Badger mumbled. 'It's only natural, isn't it?'

'No, it isn't,' Adder contradicted. 'Not for an animal who is supposed to be dying, and that's what I was told you were. D'you think I would have come all this way otherwise? There's nothing wrong with you. You're an old humbug, Badger!'

'There *was* something wrong with me. There was,' Badger insisted defensively. 'But, the truth is, I do begin to feel better.'

'How much of this so-called killer water did you actually drink?' Adder asked next.

'Um – I don't remember exactly,' said Badger. 'I was interrupted. I'd begun to lap and –'

Now Weasel cut in. 'So you only took a few laps? Then why all this bother?'

'How can you talk like that, Weasel?' Vixen asked. 'Badger saw the rabbit die. What was he to think? And we should be celebrating, not complaining. Poor Badger!'

'Of course, of course,' Weasel said contritely. 'I'm delighted. You know I am. We all are. I didn't mean . . . oh Badger, forgive me. It's such a surprise, that's all, after expecting the worst.'

The animals all began talking at once, congratulating Badger and each other on a false alarm. Adder remained silent. He was certainly pleased Badger wasn't going to die, but he couldn't quite manage to mask his irritation at the unnecessary journey. Then he remembered Whistler. He waited for the hubbub to die down.

'Listen, everybody,' he lisped. 'There's a message about the stream. Whistler has discovered something. He wants to tell us.'

'We can't leave here till dark,' said Toad. 'Will he stay around?'

'I'll go and see if he's waiting,' said Fox. 'It must be nearing dusk.' He went up the exit tunnel and peered out. The light was indeed fading. He saw Trey standing

by the pond-side at some distance. He was drinking.
Fox pushed his head out and called. 'Whistler!
Whistler! Are you there?'

There was no answer. Fox waited. But the heron
failed to appear.

'He must be planning to return at dark,' Fox said to
himself. He looked again at the stag and his anger
began to kindle. 'Whatever's the matter with that
creature?' he muttered. 'Will he never give up? What
does he intend to do? He can't slaughter us all. I refuse
to allow ourselves to be holed up like this for as long as
he chooses. We can do better than this! We'll soon test
his resolve.' He hurried back to the others.

'Badger, are you sure you'll be all right now?' he
asked first.

'Yes. Yes, I think so, Fox. If I could only eat
something.'

'That's just it. We're not going to stay here. We've all
got to eat. What are we thinking of, letting this deer
dictate to us?' He was trying to rouse them.

'Oh-ho, this is more like the Farthing Wood Fox,'
Friendly remarked to Charmer, his sister.

'We ought to be able to deal with this customer,' said
Fox. 'After what we've been through in the past.'

'That's the spirit,' said Weasel. 'I'm with you, Fox.'

'Me too. Goes without saying,' said Friendly.

'I'll back you up,' said Toad, 'though my contribution may be a bit limited.'

Adder brought him down to earth. 'Contribution to
what exactly?'

'I – I'm not sure,' Toad admitted. 'What had you in
mind, Fox?'

'Oh, only that we're going to leave this little refuge now. We'll go together. We're going to live our normal lives. If Trey has been injured by some of us he brought it on himself. There's every reason to defend oneself in an awkward situation. He must understand that. So – what are we waiting for?'

'I – I don't feel quite ready for a scrap just yet,' Badger said. 'I've got no strength to rely on.'

'Of course not. We weren't intending you to join in,' said Friendly. 'You must stay here and we'll bring you back something to sustain you for a while.'

'I'm so glad I was able to get you all together,' said Badger. 'What a joy it is to have such friends. Now I know we're all safe. There's only one thing I'm unhappy about: Tawny Owl's absence. He won't know about the dangers of the stream and if he should take it into his head to steal back some time without our knowledge we couldn't warn him about it.'

'No good worrying about him, Badger. He's out of reach,' said Weasel.

'If I know Tawny Owl,' said Charmer, 'the first thing he'd do on his return is to find a comfortable spot for a nap! And we all know his favoured places, don't we?'

'All right,' said Fox. 'Enough of talking. Let's face the foe and see just what that supercilious deer is made of!'

He led the way up the tunnel. Friendly, Vixen and Charmer followed directly behind. Weasel went next with Leveret and Toad and Adder brought up the rear. Outside the set it was now almost dark. The first animal they saw, sitting by the water with the utmost composure, was Plucky.

He leapt up. 'Is Badger –' he began anxiously.

'He's blossoming,' Adder drawled sarcastically. 'He simply loves all this attention.'

Plucky was quickly acquainted with Badger's recovery. He was tremendously relieved. 'What wonderful news,' he said. 'And now I've some for you. I've persuaded Trey to quit.'

'What? How? How could you –' Fox floundered.

'I told him the other stags were rejoicing in his absence,' he answered, 'and that they were becoming extremely friendly with the hinds. I didn't need to say more. You should have seen him gallop. I don't think the dust has settled yet.'

'Well!' exclaimed Vixen.

'*Very* well,' said Friendly. 'Plucky, you're a chip off the old block.'

12

A Royal Stag

The animals dispersed to follow their own immediate concerns. Chief among these was food. Plucky carried the good news of Badger to Mossy who had been racked by misery ever since he had believed he would never see Badger again. The little mole was so excited he could scarcely wait for the old animal to return to his own home.

'He's got to lie low for a bit,' Plucky told him. 'Get his strength back. Fox and Vixen are collecting food for him.'

Badger lay for a while in the deserted set without moving. The aches in his body were subsiding and the dominant discomfort he felt was still his sore, parched throat. In the end he had no recourse but to stir himself. He lumbered slowly out of the underground chamber and into the tunnel, and from there very, very slowly towards the set entrance. He knew nothing about

Plucky's clever trick on Trey but he was so desperate for water he no longer cared whether the stag was waiting in ambush for him or not. He sniffed at the night air. He could detect no deer odours. Painfully Badger forced his weak, quivering legs over the short stretch of ground to the Pond. He fell on his face in the cool water and gratefully let it wash over him, gulping it down in great draughts. He lay still for a while. It was bliss in the refreshing water. There was no sound nor sight of the stag and Badger was in no hurry to move. What a lucky escape he had had! If he hadn't come across the rabbit he would surely be dead by now. As it was, he had come pretty close to it.

He wondered what Whistler had managed to find out about the stream's danger. Whatever it was, it would be something beyond the scope of mere beasts and birds to rectify. He hauled himself out of the Pond, deliciously wet, and tottered back to his temporary base. Moments later Fox and Vixen returned, carrying roots, tubers and a variety of carrion in their jaws.

'Eat, my friend, eat,' said Fox when he had deposited his load on the hard-trodden earth. 'We want you back with us in our corner of the Park. And your path is clear.' He told him about Trey's abrupt departure.

Badger began eagerly to eat. Fox was amused and approving. 'Badger – the great survivor,' he joked. He and Vixen were supremely happy at their old friend's good fortune.

Badger despatched a succulent root with relish. 'I've had an idea,' he said suddenly as if he had surprised himself. 'There may be a way we can rid ourselves of the stag's threat permanently.'

'We're all ears,' Fox told him interestedly.

'We could make the stream our ally.'

Fox wasn't sure if he understood Badger's suggestion correctly. 'You're not thinking we should persuade Trey to drink from it, are you?' he asked.

'Of course that's what I'm thinking. He's not aware of its danger as far as I know.'

Vixen wouldn't hear of it. 'That's not like you, Badger. It would be an act of betrayal. We've never acted treacherously towards another creature.'

'He's made himself everyone's enemy,' Badger pointed out. 'We had no quarrel with him.'

'That's true,' said Fox. 'But, my dearest Vixen, your heart's in the right place. Trey has no wish to kill any of us; only to dominate the entire Park. So how could we plot his death?'

Badger relented. 'You always were a wise counsellor, Vixen. I bow to your better nature. But I think you're wrong about the stag. After our recent tussles with him I'm sure he'd do anything within his power to avenge himself and it may be some creature will lose its life. I'm not known as a belligerent animal, but if it's a choice between Trey's life and one of my friend's – well, I'd adopt any means to save a friend.'

'It hasn't come to that yet, Badger, thankfully,' Vixen said. 'He's preoccupied with watching the other stags at present. Perhaps we'll have no further brushes with him.'

'I doubt that,' said Badger bluntly. And there the subject was left.

Fox wanted to know more about the stream's mystery and so he sought out Whistler.

'I've been trying to locate some of you,' the heron said petulantly. 'Adder was little help, though I asked him to be. I'm afraid I'm not as stealthy as he and I alarmed him. I wanted you all to know that I've found a clue to the stream's impurity.'

'What is it?' Fox barked. Whistler's long-winded manner could sometimes be infuriating.

'Outside the Park where the stream is joined by a ditch, humans have left their debris. We all have good cause to know how careless humans are about tainting the land. No doubt they're as mindless about water. The rubbish, whatever it is, has contaminated the ditch and the water from the ditch flows into the stream. So it seems very likely to me that –'

'Yes, Whistler,' Fox cut in. 'I understand your drift, and it all sounds very feasible. What made you investigate this?'

'The stream was my chief source of food,' the heron explained. 'Naturally I've wondered why there have been no fish. Now I have to fly a distance to feed. It's very inconvenient. But I think the damage to the stream must be irreparable. It's completely devoid of life.'

Fox pondered the cruel thoughtlessness of humans. 'They poisoned the Great Stag,' he murmured. 'Thanks to them, we have Trey in his place.'

'Countless smaller animals have died there too,' Whistler remarked. 'The entire surroundings have become barren.'

'Even Badger was nearly killed,' Fox growled.

'Wildlife is helpless in these situations,' Whistler said. 'We're at their mercy.'

'I wonder the Warden isn't suspicious, with all these deaths occurring,' Fox mused. 'The carcasses are removed, aren't they?'

'I believe so,' Whistler said. 'The larger ones, certainly.'

'Then he must know something is wrong. *He'll* come to our aid. He cares for us.'

'A heartening notion,' Whistler commented. 'But what of the smaller carrion, such as mice and voles? And songbirds?'

'What do you mean?'

'I don't think the Warden would gather *them* up. They'd be less detectable. So they may be taken by predators such as yourself.'

'I don't hunt or scavenge anywhere in that vicinity,' Fox told him. 'Nor do any of my relatives. But I see what you're driving at. If the little animals are poisoned they in turn may poison those that feed off them?'

'Exactly,' Whistler intoned solemnly. 'So the deaths could become more widespread.'

Fox shuddered. 'All because of one act of carelessness,' he said angrily. 'Will they never learn?'

'Learn?' Whistler echoed. 'You said it yourself, Fox. They don't care.'

The animals became more discerning than ever in their eating habits. The time of the rut was approaching and Trey's main concern continued to be potential rivals amongst the other stags. This allowed the hunting animals a breathing space which enabled them to range across the safer parts of the Reserve without fear of hindrance.

Badger recovered sufficiently during this time to be able to return to his old set. Mossy was so delighted to have him back as neighbour that he made Badger a present of a large heap of the plumpest worms and then they celebrated together.

The animals' enjoyment of complete freedom of movement again was to be short-lived. By September Trey's challenging bellows began to boom through the length and breadth of the Nature Reserve. The Farthing Wood community, like all the other inhabitants, listened and marvelled at their power. And they wondered. They wondered if there would be any answering challenges. They recalled the other stags' responses to their suggestions that Trey wanted to drive them out and most of the animals were not very hopeful.

However, as autumn advanced, there *were* other calls and challenges. Other stags roared because it was in their nature to do so at this time. If a challenge was offered them, they had to take it up. Now Trey came into his own. His calls were defiant, scathing, dismissive of any competitor. His were roars of confidence and supremacy. And, pretty soon, the crash of tangling antlers marked the beginning – and end – of the stags' rivalries. Those bold enough to respond to Trey's taunts became acquainted with his massive strength and force. None fought for long. Even as they locked antlers they were pressed backwards, pushed aside, tumbled, glad to wrench themselves free and be chased far away from the proximity of the hinds. The dominance that Trey had threatened and of which he had long boasted was confirmed. The hinds were his for the taking. He was a royal stag.

The Park fell quiet again. The mists of early autumn rose in the evening and in the still air the Reserve was shrouded secretively. An atmosphere of expectancy pervaded the whole area as if it were on edge, waiting for something to happen. . . .

Trey paced his domain in lordly manner. White Deer Park was his kingdom and the inhabitants his subjects. He really believed all were under his rule and he meant to have none stepping out of line. He hadn't the sense to realize that the birds who nested in the Park were as free of his decrees as the air they flew in. As for the animals of Farthing Wood, they were free in another sense. They had freedom of spirit and no creature, not the Great Cat who had terrorized the Reserve, nor even Man himself, had ever managed to break that. And, as White Deer Park held its breath, it was to be Nature who would demonstrate to all her creatures the real meaning of dominion.

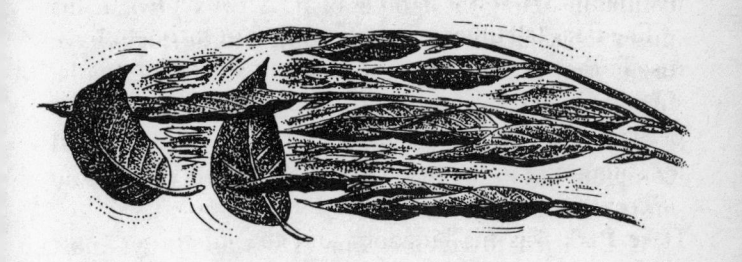

The Hurricane

Tawny Owl was trapped in Farthinghurst. He was
unable to stir from the protection of the Great Beech
that had, through force of circumstances, become his
permanent home. His movements were restricted to an
awkward shuffle along the branch he used as a perch.
Weighed down by his cement shackles he couldn't fly
and it was as much as he dared do to put one foot in
front of the other as he waddled miserably along the
branch and back again. Even those exercises had to be
rationed as he was constantly afraid of toppling over
and plunging to the ground. And that really would
have been the end of him. But there was one blessing for
poor Owl and her name was Holly. The female owl
may have led him a bit of a dance at the outset, and
indeed had unwittingly brought about his present
dreadful situation, but since then she had more than
made up for it. All through the remainder of that

summer she hunted and caught food for both of them. She never questioned the necessity for this, nor did she complain about the labour of it. Tawny Owl in his misery was not always as appreciative as he might have been. And this was because in his heart of hearts he blamed her for his misfortune.

'I don't feel like a bird any longer,' he would complain to her. 'A bird who can't use his wings is no more than a – a freak!'

Holly tried to comfort him. He was always most miserable when the weather had been dry for a long spell. Since he couldn't leave the tree to drink from a pool or puddle, he had to rely on catching raindrops or dew as it dripped from the leaves of the beech. His thirst was rarely satisfied adequately and he suffered a great deal.

'My body's drying up,' he would moan. 'I should be stuffed and put in a glass box.'

'There will be more rain in the autumn,' Holly would say soothingly. Sometimes she gathered earthworms for him as the moistness of their bodies helped to keep him lubricated.

Tawny Owl had given up all hope of ever seeing White Deer Park again. The ironic situation might have amused a more cheerful creature than he. For he had found his mate, yet was unable to return home with her in triumph. To Owl the bitterest irony of all was that he alone of all the Farthing Wood party who had travelled to the Nature Reserve had actually found a mate from Farthing Wood itself. All the others who had paired long before had found theirs in White Deer Park. Even Fox had found his Vixen during the journey. And Tawny Owl, after the taunts he had received, was beside himself with exasperation that he wasn't able to boast about this to his friends. He longed to triumph over them.

Holly had tried to remove some of the cement from his wings by pecking and tearing at it, but this had proved very painful for him and when he had attempted to do this to his feet the discomfort was so intense he had to give up. Filled with anguish, Tawny Owl had eked out his existence from day to day and week to week with only Holly's companionship to comfort him.

By early autumn one problem at least was alleviated. There were frequent outbursts of heavy rain allowing plenty of water to drip from the tree. There was so much water in fact, that Tawny Owl was often unpleasantly wet. There was nowhere he could take shelter and he yearned for a hollow oak and wings that could carry him there. As time went on he became more and more disconsolate.

'Why bother to bring food for me?' he said to Holly one evening. 'You're only prolonging the agony. I might as well starve and get it over with.'

'That's no way to talk,' she told him. 'Things are bound to get better eventually.'

'Oh yes? And how will they?' he demanded. 'Am I suddenly going to shed these old wings and grow some new ones, like Adder sloughing off his skin?'

Holly had no answer. She simply wished to cheer him up. It was becoming increasingly difficult to do so.

While she was hunting, Tawny Owl used to shuffle up and down the branch that had become his prison.

He ceased to be so careful with the way he placed his feet. 'What difference would it make if I did fall?' he would mutter to himself. 'It would be an end to this misery.' But somehow he never did tumble off and, despite his words, he still preserved deep inside a faint hope that one day, some way, he and Holly would enter White Deer Park together.

The periods of rain increased in length and intensity, exceeding even those during the wet spring. Underneath the beech the ground was sodden. Pools of water appeared in the gardens nearby. The soil couldn't absorb them. The pavements and roads of the Farthinghurst estate streamed with water. Tawny Owl, hunched and shivering, wondered how much more he would have to bear. Holly found the mice were thin on the ground.

'Better try your luck at fishing,' Tawny Owl joked feebly. 'It would be more suitable.'

Holly began to catch more small birds and sometimes insects. She was very adaptable. During the day she sheltered elsewhere from the incessant rain. But at dusk she faithfully returned to Tawny Owl, and during the dark hours she kept him supplied with a share of her catch.

One night, after the two birds had eaten frugally, Holly kept flitting from one branch to another restlessly. She couldn't keep still.

'What's the matter with you?' Tawny Owl asked her testily.

'I feel ill at ease,' she replied.

'Why?'

'I don't know. There's something. . . . Something's going to happen,' she finished.

Her unease eventually communicated itself to Tawny Owl. And there *was* something in the atmosphere. It was charged with a kind of menace. They noticed other birds – starlings and songbirds and suchlike who would normally be safely roosting – stirring from their sites and calling and moving about in a jittery way. The gregarious starlings bunched together as if for reassurance. But it didn't help them to settle and they wheeled about, coming to rest around the roof-tops, then taking off again uncertainly. Sparrows chattered nervously. Small nocturnal mammals scuttled for cover deep inside their bolt-holes. They sensed a great danger was hovering and they instinctively tried to bury themselves away.

It began as a breeze that rustled the vegetation. It was a steady rustling that made the leaves and twigs of the Great Beech quiver. The owls listened. The breeze didn't die away, then return in fits and starts like the usual night breezes to which they were so accustomed. It persisted, as if it were toying with a few ideas before really making its mind up. Then it stiffened, growing rapidly in strength until, with a sudden explosion of force, it roared with a malevolent snarling anger. The beech tree rocked and shuddered. Holly fluttered to a new perch. Tawny Owl could only cling on grimly. But the wind hadn't yet reached its full fury. It expanded into a whirling, devastating violence that battered everything in its path, contemptuous of any resistance. The noise of it was terrifying – a high strident howl that every so often rose to a scream as a gust of unprecedented power tore at the landscape. There had never been anything quite like it before. It was a wind of hurricane force.

The human population of Farthinghurst awoke in darkness as their homes buckled and shuddered. Glass shattered, tiles crashed; fencing, sheds and outhouses were ripped to pieces. Chimneys toppled, roofs caved in and some old or badly constructed buildings collapsed entirely. Everywhere, through the roars and shrieks of the wind, was the sound of destruction. Human ingenuity counted for nothing in the face of this onslaught. Man-made things were as vulnerable as those of Nature's making, rooted in the soil. All life, from the lowliest insect to human beings themselves, were reduced to the same insignificant level before such elemental ferocity. Each could only cower helplessly while it raged.

In the early hours of the morning the storm reached its height. Animal cries of panic were drowned by the deafening roar. Every building rattled and vibrated. Broken materials were bowled along or hurled through the air like pieces of paper. Small plants were flattened. Saplings whip-lashed demonically. Only bushes and shrubs with tightly-knit masses of twigs and leaves could partially withstand the blast. Into their midst burrowed countless terrified birds. In Farthinghurst there were no large trees remaining save the Great Beech. The beech bore the full brunt of the storm's force. Its great branches with their heavy load of foliage bent and groaned and cracked beneath the weight. The roots, loosened by days of rain that had drenched the ground deep down, began to lose their grip. As the tree swayed and shifted, then leant before the assault, Holly abandoned it altogether. She was too frightened to think about anything except her own preservation. She knew the tree was no longer safe. As she left her perch she was caught up in the storm's cruel grasp and tossed like a speck through the air. Her wings spread, she was driven along at tremendous speed until finally she was dashed against a tall hedge. Shaken but otherwise unhurt, she pushed herself into the hedge's denseness like any tiny wren or tit.

Tawny Owl, talons locked as best they could on the splintering branch, waited for the end. The great tree which had withstood scores of lesser storms without damage seemed to heave a last great sigh. Then slowly it gave way. It was as if a giant hand had been plunged into the beech's glossy green hair and was pulling and tugging at it until the whole body underneath lost its balance. The tree toppled, the roots torn from the earth and, with a mighty crash, the last survivor of Farthing Wood prostrated itself on the soil that had nourished it for so long. Tawny Owl was hurled to the ground, yet the force of the wind blew him away from the colossal weight of the beech. As his body struck the soft earth the breath was driven from his lungs. But the brittle cement that had trapped his wings and talons was shivered into pieces. Bruised and gasping for air, it was some time before the bird realized he was free. He lay like a piece of rubbish himself amongst the miscellaneous debris scattered by the hurricane. At last he stirred and instinctively struggled to his feet, flapping his wings as he did so. His shackles had been unloosed. He found he could fly once more. Yet, ironically, flight now would put him into greater peril than before. He scurried for shelter, bumbling into a small conical cypress that grew in a corner of one of the neighbouring gardens.

Towards daylight the hurricane passed, leaving a scene of destruction in its wake. There was damage everywhere and the countryside round about was changed forever.

Thus the last vestige of Farthing Wood was finally obliterated from the map. Now the Wood only lived in the memory of those who had known it.

14

Dependency

Tawny Owl's first thought, as he nestled amid the thick feathery foliage of the cypress, was for his friends in White Deer Park. He wondered how they had fared during the great storm. Now he knew he could fly back to them, he was eager to begin the return journey and this led him to his second thought which was for Holly. He was glad she had left the Great Beech in time, and could only hope she had managed to find safe shelter somewhere. The wind gradually eased and Tawny Owl looked out through the greyish light at a bruised and battered world. The beech lay motionless along the ground like a slaughtered Goliath. Only the dead leaves on its boughs rustled in the strong air currents that were the aftermath of the hurricane. People were already out of doors, surveying the damage to their property and their neighbours'. Tawny Owl decided to quit his refuge.

He flew up and away and began to call for Holly from the wing. Fragments of cement still clung to his plumage and talons but he was oblivious to them. Soon his cries were answered and he saw Holly emerge from her hedge and fly up to meet him. They were both filled with relief to see that the other had survived. Holly began to question Owl about his miraculous return to flight.

'I have the storm to thank for that,' he told her, 'but there's no time to explain now. We mustn't loiter here any longer. We have a journey to make. Follow me.'

Holly willingly tucked herself into his slipstream and they flew away from Farthinghurst and its shocked and dazed human occupants. Tawny Owl led the way back to the countryside, high across the roads and the marsh towards the place where he had conversed with the squirrels. Everywhere there were changes. Everywhere trees were down; others leant at crazy angles against sturdier neighbours; others again had remained upright but with gaping wounds where huge branches had been ripped off by the butchery of the storm. Tawny Owl couldn't recognize the tree where the squirrels had had their home. It may have survived; it may have fallen. It was impossible to tell. He wondered how much White Deer Park would be altered.

The birds continued to fly throughout the early part of the morning. Tawny Owl wanted to press on while there were not too many humans around. Their numbers were increasing all the time as the morning grew lighter. Tawny Owl knew he and Holly would have to hide themselves away before too long. He was able to steer them towards the orchards, despite the changed aspect of the terrain. Many fruit trees had been uprooted or damaged. The two owls sailed overhead. Neither passed a word to the other. Tawny Owl needed to concentrate on navigating their route. He was searching for Rookery Copse. Holly was content to be led for the moment. She had no regrets about leaving Farthinghurst and considered they had both been very fortunate to emerge from the ordeal of the storm without mishap.

The first clue Tawny Owl had that they were near the copse was in the sky itself. Ahead of them in the distance a dark cloud of uncertain shape moved erratically, now in one direction, now another. It didn't take Owl long to realize that the cloud was made up of birds. They were rooks, dispossessed and disorientated by the events of the night. They wheeled about uncertainly, crying their harsh cries of distress and lament. And soon Tawny Owl saw what was left of the copse. At least half the trees in which the rooks had faithfully built their nests season after season were flattened. The old regular outline of the group of tall trees was punctured by great gaps where the storm had wrought its work. The rooks were in turmoil. Their world was turned inside out. Some of them from the living cloud landed briefly on a branch here and there but took off again almost immediately. The others would follow suit and this descending and ascending and wheeling about went on continuously. The rooks were caught up in a mass panic where none of them knew what had happened or what to do. Rookery Copse had become something different and it was something they didn't understand.

Mindful of his reception there on his previous journey Tawny Owl decided to leave the troubled birds to their own devices. Despite his rough treatment by the rooks he felt a tremendous sympathy for them. All over the countryside, he now realized, wild creatures would find their homes destroyed; their territories strange and unfamiliar. Now, more than ever, he longed to reach White Deer Park again. He was afraid of what he would find but he knew he wouldn't be able to rest properly until he saw it with his own eyes. A little further on he flew down and landed in a dead elm which, killed long ago by disease, had with a strange irony withstood the blast of the hurricane when so many healthy trees had succumbed. Holly perched beside him.

Tawny Owl spoke first. 'You may as well discount what I've told you about White Deer Park,' he said, 'because it will probably look quite different now.'

'Yes,' Holly agreed. 'I've been thinking the same thing. Unless the storm missed it?'

'I don't think we can depend on that,' he answered morosely. 'How I wish we could!'

'It'll still be a Nature Reserve, though. Won't it?'

'Oh yes. *That* won't have changed.' Tawny Owl was about to add that his friends would still be there, too, but he choked the words back. How did he know if they would be? He had been away a long time. And the hurricane must have claimed lives wherever it had passed. 'I'm eager to get back just as quickly as we can,' he told Holly instead. 'But it's a long journey and we have to be wary, because there are bound to be many humans about. I think we should look for a place to roost soon; then we can continue when it's dusk.'

'I'm not a bit tired,' Holly informed him. 'We can fly for as long as you like. I leave it to you as the senior.'

'How very diplomatic,' Tawny Owl remarked wryly. 'Well, come on, then.'

The two birds left the bleached skeleton of the elm tree and continued their flight. Tawny Owl was bemused by the tortured features of the scenery. He felt as if he were flying over a new land. He tried to ignore the devastation beneath them. He knew they were on the correct course for the river: he had been able to gauge their direction from the ruined copse. But every so often the cries of wounded or homeless beasts and birds could be heard as the owls travelled past. Sometimes they saw bodies crushed by the force of the storm, lying where they had been hurled. He saw a badger who had been trapped by a fallen tree. And birds – birds everywhere bemoaning their lost nest sites and broken communities. It was then that Tawny Owl feared for his friends and wished fervently that he had never left them. For, whatever horrors they had suffered during the storm, at least he would have been there to share them. That was how it had always been. They had shared all kinds of experiences and hardships and had been able to help each other through their difficulties.

Holly guessed the content of his thoughts every time they became witness to some fresh tragedy. She had no-one to mourn for; she had lived a generally solitary life. Companionship was a new enjoyment for her and the more she appreciated it the more she understood Owl's concern.

'Look out for a likely spot to rest,' Tawny Owl called behind him. He knew the river was not too distant. They were flying over meadows.

Holly scanned the area. There were few trees of any size. But she spied an elder tree which, though not tall, was festooned with a thick cladding of ivy. She thought this might suit their purpose. She flew alongside Tawny Owl. 'Down there,' she indicated. 'There's plenty of cover.'

'Perfect,' he said and they skimmed down together.

There was plenty of space amongst the thick tendrils of the creeper to hide themselves, and they were confident they would be secure. Not that there were any humans in the vicinity. It wasn't a time for people to be out sauntering and taking the air. There were far more important and pressing concerns that day for everyone.

Tawny Owl could hardly wait for dusk. For the first time in many weeks he was looking forward to hunting for himself. Holly had fed him like an invalid for so long he had come to feel quite subservient. He dared not tell her that after their long flight he was well-nigh exhausted. His wing muscles ached abominably. But he told himself he would be more than ready after a good rest. So Holly's next words came as a shock.

'I'll carry on being the provider,' she announced. 'You don't need to pretend any longer to be a bird of prey.' It sounded as if she thought he had become actually incapable of hunting.

'But – but –' he spluttered, so taken aback he couldn't find an adequate response.

'No "buts",' she said firmly. 'I can easily catch

enough for both of us, as you know. You need all the rest you can get. It's a wonder a bird of your age has come through such experiences as you've had at all.'

Tawny Owl was dumbfounded. He couldn't conceive that Holly spoke from kindness and suspected she was insulting him. This was not the sort of association he had wanted to impress his friends with. Why, it was worse than solitude.

'Look here,' he finally managed to say, 'I'm not quite in my dotage yet, you know. I'll admit I'm very tired. It'd be surprising if I weren't. But my hunting days aren't over by any means.'

Holly was amused. 'It's all *right*,' she insisted. 'I understand how you feel. It must have been a humbling episode for you in the beech when you couldn't fly. But it really doesn't matter. I don't mind in the least. I'm younger, fitter, and I can do all that you used to do.'

Used to do! What did she think he was – senile! Oh no. He'd show her. But he smothered his indignation for the present. He decided actions were more telling than words. However, in a short while, both he and Holly were asleep.

Holly awoke first and left the mantle of ivy without disturbing Tawny Owl. It was quite dark and she spread her wings and began to search the meadows. A light shower of rain was falling. Eventually the raindrops which penetrated the ivy aroused Tawny Owl. Realizing his companion was absent he pushed his head out of the creeper and looked for her. At that moment Holly was swooping on a shrew. Tawny Owl saw her pounce and he struggled free of the ivy tendrils and launched himself into flight. He wanted to get clear away before the female owl might return with her kill.

He was surprised to find his flight muscles were painfully stiff. After such a long period of disuse, he had overtaxed them on the first lap of the journey from Farthinghurst. But he bore the aches and soreness with determination. He had to make it clear to Holly at the outset that he could resume catching his own food. The trouble was, his whole body felt incredibly tired and feeble. It was as much as he could do to flap his wings occasionally, merely to keep airborne. So how was he to hunt? He had no speed now and no agility to rely on. Even if he saw some likely prey he doubted if he could direct his exhausted body with sufficient accuracy to make a kill.

'This is absurd,' he spluttered, angry with his physical shortcomings. 'Am I to remain dependent on another? Unthinkable, unthinkable. . . .'

He had to try. Fortunately his eyesight had lost none of its sharpness. He flew over some fields well away from where he had seen Holly pounce. There was no dearth of small creatures running on their habitual paths through the grass-stems. He looked hard for an animal that might be a little slower, a little older, a little more accessible. The diminutive creatures scurried about busily, pausing occasionally to sit on their hind legs to nibble at a tasty morsel or to look and listen for danger. Tawny Owl flew up and down, unable to decide on his target. His wing-beats became more and more laboured and gradually decreased in frequency. His body dropped steadily nearer ground level. And the nearer to the ground he became the more detectable was his presence to the voles, shrews or wood mice he was hoping to catch. He soon realized that, unless he selected his quarry quickly, he would lose all opportunity of a capture. Most of the animals were running for the shelter of their tunnels. He did see one, however, who was very absorbed with some particularly appetizing seeds. Tawny Owl lowered his talons and plunged towards it. The wood mouse seemed unaware of his approach. Tawny Owl struck it, grasped it in his beak and prepared to take off again. The mouse was dead. He had made his kill and he was filled with a mixture of pride and relief. But now he found his wing muscles were too stiff for him to achieve lift-off. He needed to beat his wings quickly to get airborne, using what air currents were available to do the rest. But the muscles were so tired and sore that he could only manage a couple of quick beats and these were no use at all. Tawny Owl realized he couldn't get off the ground.

He dropped the mouse. 'Now I really am stuck,' he murmured to himself. 'I can't even get back to the roost.' He began fatalistically to tear at the mouse carcass. At least he could eat where he was. Then all at once he stopped. He knew Holly would eventually come looking for him. He would need a longer rest before he could fly again. And it was important to him that Holly should see that, although he had over-stretched himself, he had not entirely wasted his efforts. So he left the rest of his kill untouched as a sort of trophy to display to her.

Holly was a long time making her appearance and Tawny Owl had grown horribly hungry in the meantime. So when he finally saw her gliding above he called to her in all humility, desperate to break his fast: 'Here! Here I am!'

Holly's scolding began before she reached the ground. 'What did I say to you, you silly old bird? I've been searching for you for ages. I've caught enough mice to feed a brood, let alone just the two of us.' She landed and noticed Owl's catch. 'And is that all you exhausted yourself for? Some other predator's leavings? Now what is to happen? Are you going to stay here in the open in broad daylight?'

'I caught this, I caught it myself,' Tawny Owl protested feebly. But it was no use. Holly wasn't listening.

'I'll go back and fetch some better food for you,' she told him. 'You'd better eat heartily and build up some strength. You'll need to exercise those wings before much longer or I don't know what might happen to you. And in future,' she nagged him, 'you want to pay more attention to what I say. You've made a real fool of yourself – and at your age too! I shall have to keep watch over you now, just as if you were a helpless chick.'

She flew away, back to the elder tree, to fetch the food. She didn't wait for a reply. Tawny Owl groaned. By trying to assert himself he had ended up becoming more dependent than ever.

15

No Contest

In White Deer Park, in the last few days before the hurricane reached it, Trey had followed up his triumph by establishing his rule over the whole herd. The other males largely kept their distance but the dominant stag couldn't be in all places at all times and so they were able on occasion to rejoin the hinds. The females were quite content with the situation. When Trey was around, which he generally was, each seemed happy enough to be part of his harem. He was the finest of the stags by far and they recognized his superiority.

The other animals often saw him leading the herd to drink at the Pond. The hinds grouped around its fringes and drank together whilst Trey kept watch for any possible interference. At these times it was not advisable for any creature of the Park to approach too closely. Trey would exercise his self-appointed authority over the Nature Reserve by chasing it away.

He was very jealous of his herd's rights to have exclusive and uninterrupted use of the water. The other inhabitants wondered how much further he would attempt to rule their lives when his present absorption with the hinds was over. He had given them plenty of indications and they tired of seeing him stepping regally along the boundaries of the Park, his head with its heavy burden of antlers held high, and his haughty glance sweeping over the length and breadth of the Reserve.

'It seems his vanity knows no limits,' Fox remarked when the animals were gathered one evening. 'But his legs bear the toothmarks of Plucky and Badger. He's not unassailable.'

'Let sleeping dogs lie,' Vixen counselled. 'He doesn't impose himself on us at present.'

'We've always been free to visit the Pond whenever we needed,' Fox replied. 'All of us. These days, Toad's the only one who's allowed free rein because he's small enough to be overlooked.'

'If only Trey would go and drink from the stream,' Weasel growled, 'it would solve all our problems.'

'It's hardly likely,' said Friendly, 'when every other creature in the Reserve avoids it.'

Adder was bored with this continuous topic of water, perhaps because as a reptile he didn't understand the mammals' preoccupation with the need to drink. 'There's plenty of rainwater lying around now,' he hissed. 'Enough for all the animals in the Park to make use of. Why this constant obsession with the Pond?'

'It's symbolic,' Weasel told him.

'Symbolic of what? Only of unending chatter as far as I can see,' the snake contended.

'It's symbolic,' Weasel intoned slowly, 'of the way our freedom to roam has been blighted by this stag.'

'Oh – oh. Round and round we go,' Adder rasped and coiled himself up as he spoke, so that the others weren't sure if he was being sarcastic or commenting on his own activity.

Weasel, however, was goaded. 'He's right, you know,' he said. 'I can remember days not so very long ago when we did more than just talk.'

'Yes,' said Fox. 'We were young and vigorous then.'

Weasel drew himself up. 'We're still the Animals of Farthing Wood,' he said proudly. 'We've got the better of many a foe in our time. And you said yourself Trey isn't unassailable.'

Fox was interested. 'What do you propose, Weasel?'

'I propose,' he answered, 'that we stand up for ourselves, just like Plucky and poor old Badger.'

'We don't want to meddle with Trey,' Vixen cautioned. 'He's a youthful beast and a strong one and all our wisdom and guile may count for nothing against that.'

'I'm not advocating meddling with him,' Weasel assured her. 'I don't want anything to do with him, personally. But if he continues to meddle with our liberty within the Reserve then, as I say, I think we should stand up for ourselves.'

'Bravo, Weasel. Well said,' Friendly commented. 'Father, why don't you lead our party down to the Pond to drink, just as the stag does with his herd?'

'That's provocation,' said Charmer.

'That's right,' agreed Friendly happily. 'Well, Father?'

'All right,' said Fox. 'It's worth a try. We'll browbeat him. He can't intimidate a whole group of us. He'll have to concede. And, once he's done so, perhaps we shall be allowed to carry on our lives without this constant fear of hindrance.' There was the old authority and determination in his voice.

'We can't travel around in a big group all the time,' Leveret pointed out. 'Supposing he tries to pick us off one by one?'

'We've no reason to fear that,' Fox encouraged him. 'He's shown no sign of it so far. I don't think he's vindictive enough.'

'Nor sufficiently clever,' Weasel added.

'Well, no time like the present,' Fox said confidently. 'I feel two seasons younger already. Who's coming?'

There was a general chorus of support.

'Good,' Fox said. 'Only Badger must stay behind. And Mossy can keep him company.' He turned to the mole. 'Will you make certain he remains in his set?'

Mossy assured him he would.

'Apart from you, then, it's the whole party?' Fox summed up.

'Except for Tawny Owl,' Whistler reminded him.

'I begin to believe we shall never see old Owl again,' Fox said sorrowfully. 'I'm afraid something must have happened to him.'

The younger foxes looked uncomfortable as they always did when Tawny Owl was mentioned.

Fox noted their discomfort and relieved them of it. 'Follow me, then, all of you,' he cried and, quitting the Hollow, set off in the direction of the Pond.

Beside himself and Vixen, only Weasel, Whistler and Leveret were also of the old Farthing Wood contingent. Toad was already at the Pond, Tawny Owl was absent, Badger too feeble, while Adder showed no sign of wishing to uncoil himself. So it was just as well there was a good number of Fox's and Vixen's descendants to bolster the throng: Friendly and Charmer, Pace, Rusty, Whisper and Plucky. Mossy hurried to Badger's set to acquaint him with the animals' move. His short legs were not any swifter overland than his father, Mole's, had been. So an appreciable period had elapsed before he dug himself into the familiar darkness of his labyrinth of tunnels that connected with Badger's home. The old animal took the news badly. He was hurt.

'So they don't think I can contribute anything any more?' he mumbled. 'How could Fox be so unkind?'

'No, no, he meant to be quite the opposite,' Mossy asserted. 'He wants to protect you, I'm sure.'

'Protect me? Nobody needs to protect me,' Badger declared. 'I can look after myself.' He began to lumber up the tunnel.

'Where are you going?' cried Mossy in alarm. 'Fox is relying on me to –'

'To keep me out of it? Oh no. That'll be the day,' Badger growled. 'Where the Farthing Wood animals go, *I* go.' He was quite obstinate. He turned his back on Mossy and headed for the exit. Mossy was powerless to stop him.

'Oh dear,' said the mole. 'I've done this all wrong. Whatever will Fox think of me if Badger's hurt?'

But Badger had no intention of getting hurt. He'd already survived one brush with the royal stag, as well as a near poisoning and he didn't think Providence was against him. As he passed the Hollow he saw Adder enjoying his solitude.

'What are you doing here at such a time?' he demanded.

'Being more sensible than you, by the look of it,' the snake answered, quite unruffled.

'Come on, Adder. We're all together in this.'

'Oh no, Badger. Quite the reverse. We're *not*.'

'Have you forgotten the Oath?'

'No, of course not. But whatever happens at the Pond would have happened anyway long before I could have got there.'

Badger saw the sense of this and realized the same could apply to himself. 'All right,' he said. 'Well, I'll see you later.'

'I certainly hope so,' Adder replied. 'But if you must go, go carefully, Badger. There's something in the air tonight.'

Badger's senses, blunted by age, had not detected anything unusual, besides which his thoughts were thoroughly absorbed with the affront dealt him by his friends. He stumbled along on the trail of the other animals, determined to play his part in the Pond scenario.

The night was well on when the others brought themselves within sight of the expanse of water. As if Fate had ordained it, the first thing they noticed was that the Pond was ringed by the ghostly white blur of deer jostling for positions to drink. Fox's eyes searched for Trey's figure. And there he was, a short distance from his minions, keeping watch over the area. Fox saw the stag's head turning this way and that as he craned his long muscular neck for intruders.

'He's there all right,' he remarked needlessly, for all of them had seen Trey.

The animals bunched together. Whistler landed in their midst. 'What — what do we do now?' Leveret whispered nervously.

'We go forward, of course,' Weasel snapped. 'To drink.'

'Yes, but we won't go blundering straight in,' Fox qualified his answer. 'We've got to be clever about it. The most important thing is that we stay in a tight group.'

'There's room at the far end of the Pond for us all,' Whistler pointed out. 'Well away from where the stag's taken up his station.'

'No, Whistler, that's just what we don't want,' Fox told him. 'It would be too blatant and would only stimulate Trey into immediate action. He'd come charging at us at once, assuming we were out to challenge his authority.'

'But we are — aren't we, Grandfather?' Pace asked.

'There are ways, Pace, of doing these things,' Fox told him patiently. 'An animal of Trey's size galloping at full-tilt would scatter us irretrievably. He'd have won his argument before we'd even begun. No, we're going to, quite literally, fox him.'

The animals enjoyed the pun.

'How do we do that?' Whisper asked.

'By doing what he'll be least expecting,' Fox replied.

'We're going to march right up to him and confront him. He won't be quite sure how to take us.'

'Lead on then, Fox,' said Weasel. 'If anybody can pull this off, you can.'

The animals trod quietly but deliberately forwards, heading directly for the imposing figure of the royal stag. In the darkness it was a while before Trey picked them out. He began to toss his head in a threatening manner. But the collection of animals kept on coming. From the edge of the Pond, amongst some rushes, Toad watched their progress. 'It looks like a deputation,' he marvelled to himself.

'What's this?' Trey bellowed to the approaching group.

Fox waited until they were near enough for him to answer without being required to raise his voice. 'It's a drinking party,' he replied quietly.

Trey's eyes roved over the animals appraisingly. He wasn't sure why they had gathered together but he didn't see anything to test his strength. 'Where are you heading?' he enquired, though he knew the answer.

'To the water,' Fox said.

'There are many suitable puddles all around you,' Trey told them.

'Ah, but they're not suitable for the deer herd, it seems,' Fox said coolly.

'Of course not. The Pond's our source of water.'

'Well then, it shall be ours too,' Fox stated. 'There's plenty of room for each of us and we shan't disturb the hinds. Come on, everyone.'

The band of animals followed Fox and Vixen without a word. They passed Trey and went on towards their destination. For some moments the stag stood stock still. The presumption of the motley group took his breath away.

As they reached the Pond Fox whispered: 'Get in amongst the hinds.'

The animals did as they were bid and pushed themselves between the bulky bodies of the deer as they drank. Some of them got underneath the long legs of the females and in that manner threaded their way through to the water. By this time Trey had identified Plucky, the young fox who had dared to intervene when he had been teaching the old badger a lesson. The sight of this particular animal boldly defying his presence and actually mingling with his hinds galvanized the stag into action. He dashed across the short distance to the Pond, intent on proving his mastery once and for all. But all the animals in Fox's band had become so intertwined with the female deer that Trey was unable to attack. He snorted furiously and galloped up and down looking for an opening.

The hinds had made no objection at all to the smaller animals' presence at the waterside. They were quite used to the existence of foxes and other creatures in the Park. They had always been around and they had no fear of them. Indeed Fox and Vixen, Badger and Tawny Owl were well-known to them and held in high esteem. Trey was unique amongst all the deer in his arrogant attitude and the antipathy he aroused in the other inhabitants of the Reserve. So, while he sought angrily for one of the Farthing Wood band who might have exposed himself to attack, the female deer were welcoming their company at the pondside and docilely engaging them in conversation.

Trey's exasperation was overwhelming. Toad watched his antics with the greatest enjoyment. 'Trust old Fox,' he chortled to himself. 'He's left the stag helpless.'

The animals were free to drink for as long as they chose. Yet many of them were not drinking at all. Their trek to the Pond to confront Trey had been a gesture of independence and the fact was that they hadn't really needed the Pond's water to quench their thirst. Led by Fox, they had been out to demonstrate that they meant to go on using it when the need *would* arise. When the stag realized that they were not drinking, his anger bubbled over. Ironically, the very thing he had been trying to prevent now incensed him the most. He knew their intention had merely been to best him. He roared at his females who were displaying every token of friendship to the other beasts.

'Cease your prattling,' Trey boomed, 'and step away!' He wanted to get at Fox himself now. He knew all about his legendary cunning and he couldn't allow Fox to make a fool of him in front of his harem. The stag was simply seething with rage. Flecks of foam flew from his lips.

The hinds turned to look. Trey pranced about, unable to keep still. Some of the other stags who also used the Pond were hovering not so far off, relishing their conqueror's discomfiture. The females were in no hurry to move. Nothing would have persuaded them to put Fox and Vixen in danger.

'Step away, I say!' Trey roared. 'Or you'll rue the

consequences!' His threats were idle. He couldn't harm his own herd.

A wind blew across the Park, a wind of ill-omen. All the animals – the hinds, the other stags, the Farthing Wood community and its younger relatives – were aware of it. They paused from their activities, raising their heads to look for its meaning. The foxes snuffled the air. Whistler flew over the Pond croaking a warning and birds clustered in the sky in nervous knots. Only Trey, obsessed as ever by his own importance, failed to notice. But his bellows and ranting were ignored.

'We need to find shelter,' said Vixen. 'There's a storm brewing.' Even as she spoke the wind began to moan in the nearest tree tops and send wide ripples chasing each other across the surface of the Pond.

Fox quickly began to round up his group, heedless of the fact that they had now to leave the protection of the clustered female deer. There was a greater danger to pay attention to. The hinds milled around uncertainly.

'Remember the place where Badger thought he was dying?' Fox asked his friends. 'We must go there now. There's no time to get back to our own homes.'

Plucky knew the way to the deserted set better than anyone. It was he who had first discovered it. He trotted off, calling over his shoulder. 'It's in this direction.'

Trey saw his opportunity. 'You've taken one chance too many this time,' he said savagely and began to charge at once, his great antlers lowered.

'Plucky! Plucky! Take care!' Vixen cried and she was only just in time.

The young fox sidestepped the stag's impetuous rush

which carried the foolish animal some distance past him, towards the rest of the group.

Fox was scornful. 'The mighty stag!' he scoffed. 'You call yourself the overlord of the Reserve. Yet you don't seem to have any regard for the danger your own herd is in.'

Now the wind was beginning to howl and strong gusts whipped at the sedges and rushes by the Pond. Trey's anger was cooled, despite himself, by the jittery behaviour of the hinds. They sensed the storm and were fretful, lacking direction.

Fox turned his back and led the animals after Plucky. One by one they entered the set, gaining comfort from each other's company. Whistler joined Toad amongst the rushes.

'No contest,' Toad remarked. 'The Pond's ours again.'

They watched Trey gathering the hinds. Presently the herd moved away from the water's edge.

'They'd be wise to stay in the open,' Whistler commented. 'I hope he has the sense not to lead them under the trees.'

The other stags moved away as Trey approached. The strength of the wind increased in power with every passing minute. In a patch of woodland, not too far distant, Badger urged his ancient limbs to greater efforts. He had travelled too far from his own set to be able to return in safety. He could think only of the alternative shelter where, unknown to him, his friends were already assembled. He was between the two and he knew he had put himself in the greatest peril.

16

Storm Over the Park

In the teeth of the wind the deer herd stood on the open grassland. The other stags wandered ever closer, desiring the reassurance brought by a mass of animals. Trey, however, would only allow them within a certain radius of the hinds. If they overstepped this invisible boundary he corrected them. Some of the males lay down. The vicious wind grabbed at their heavy antlers, threatening to pull over. The females milled about uncertainly. Trey planted his feet farther apart as he battled to withstand the full force of the wind.

The hurricane quickly reached a crescendo. It became impossible for any of the deer to stand against it. The hinds lay down and gritted their teeth, sheltering their youngsters as best they could. Even Trey succumbed and now all thought of rivalries and possession was forgotten in the maelstrom of air that whirled across the Park. The herd, including the other males, instinctively bunched into a tight-knit group. They listened to the crack! crack! of shattering branches from distant trees. There was a creaking, tearing, ripping cacophony, punctuated by crashes as the root systems of mature specimens in the patches of woodland were loosened from their moorings in the saturated soil and their trunks and branches hurled earthwards. One after another was destroyed. Above the boom of the trees smiting the earth like blows from a steam hammer, the screaming, shrieking wind was the dominant sound. It seemed to laugh and mock at the havoc it caused. The terrified wildlife population of the Nature Reserve cowered in their tunnels and holes or took shelter where they could. Some of them left the Park altogether for the open downland as portions of the boundary fence were torn down, leaving escape routes to the world beyond for those who were driven to take them.

In the abandoned set the community of Farthing Wood animals huddled together, almost too frightened to speak. Every tunnel, every chamber of the underground system was occupied. Fox managed to voice his thoughts to Vixen. 'I'm so thankful that Badger is safe inside his own set.'

As he said it, in that other part of the Park, Mossy dug deeper into the ground while the tempest raged and roared. He had waited for Badger's return when the wind first sprang up, thinking to return would be the old creature's first reaction in the storm. But, as time went on and the storm increased in intensity with no sign of Badger, Mossy began to fear the worst. How he rued his own action in Badger's departure. For, innocent though it was, if he hadn't brought the message from Fox, Badger would have known nothing of the animals' expedition to the Pond and would have been quite happy staying put. So Mossy trembled for Badger so exposed to the power of the elements and longed for a miracle to preserve him. The little mole buried himself deeper and deeper to escape the terrifying noise. As he paused from his efforts, suddenly the whole labyrinth of tunnels and passages shook under the most almighty blow which reverberated underground like an earthquake. Mossy thought the world had fallen in on top of him and indeed, in some respects, his own subterranean world had done so. One of the larger trees in the wooded area where Badger had constructed his home had fallen directly on the set and smashed through the system of passages into the heart of his living quarters. Thus unwittingly Badger had saved himself by his determination to defy Fox's advice.

Yet now, with every faltering, stumbling step he took across the Park, Badger was still risking death. All around him heavy branches, snapped by the wind, were falling to the ground with their heavy loads of twigs and leaves. As he scuttled free from one dangerous spot another bough would break and bar his way. When the trees themselves began to fall he knew he must attempt to get into the open. But his progress was constantly impeded by the huge obstacles which littered every portion of the woodland.

'It looks as if I escaped being poisoned only to be flattened by an oak,' he muttered grimly. 'If that's to be my fate I wish I'd died earlier because now I'll never know if the others survive.'

Somehow he struggled on. The horrific howl of the storm accompanied him every step of the way. Badger pulled himself over or under branches, making a circuit of the larger uprooted trees. Some of these had not been torn entirely free from the soil and still quivered as if in their death throes. At last he saw light ahead at the edge of the woodland. It was so dark under the trees that even a slight lessening of the gloom was markedly noticeable. Clouds raced at breakneck speed across the sky, obliterating the moon and stars. But as Badger – panting, exhausted, terrified – pulled himself over the last hurdle of a mass of flattened vegetation, the hurricane strength of the wind was dropping. Badger forced himself on, putting sufficient distance between himself and the horrible sound of crashing trees. Eventually he could go no further. His shaky legs gave way beneath him and he lay, quite helpless, with the storm roaring overhead. The worst of it, however, was past.

When Trey became aware that the storm's force was slackening he scrambled to his feet to survey the herd. A few metres from where the deer were gathered was a crumbled piece of fencing which had once marked the limit of the Nature Reserve. Next to it a hefty Scots Pine, not quite ripped from the earth, leant at a crazy angle and swayed threateningly with every gust of air. Trey saw the wide gap in the boundary fence and he saw the males of the White Deer herd dotted amongst his hinds. He tossed his great head, almost in defiance at the storm's diminishing power. He was once again the royal stag, jealous of interference. The other males stirred as they saw him towering over the herd. Some of them remembered the tales of how Trey had sworn to drive them from the Park. One by one they stood up, uncertain of their next move. They were not long in noticing a ready-made exit close at hand.

Trey now decided to rid himself of their competition for good. He began to see a way of doing it, thereby fulfilling Fox's prediction, though without realizing it himself. It was growing light. The wind still buffeted the males' antlers, making it hard for them to keep their balance.

'Begone,' Trey ordered the stags. 'The danger is over. Move away from my hinds, I say.'

The males extricated themselves from the herd and wandered off a little way. Trey wasn't satisfied. They hadn't moved far enough. Something about the way the other stags still seemed to be hovering in hope near his females aroused his anger once more.

'*That's* the way, over there, through that gap!' he ordered them.

When they looked at the broken fence and back at Trey in disbelief he began to hustle them.

'I want no rivals near, do you hear? Go now of your own volition or be driven out!' And, to hasten their departure, he cantered towards them with lowered antlers.

Some of the inferior stags took him at his word and actually ran through the gap out of the Park. The hinds watched in amazement. The stouter males saw no reason why they should be forced from their home. But Trey meant to do just that. As they hesitated he singled one out and charged at him. The animal put up no resistance. In a moment he had joined those who had already left. The remainder were not so easily cowed. They realized that if they didn't make a stand now Trey would have the Park to himself indefinitely. As he ran at them they ducked and weaved and sidestepped in any direction but the one in which he intended they should go. His temper flared. He managed to connect with one stag, butting him and bowling him over. The deer leapt up and ran for the opening. Trey scented victory. He chose another target, a particularly sturdy animal, and gave chase. The two stags went round and round, this way and that. The others looked on in suspense. Trey drove the other male close to the leaning pine. The stag stumbled over the broken fencing, was momentarily overbalanced, and a gust of wind did the rest. He went sprawling. As he fell he smashed against the pine tree which began to rock ominously. Trey, carried forward by the impetus of his charge, was unable to pull up. As the huge tree teetered Trey was underneath it. Even as he turned to avoid it the pine lost its tenuous grip on the soil and fell. It fell directly on to the royal stag, pinning him down beneath its weight. The mighty overlord of White Deer Park lay motionless. The other stag regained its feet. Then the herd mingled around Trey, looking in horror and awe at his stricken body. The males outside the Park returned to gaze at the sight. Trey looked at them helplessly through glassy eyes. His tongue protruded from his muzzle. Blood flowed from his open mouth and collected in a pool under his head.

Dawn broke over the shattered Nature Reserve.

Many trees had fallen. Many lives had been lost. In the Hollow, Adder uncoiled himself and slid away. During the passing of the storm he had not stirred a fraction.

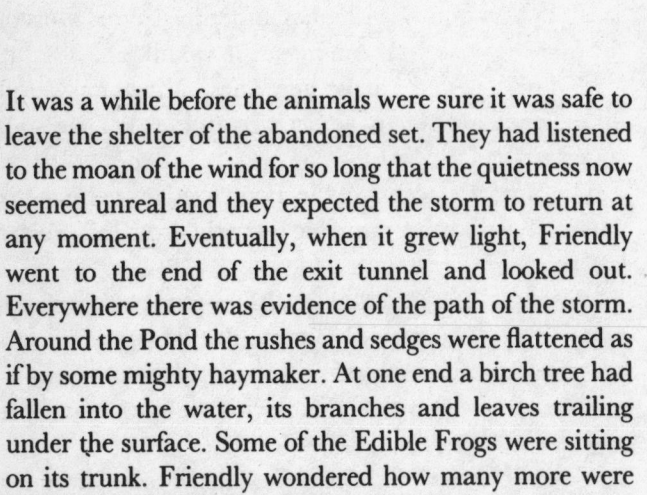

17

Homeless

It was a while before the animals were sure it was safe to leave the shelter of the abandoned set. They had listened to the moan of the wind for so long that the quietness now seemed unreal and they expected the storm to return at any moment. Eventually, when it grew light, Friendly went to the end of the exit tunnel and looked out. Everywhere there was evidence of the path of the storm. Around the Pond the rushes and sedges were flattened as if by some mighty haymaker. At one end a birch tree had fallen into the water, its branches and leaves trailing under the surface. Some of the Edible Frogs were sitting on its trunk. Friendly wondered how many more were squashed underneath. As he looked further afield he could see a wooded area thinned out by the hurricane's savagery. He hurried back to the others.

'It's – it's changed,' he whispered. 'Everything's changed.'

Now all the animals wanted to look. They left the abandoned set and sat in a group around the entrance hole, not quite believing what they saw. The older animals were reminded of their past.

'It's just like Farthing Wood when the bulldozers came,' Fox said sorrowfully.

Weasel tried to raise their spirits. 'But there are many trees still standing or – or – leaning. . . .'

Fox recognized a new danger here. 'We must avoid the wooded areas as much as we can now. Listen! I can hear them creaking.'

Leveret, whose home was in the open grassland, said: 'What about your homes under the trees?' Most of the foxes' earths were amongst the woodland.

'We may have to make new ones,' Vixen answered him. She shook her coat. 'Let's go and see if Toad's all right.'

The animals went to the Pond's edge, calling his name. Toad came crawling eagerly from his rushy bower.

'What a night,' he croaked. 'I thought it would never end. Whistler kept me company. But he's gone now to examine his nest. Fox,' he enthused, 'it's marvellous to see you all safe. I watched you with the stag. How cool you were!'

'Hm. No sign of the deer,' Fox answered. 'I wonder how they fared?'

'The main thing is, *we've* all come through,' Toad said happily. 'But where's Badger?'

'No need to worry about him. He's safe in his own set,' said Friendly.

The animals realized that their priority now was to see how their own homes had suffered.

'Remember, everyone,' said Fox, 'the trees! Tread carefully and avoid creakers. Good luck.'

They left Toad by the water and went their own ways. It was Fox and Vixen who found Badger. The old animal had rallied with the daylight and was creeping about, not sure whether to continue on to the Pond or retrace his steps. The sight of the pair of foxes put new heart into him. He was eager to know whether they had encountered Trey, but first he had to explain to his astounded friends what he was doing there.

'Foolish but loyal creature,' Fox commented warmly. 'And there we were, all of us, congratulating ourselves you were out of harm's way.'

'I did take a bit of a risk,' said Badger. 'Mole tried to prevent me, but I thought you might need me. Did Trey make an appearance?'

'Oh yes, he was there. But we soon dealt with him.' Fox described their tactics. 'I don't think he'll be bothering us so much from now on.' He didn't know how right he was.

'Are you heading homeward?' Badger asked.

'Yes.'

'Will you walk with me? It may take you a little longer because we have to avoid that stretch of woodland – it's full of debris – and, well, I may be rather slow.'

'Of course we'll go with you,' Vixen answered. 'What an unnecessary question. We'll see you to your set.'

'No need to come all the way,' Badger said, keen to

retain some semblance of independence. 'Just as far as your own earth.'

They set off. Badger was indeed slow but the foxes were patient and made no attempt to hurry him. As they progressed they constantly saw new areas of destruction. They discussed the changed aspect of the Park. At one point they spied the Warden in the distance doing his own round of damage inspection. The sight of the man always inspired confidence amongst the animals.

'He'll make it all right again,' Badger murmured trustfully.

'It'll never be quite the same,' Fox contended. 'Remember Farthing Wood. When trees are down. . . .' He left the rest unsaid.

'It's still the Park,' Vixen commented. 'The animals' Park. No human dwellings. We'll get used to the changes.'

As they travelled Whistler was flying to meet them. He had seen Trey's body from the air and so, for the second time in a season, the heron was the first to bring news of the fall of a dominant stag. He scoured the Reserve for a sight of Fox. Presently the three animals heard the well-loved whistle of the bird's punctured wing. With a few mighty flaps Whistler came to rest on the ground a metre or two ahead of them.

'Astonishing news,' he greeted them. 'Our tormentor is a victim of the storm. He's lying by the perimeter fence, crushed under a tree.'

'Trey?'

'None other.'

'Is he dead?'

'Not dead, but utterly helpless.'

Fox and Vixen exchanged glances. They were stunned. Yet they had mixed feelings about the news. Badger, however, had a look of satisfaction.

'The stag has made his last patrol of the Park,' he remarked. 'So that's one of our troubles removed.'

Fox looked doubtful. 'Where is the rest of the herd?' he asked Whistler.

'Milling around the fallen leader,' the heron replied. 'They seem to be in some sort of confusion.'

'Well, it's no concern of ours,' said Badger. 'We have other matters to think about. We don't even know if our homes have survived.'

'Whistler, forgive us,' said Vixen. 'Your news drove every other thought out of our heads. Did your nest survive?'

'No. It's wrecked,' he replied. 'But nests are easy to replace. Not so the trees that supported them.' He left them then to give the news to others of the community.

'Many homes must have been destroyed,' said Badger. 'The birds and squirrels will have fared worst.'

'I – I wonder if Owl survived,' Fox murmured. 'I don't think we'll ever know. Oh, I do yearn to see that poor pompous old bird!'

'Me too,' Badger echoed. 'It just hasn't been the same without him. Even if he is so quarrelsome at times.'

Fox was amused in a sad kind of way. 'I bet Weasel misses their arguments,' he ventured to say.

The sun was well up when they approached Fox and Vixen's earth. They went very warily under the trees. But the foxes were fortunate. Their earth was situated in a copse of immature trees which, with their more flexible trunks and branches, had survived very much better than many of the larger specimens.

'We're lucky,' Fox said to Vixen. 'May you have the same luck, Badger, old friend.'

'We shall see, we shall see,' Badger replied as he trudged on, leaving them behind. He crossed the open space between the foxes' copse and the sloping piece of young beech woodland within which his set had been excavated. He soon noticed that, just as elsewhere in the Park, this patch of woodland was altered beyond recognition. Many well-grown trees had met their deaths during the hurricane's brief but imperious rule. They lay, spanning the ground amongst the litter of branches and brushwood. Badger paused to listen for the tell-tale creaks that might herald the imminent fall of those weakened trees not yet entirely prised from the ground. There was nothing immediately noticeable. He loped his way anxiously around the obstructions in his path. He was not far now from his set. A little farther – and he stopped dead in his tracks. He stared at the crater in the ground which was all that was left of his home, crushed beneath the impact of the fallen tree. Badger was rooted to the spot.

'My – my home,' he whispered. 'I have no home.' Over and over again he muttered the last words. Then, all at once the realization came to him of his narrow escape. He knew that there was no question but that he would have been killed had he stayed where Fox had wanted him to. He recognized the irony of Fox's parting wish. For, despite his new homelessness, Badger *was* lucky. Very lucky indeed. He continued to gaze at the smashed set, wondering how or where he would be able to construct a new home at his advanced age. The thought was not in his mind for long. He had suddenly remembered Mossy.

'Oh! Oh!' he wailed. 'Mole! What's happened to you? Are you buried in there or – or – there at all,' he finished in a whisper.

But Mossy was above ground. After the tree's crash he had surfaced from one of his network of tunnels and he had been timorously waiting and keeping a look-out for Badger ever since. Now he heard his voice and he slowly struggled over the broken and cluttered terrain towards it.

He began to call. 'Badger! Badger! You're safe!'

Badger's head turned at the sound. He saw the little velvet-clad creature pushing through the debris. The two animals rejoiced at the sight of each other.

'Oh Badger, thank goodness you didn't listen to me,' Mossy said fervently. 'Your stubbornness saved you.'

'It did indeed,' Badger replied. 'And your tunnels and home – are they intact?'

'Pretty well,' Mossy said. 'But, poor Badger! Where will you live now?'

'I've no idea,' the old creature admitted. 'I'm a bit long in the tooth to be digging a new home.'

Mossy was silent. He couldn't offer any comfort.

'There's one consolation, though,' Badger went on. 'The Park's ours to roam again. With the threat of Trey removed, I could live – well, just about anywhere. Only, I'd like to be near you, Mole. And *you* live here.'

Mossy was eager to hear about the stag and the rest of the animals. Badger soon told him what he knew.

'Now, what do you think about my idea?' the old creature prompted as soon as the mole was acquainted with events.

'I – I – don't know,' Mossy answered, 'if it would be possible for me to – er – move home now.'

'Oh.' Badger looked crestfallen.

'You see, I have family ties like everyone else – well, *almost* everyone else,' Mossy corrected himself hastily, 'and – and –'

'Of course, I'd forgotten; don't give it another thought,' Badger said at once, kindly. 'I'll manage. Don't worry.'

But Mossy did worry. 'We could stay close anyway, couldn't we?' he offered.

'Well, no, I don't see how we can really,' Badger replied doubtfully. 'You see, the only place I think I can go now is back to that empty set by the Pond. Ah me, I seem to spend all my time going from one end of the Park to the other.'

Mossy was at least cheered by Badger's prospect of ready-made quarters. But he knew they would be distant from each other now and that there was no help for it. The two animals looked at each other sadly.

'Well, well, I'd better be going, Mole,' said Badger. 'I wish I'd stayed where I was, out in the open. I was more than halfway there already.'

'Oh Badger, won't you rest awhile?' Mossy beseeched him. 'You look *so* tired. I'll bring some worms for you. I've plenty to spare. You could at least wait until nightfall before setting off yet again?'

Badger didn't need much persuasion. 'Yes, yes, it would make sense,' he agreed. 'I'll just lie down here for a bit against this tree' – he referred to the one that had smashed his set – 'and have a nap while you rustle up some titbits. And thank you, Mole.'

Fox and Vixen had not been able to put Trey out of their minds. He had made himself their enemy, yet the thought of the stag lying in agony under the crushing weight of a tree niggled at their consciences.

'I suppose he will be found by the Warden,' Vixen conjectured.

'Maybe not for hours – or days,' Fox commented. 'He may be examining quite another section of the Reserve. Look, Vixen,' he said with sudden resolution, 'we can't leave it like this. I feel I want to see for myself what can be done.'

'I'll come with you,' Vixen said, almost with relief.

They headed in the direction they thought most likely to bring them to the wounded stag. They knew he was by the perimeter fence and they guessed it would be at a place not too far from the Pond. In the end they were guided to him without difficulty because they came across the rest of the deer.

Trey had been lying in anguish for a long while. The herd had been unable to help him and he watched the foxes arrive (as he thought) to gloat, with a bitter expression. 'You!' he gasped. 'Couldn't you have . . . left me . . . to my doom?'

'We may be able to help,' Vixen said. 'It's not our way to turn a blind eye to any creature in such terrible distress.'

'What can . . . you do?' Trey panted. 'Puny creatures. . . .'

Vixen ignored his gibe. 'What do you think, Fox?' she asked her partner. 'He'll surely die if that tree isn't moved.'

Fox was racking his brains. He glanced at the other stags who stood about, none of them offering any suggestions. One of them said, 'He's as good as done for. It's only a matter of time.'

'Perhaps not,' Fox said slowly. He was studying the size of the males, their likely strength and the possibility of their using their great antlers. He came to a decision. 'There's only one chance,' he said briskly. 'You males must line up here by the felled tree. Then you must bend your necks and press your antlers against the trunk – all of you, together. You have to try and push it off him.'

The stags muttered amongst themselves.

'Why should we?' asked one bluntly. 'Trey was no friend to us. His day is over.'

'What's *your* interest in helping him?' another one challenged Fox. 'Why do you ask this of us?'

'I'll tell you why,' Fox answered softly. 'Because I picture myself under that tree. It's not difficult to imagine how the poor beast must be suffering.'

His words had a noticeable effect on the male deer. They looked crestfallen; some, a little ashamed. They came forward. Trey watched them in disbelief. He didn't know what to make of Fox, but his pride came to the fore.

'Leave me . . . be,' he whispered. 'I don't ask . . . your help.'

Fox ignored him. The stags hesitated, then continued. Even now some were still in awe of their maimed leader. They set their heads to the bole of the pine and, each straining to his utmost, pushed against the weight of the upended tree. Trey groaned, then bellowed with pain as he felt it shift.

'Harder!' Fox urged. 'It's moving!'

Suddenly the tree half-lifted and then rolled over, leaving Trey free, his gashes and wounds exposed to the onlookers' gaze. He struggled to raise himself but, racked with a terrible agony, fell back again. His crushed and broken limbs could no longer support him. His efforts had exhausted him and he was unable to stir. The other deer backed away, appalled at what they saw.

'We can't leave him like this,' said Vixen.

'Only human intervention can help him now,' Fox replied grimly. 'We must search for the Warden.' He turned a look of compassion on Trey and a flicker of recognition momentarily lit up the stag's glassy eyes.

The foxes moved away. They had not gone far when the human figure they knew so well suddenly confronted them. The Warden had heard Trey's roars of pain and was already on his way to investigate. He recognized the pair of foxes and, for a second, three pairs of eyes met. Then the man went on, leaving Fox and Vixen with a strange feeling of comfort and well-being. They saw he was heading for the wounded beast.

'Do you think there's anything even he can do?' Vixen whispered.

'He has his means,' Fox said. 'Humans have great powers.'

Later, that evening, after his rest, Badger left the

regretful Mossy and stumbled away into the darkness. Mossy wondered when he would see him again and Badger, for his part, had much the same thoughts in his own mind. The old animal didn't hurry himself. A new, lighter wind had sprung up, but a chilly one with the feel of late autumn about it. Badger was wary of any wind now that might dislodge the 'creakers' Fox had warned about, so he kept to the open as far as he could. It was a sensible precaution but one that, unfortunately, made his journey to the substitute home much longer, and this delay was to prove crucial.

18

The Missing Ones

The damage caused by the hurricane throughout the Reserve was extensive. Badger, of course, was not alone in having his home destroyed. And, by the time he had hauled himself to the Pond and crept round its edge to the abandoned set, a whole family of badgers had forestalled him. The set was already tenanted. Badger smelt the smell of his own kind as he snuffled the air. He guessed at once what had happened. At the entrance hole he stopped and listened. Animated badger voices – some young, some older – were all chattering about their luck in finding this new home. Badger sighed. They had beaten him to it, and he had to acknowledge that the extensive tunnels and chambers were more suited to a family than to one ancient, solitary animal. He trudged to the Pond to drink.

Lost in his mournful reflections on the situation, he was unaware that another badger was drinking, only a metre or two away. But she, however, had noticed him and, so familiar a figure was the Farthing Wood badger, she knew at once who he was. She lost no time in trotting to his side.

'It's a pleasure to see you,' she said sincerely.

'Oh!' said Badger with a start. 'Is it?' He looked at the young female.

'What a terrible storm,' said the female. 'I've moved my family here. We lost our old place.'

'Yes. So I gathered. I'm also homeless,' Badger confessed.

'You? Oh no. That's dreadful. But wait – were you –?'

'Yes,' Badger interrupted her. 'I came here on the same quest. But you stole a march on me,' he joked. 'I've no complaints; don't feel bad about it. There's too much space to be wasted on one old male.'

'Oh, but you have to have shelter too,' the female replied feelingly. 'There's plenty of room for one more. Please – we shouldn't care to leave you out in the cold. Do join us. We shan't interfere. You can keep yourself to yourself. And we –'

'No, no, I wouldn't dream of it,' Badger refused. 'You're very kind, I'm sure. I do appreciate it. But I'm not used to sharing. Really, I wouldn't care to start now. I'll be all right. I'll find something.' He had already begun to move off.

'Please,' the female badger called after him. 'Don't go. I'm sure we could work something out quite to your satisfaction.'

'I'm touched by your kindness,' said Badger, but he

didn't turn back. 'Please don't concern yourself about me.' He even increased his pace.

The young female stood looking after him. 'Poor old fellow,' she murmured to herself. 'I do believe he was a little afraid of me.'

'No home now, no home now, not anywhere,' Badger muttered as he wandered about. 'What can I do? I can't live out in the open. Perhaps there's a hole somewhere I can tuck myself into.' That was the best he could hope for. Just a resting-place; a refuge. He didn't expect to find himself a proper set. And, as he wandered and searched and searched and wandered, even the modest demand of a small hole seemed unattainable. The prospect of wandering right through the dark hours without discovering anything seemed a real possibility, as the areas Badger dared to search were limited because of the risks under the trees.

For the first time in his long life Badger came close to despair. He tried reminding himself that, during the animals' long trek from Farthing Wood, he had had to rest and hide in all kinds of unusual places. But he had been younger then, more adaptable and, above all, not alone. Now he was aware of an awful loneliness and he really was too old to cope with this sort of disruption to his life.

'What a way to end up,' he murmured self-pityingly as he sought in vain for a shelter of some kind. He got in such a state that it rather turned his head and he didn't realize where he was going. He wandered through one of the gaps in the broken perimeter fence and out on to the open downland. He didn't know where he was and he went on, blindly searching, as if he were still within the Park. In the end weariness and hopelessness took their toll of the old creature and he simply lay down where he was and went to sleep. Even the cold wind failed to disturb him.

When daylight broke over the grassy expanse Badger woke up, thinking momentarily that he was safe inside his set. His eyes soon told him differently and, with an awful shock, he realized he was no longer even in the Nature Reserve. He felt as if he were in a sort of daze. Nothing seemed quite real any more. He didn't know why he was standing alone on the downland or how he had got there.

'No point going back to that place,' he told himself as he stood looking towards White Deer Park. 'Nowhere for me there.' The rigours of homelessness and solitude had scattered his wits. 'Only one home for old Badger,' he decided as he remembered the comforts of his ancient family set in Farthing Wood. '*That's* where I'll go. Nobody else knows about it. It'll be just for me, like always.' And at that moment he really did believe the set was there waiting for his return.

'Now, let me see, which direction would it be? It's a long way, I know.' He looked about him and settled on his course. Some dim recollection of the way the animals had travelled prompted his decision. 'Hm, yes. I think this is it,' he mumbled as he set off again. 'Toad will know anyway. When I see him he can remind me.'

The cold wind ruffled his bristly coat. Under other circumstances Badger would have known perfectly well that Toad, in such temperatures, would be driven to begin his hibernation. But that sort of reasoning was beyond him now and so, in this sorry state of mind, he went on.

During the next few days the animals speculated about the White Deer herd. The Warden had taken charge of Trey and Whistler had reported that the stag had been removed from the Reserve. 'I doubt if he will be seen again,' he said. 'His injuries were so severe.'

'Only time will tell,' said Fox. 'We did our best for him, at any rate.'

'And if he doesn't return, who will be his successor?' Weasel wondered. 'Let us hope it will be one who recognizes that the Park is for all of us.'

'We can almost depend on that,' said Vixen. 'The blood of the Great White Stag, our friend, is in most of the herd. Trey was not typical. The others are unlike him. They're altogether milder creatures.'

The inhabitants of the Park became used to the presence of men brought in to remove dangerous and fallen trees and to repair the all-important Reserve fencing. The sound of mechanical saws became a regular feature, together with that of hammers and motor vehicles. Naturally the animals kept well away from any human activity but, as time went on and much of the wreckage was cleared away, they were struck constantly by the new look of the Park that was their home. New vistas, new clearings were opened up. The familiar terrain became unfamiliar and for a while the Reserve's inhabitants all felt strange; as if in some way they had been displaced. However, there was one piece of good fortune that resulted from the storm.

On his rounds of inspection the Warden had covered

every corner of White Deer Park. In this way he had discovered the poisonous containers that had been dumped some time ago into the ditch which led into the stream from outside the Park's boundaries. In no time at all these dangerous items had been disposed of, yet it would take a while longer for the water to be rid of its pollution and run clean again. All aquatic life in the stream had been killed. It became the Warden's responsibility to monitor the level of toxicity in the water so that eventually, once the stream was healthy again, re-stocking of fish and other small fry, as well as some vitally necessary vegetation – water-weeds and suchlike – could go ahead.

The ever watchful Whistler kept his friends up to date with events. 'He's testing the water,' he guessed. 'He cleared the rubbish out of it. I think he's trying to make the stream well again.'

Another time the heron notified them, 'The Warden's taking some water away with him. If he's going to drink it, it must be pure.'

'Take care,' Fox warned him. 'Don't risk yourself too soon.'

'There's no danger,' Whistler answered. 'I shan't go close to it until the fish return. Then I'll know the stream runs clear once more.'

But the stream was not the animals' main concern. Their chief worry now was the disappearance of Badger.

No-one knew where Badger had gone. Fox and Vixen had soon found the crushed home of their old friend and had been pointed in the direction of the abandoned set by Mossy. But when they discovered the family of strange badgers in residence, they turned their attentions elsewhere. A meeting was held in the Hollow and everyone was asked to comb each likely spot for a sign of the missing animal. Of course every one of them drew a blank.

Fox feared for the worst. 'I'm afraid we've lost him,' he said to Vixen brokenly. 'He can't be in the Park any more. We've looked everywhere. There's just nowhere else. He's gone outside it, I know he has.'

Mossy was distraught. 'He couldn't find a home, he couldn't find a home,' he kept chanting in his misery.

'*We'll* find him a home all right,' Plucky declared. 'It only needs a few of us to drive out those usurping badgers. We'll save the set by the Pond for *our* Badger.'

'No, no, we certainly shan't,' Fox, his elder, corrected him. 'Your heart's in the right place, Plucky, I know. But the set was never Badger's own. The other animals have just as much right to it. They've settled there and *we* shan't disturb them. Oh, if I could only find the dear old creature I'd dig him a home myself. Yes, if it took all my strength I'd do it.'

'You wouldn't do it alone and you know it,' Vixen told him. 'I have claws too. Do you think I wouldn't want to help?'

'Of course you would,' Fox said. 'But what's happening to us? First Tawny Owl and now Badger. We're losing each other and – and I don't think I can put things right this time. I just can't bear it, Vixen.'

'If Badger's gone outside the Park, then why don't

we go after him?' suggested Weasel. 'He's not so swift-footed that we couldn't soon catch him up.'

'Yes, and which direction would we go in?' Adder demanded. 'Would we all go crawling about over the countryside together? Or take different paths? That way there'd be more than just Owl and Badger numbered among the lost. As it is, if I don't get underground soon I shall be lost anyway. Lost for good if the frost gets to me.'

'Nobody's asking you to hang around,' Weasel pointed out.

'Thank you for your civility,' Adder hissed. 'D'you think I can sleep the winter away without knowing if Badger will be here to greet when I wake again?'

'Well, well, you snakes must become more senti-mental as you get older,' Weasel remarked. 'I've never known you admit to such feelings before.'

'Never you mind about that,' Adder rasped, his demeanour resuming its usual mask of nonchalance. 'I think it was you who was instrumental in driving out Tawny Owl from amongst our company?'

'Never!' Weasel cried. 'Not I! I'd never do such a thing. I acknowledge I may have pulled his leg once or twice but how could I have foreseen the consequences? Why, I've never ceased to rue the day he left. All I want is for us all to be together again especially as – well' – here his voice dropped, even trembling slightly – 'as we all grow older.'

Whistler said, 'I'll fly a reconnoitre now and again. But you know I had no luck seeking out Owl. It may be as unrewarding looking for Badger.'

'There's one advantage,' said Friendly. 'Badger's on the ground. Easier to spot an animal than a bird.'

'I'll do my best,' Whistler promised.

Fox turned to Adder. 'Please don't put yourself at risk,' he advised the snake. 'Toad's already slumbering in his winter quarters. We don't want any more losses.'

'I'll wait awhile,' Adder said firmly. 'There have been no frosts so far. And one thing's for sure. There is no dearth of leaves to bury myself in at night.'

'If you should need extra warmth,' Vixen offered graciously, 'our earth can be the cosiest of places. . . .'

Adder's tongue flickered busily. He was strangely moved. 'D'you know, Vixen,' he said softly, 'that sinking my fangs into that horse's leg, so long ago now, is something I've always considered as one of the best things I've ever done in my life?' The snake's red eyes seemed to glow particularly brightly for an instant and Vixen didn't fail to notice.

'I've never forgotten it,' she whispered, 'and I never shall.'

Whistler began flying over the downland the very same day. His eyes scanned the mass of green for a flash of black and white that would reveal Badger's where-abouts. No other animal had that unmistakable colouring. But while the heron coasted and soared on his broad wings, Badger had paused to rest in the shadow of a large building. He had made uncertain progress but the church under whose walls he now lay sleeping was the first positive reminder to him that he had chosen the correct route. Just like Tawny Owl before him, it was the one recognizable landmark for him in that region. And, even as he snored in the open with his back pressed against the stonework, Tawny Owl and Holly were heading for the very same building from the opposite direction.

19

Home

Tawny Owl's journey back to White Deer Park had not been the happy one he had planned. Holly had taken charge of all hunting activities since he had exhausted himself on the first stage of their flight. She had nurtured him with the plumpest of the prey she had caught, almost as if he were a fledgling. Much as he enjoyed these tasty meals, Owl was only grudgingly grateful as, with each day, he felt he was losing more of his independence. Holly also made sure he didn't overtax his stiffened wing muscles, and of this he was quite glad since as soon as his strength returned fully he intended to end his reliance on her. The only function left to Tawny Owl now, over which Holly could exert no control, was his navigation of their route. One by one the major features of the journey – the river, the area of the Hunt, the motorway, the town – were marked and passed. Now Owl set their course for the church.

Sometimes, when Holly had been particularly irksome, he wondered about leaving her in whatever roost they had chosen that day, and then flying away as she slept. There were occasions when he definitely wished to be rid of her. But something always held him back. He would remind himself that he would lose the very thing for which he had left White Deer Park in the first place – a mate. And he was conscious of the fact that he did owe a debt of gratitude to the female owl. She had kept him alive when he had been trapped in the beech at Farthinghurst. So they stayed together and now they neared the end of their journey.

Holly was constantly asking about when they would arrive. Tawny Owl always replied that, once the church was within their sights, they were as good as home. When at last he spied the building ahead, feelings of excitement, relief, anticipation and also uncertainty flooded over him. All along he had dreaded finding what the storm had done to White Deer Park. And now that moment had almost arrived. The two birds flew straight to the church and Tawny Owl, remembering the indignation of the colony of belfry bats, led Holly to the nave roof instead where they perched side by side.

'So this is it at last,' Holly breathed. There was no mistaking her own excitement. The stars shone brilliantly in the wide expanse of sky. It was a perfect night for hunting. 'I'll waste no time,' she said to Owl. 'The sooner we eat the sooner we can complete our journey. And, just think, the next time I hunt it will be in the Park itself.'

Tawny Owl flexed his supple wings. 'Yes,' he said.

'This is the last occasion when you bring me my food. You must stop treating me like an owlet.'

Holly looked at him askance. She guessed his thoughts. 'There's no need for your friends to know about our arrangement,' she said archly. 'I'm sure they don't watch you hunt?'

'Well no, but –'

'Very well then,' she interrupted. 'I can go on looking after you just as before. You should be grateful to be relieved of the tedium of hunting. You'll have a most comfortable and cosseted old age, I promise you.'

'Look, I don't want. . . .' Owl began peevishly, but it was no good. Holly flew away without listening just as she always did. 'How *am* I to get her to understand?' he fluted in exasperation. He watched the bats darting on their aerobatic flights from the belfry. Then he glanced down and, by the south side of the church he saw an animal stirring in the shadows. The striking striped head of a badger was illuminated by the crisp autumn starlight. Tawny Owl gasped. He could scarcely believe his eyes. In his amazement he almost over-balanced from his perch on the roof. He recognized Badger instantaneously.

'Badger! Badger!' he called and swooped down-wards.

The old animal looked up with a puzzled expression. Then he saw Tawny Owl who alighted next to him.

'What on earth are you doing?' Owl asked in an astounded voice.

'Oh, Owl,' said Badger who was still very confused, 'you shouldn't have come looking for me.'

'I didn't come looking for you,' replied the bird.

'Whatever are you talking about? I haven't seen you at all for the whole of the summer. And wherever are you going?'

'Going?' mumbled Badger. 'Oh – um – going home, Owl. Going home.'

'I should think so. But why have you left it?'

'Left what?'

'Home.'

'Well, we all left it, didn't we, when we travelled across country to the – to the. . . .'

'You're not making any sense,' Tawny Owl interjected. He could tell that something was wrong with Badger. 'Now, tell me again. Where are you going?'

Badger looked at him as if he thought it was the owl who was out of his wits. 'Well – Farthing Wood, of course.'

'FARTHING WOOD?!'

'Yes, I have to get home, you see, because I can't live out in the open. I need shelter and – and –'

'Badger, stop. It seems there's something seriously wrong. Now, what's happened? What's the matter with you?'

'The matter with me?' Badger echoed. 'Well, I should have thought that was obvious. I'm homeless, Owl. That's what I am. Homeless.'

Tawny Owl was able to put two and two together. He realized there had been destruction in the Park and now he dreaded more than ever what he was going to see. But he tried to concentrate on Badger's troubles. 'Your home is White Deer Park,' he prompted. 'Why have you left the others? Where are they?'

'Oh, they're all right,' Badger answered sensibly

enough. 'They didn't lose their homes like me. So they
– er – they've stayed put.'

Tawny Owl was moved by his old friend's sad plight.
'Dear Badger,' he said. 'You don't understand. There
is no Farthing Wood. So you must turn back and go
along with me.'

But Badger, who had almost lost his reason, couldn't
accept this. 'Of course there's a Farthing Wood,' he
disputed. 'What a ridiculous thing to say about the
place we all grew up in!'

'Oh Badger, have you no memory?' Owl cried. 'The
wood was destroyed! Why ever else would we have left
it?'

'It was being destroyed when we left,' Badger
agreed, 'but most of it was still there. Well, some of
it. . . .' He was beginning to sound uncertain.

'Well, it isn't there now,' Tawny Owl insisted in a
loud voice as though Badger might be deaf. 'I've been
there – all the way back. There's not one stick left
standing. No, not one plant. Everywhere is covered
with human dwellings. So you *must* turn back.'

The old animal seemed to be trying to register this
information. He couldn't quite grasp it. 'You – you've
been there?' he repeated.

'Yes.'

Badger was regaining a semblance of his wits. 'Is
that where you've been all this time?'

'A lot of it, yes. I've a long story to tell you.'

'But why did *you* go there?' Badger asked perplexedly
as he noticed a second owl skimming towards them.

'Here's one reason,' Tawny Owl replied as Holly

arrived, with her bill crammed with food. 'Now, why don't we all eat together?'

Gradually, with Owl's patient help, Badger's understanding began to return. He saw how his foolishness had resulted from the shock of finding himself without a home. When they were ready, they set off for the Park. Badger was very slow, but Tawny Owl was determined not to let the old creature out of his sight and was quite satisfied to fly in short bursts to accommodate his slower pace. As for Holly, for once she was content to take a back seat.

As they went, Tawny Owl was able to piece together from what Badger told him, how the hurricane had devastated the Park. He learnt of the poisoned stream, too, but that despite everything all his old companions had survived. Then he, in his turn, described to Badger his own adventures and the sad fall of the last relic of Farthing Wood.

'So you see, we only have one home, don't we?' he summed up. 'And that's White Deer Park.'

It was broad daylight as they approached the Nature Reserve. Tawny Owl sought out a suitable entry point for Badger where the fencing was not yet repaired. High in the air, Whistler saw the three travellers, flew closer to make sure his eyes weren't deceiving him and then, with a 'krornk' of utmost delight raced to rouse Fox, Vixen, Weasel and Adder.

So when Badger trudged once more into the Park, the group of friends were there to greet him and the long-lost Tawny Owl.

'I hardly dared hope for this,' Fox murmured

emotionally. 'It's a day like no other. How did you come together?'

'There's much to tell,' Tawny Owl answered joyfully.

'My heart beats for both of you,' Vixen whispered to the two lost ones. 'And, Owl, I see you've not travelled unaccompanied?'

Holly was speechless at the sight of the gathered group, so many of them seemed to her like living legends. Tawny Owl wasn't slow to notice this.

'No, I've had good company,' he said, 'though, as you can see,' he added mischievously, 'it's been difficult for me to get a word in edgeways.'

There was much amusement at his remark, though the animals did not, as yet, understand its irony. Weasel was so relieved to see the return of Tawny Owl that he was quite unable to offer him any banter.

'Well, at long last I can retire,' hissed Adder. 'Sinuous has given me up for lost. I've seen what I wanted to see and I don't wish for any more than that. Badger, Owl – I salute you, though you *have* caused me discomfort. Farewell, All. Till the spring!'

They watched him slither hastily away.

'Come, Badger, old friend,' said Fox. 'We have something to show you.' He led the way and eventually they all arrived at Fox and Vixen's earth. Next. to it there were new earthworks. While Badger looked on in wonder, clods of earth were thrown up from within this new construction which landed almost at his feet.

'It's not quite ready yet,' Fox said apologetically. 'But there's a company of busy fox paws digging away, as well as others'. You won't have too long to wait.'

'Me?' Badger murmured. 'Is it for me?'

'Of course it's for you. Who else?' said Fox. 'You're to be our near neighbour. And what could be better than that?'

'Nothing,' said Badger. 'Nothing at all.'

'It'll be your home for ever,' Fox told him. 'We shall stay close together for the rest of our lives.'

Just then Mossy surfaced from the new set. 'The foxes dig so furiously,' he said, 'I'm in danger of being buried.' He rushed to be re-united with Badger.

'I think,' said Tawny Owl to Holly, 'we can safely leave them to it for now. Animals have their own habits and we birds' – here he flapped his wings vigorously – 'we have other occupations. The story of Farthinghurst can wait. As for now, I propose we make a circuit of the Park. I haven't seen it for a while and I need to re-acquaint myself with my best hunting terrain. Come on, I'll show you around.'

Holly promptly followed him as he launched into flight.

'Well!' exclaimed Weasel. 'That's something I *never* thought I'd see.'

Other great reads ✎ *from* **Red Fox**

Further Red Fox titles that you might enjoy reading are listed on the following pages. They are available in bookshops or they can be ordered directly from us.

If you would like to order books, please send this form and the money due to:

ARROW BOOKS, BOOKSERVICE BY POST, PO BOX 29, DOUGLAS, ISLE OF MAN, BRITISH ISLES. Please enclose a cheque or postal order made out to Arrow Books Ltd for the amount due, plus 75p per book for postage and packing to a maximum of £7.50, both for orders within the UK. For customers outside the UK, please allow £1.00 per book.

NAME_____

ADDRESS_____

_____

Please print clearly.

Whilst every effort is made to keep prices low, it is sometimes necessary to increase cover prices at short notice. If you are ordering books by post, to save delay it is advisable to phone to confirm the correct price. The number to ring is THE SALES DEPARTMENT 071 (if outside London) 973 9700.

Spinechilling stories to read at night

THE CONJUROR'S GAME Catherine Fisher

Alick has unwittingly set something unworldly afoot in Halcombe Great Wood.

ISBN 0 09 985960 2   £2.50

RAVENSGILL William Mayne

What is the dark secret that has held two families apart for so many years?

ISBN 0 09 975270 0   £2.99

EARTHFASTS William Mayne

The bizarre chain of events begins when David and Keith see someone march out of the ground . . .

ISBN 0 09 977600 6   £2.99

A LEGACY OF GHOSTS Colin Dann

Two boys go searching for old Mackie's hoard and find something else . . .

ISBN 0 09 986540 8   £2.99

TUNNEL TERROR

The Channel Tunnel is under threat and only Tom can save it . . .

ISBN 0 09 989030 5   £2.99

Other great reads from **Red Fox**

It's chocks away with Biggles and his chums by Captain W. E. Johns

That air ace and intrepid adventurer, Biggles, is guaranteed to offer thrill-packed adventure. Whether he's flying for his life in the skies above wartime France, or smashing a big crime ring in India, these stories make compulsive reading.

BIGGLES LEARNS TO FLY

In wartime France, it's a case of learn quickly or be killed . . .

ISBN 0 09 993820 0   £3.50

BIGGLES FLIES EAST

Biggles is sent on a dangerous spying mission to the Middle East where the least slip might cost him his life.

ISBN 0 09 993780 8   £3.50

BIGGLES & CO.

Transporting gold proves no easy job for Biggles.

ISBN 0 09 993800 6   £3.50

BIGGLES IN SPAIN

Caught in a bloody civil war, Biggles finds himself charged with getting valuable papers back to England.

ISBN 0 09 993810 3   £3.50

BIGGLES DEFIES THE SWASTIKA

Biggles is trapped in Norway by the invasion of the Nazis and in constant danger from his old enemy, Von Stalhein.

ISBN 0 09 993790 5   £3.50

BIGGLES IN THE ORIENT

Something is attacking the pilots making the wartime run from India to China – and it's up to Biggles to find out what.

ISBN 0 09 993830 8   £3.50

Other great reads from **Red Fox**

Share the magic of The Magician's House by William Corlett

There is magic in the air from the first moment the three Constant children, William, Mary and Alice arrive at their uncle's house in the Golden Valley. But it's when they meet the Magician, William Tyler, and hear of the Great Task he has for them that the adventures really begin.

THE STEPS UP THE CHIMNEY

Evil threatens Golden House in its hour of need – and the Magician's animals come to the children's aid – but travelling with a fox brings its own dangers.

ISBN 0 09 985370 1   £2.99

THE DOOR IN THE TREE

William, Mary and Alice find a cruel and vicious sport threatening the peace of Golden Valley on their return to this magical place.

ISBN 0 09 997390 1   £2.99

THE TUNNEL BEHIND THE WATERFALL

Evil creatures mass against the children as they attempt to master time travel.

ISBN 0 09 997910 1   £2.99

THE BRIDGE IN THE CLOUDS

With the Magician seriously ill, it's up to the three children to complete the Great Task alone.

ISBN 0 09 918301 9   £2.99

Other great reads from **Red Fox**

Discover the wacky world of Spacedog and Roy by Natalie Standiford

Spacedog isn't really a dog at all – he's an alien lifeform from the planet Queekrg, who just happens to *look* like a dog. It's a handy form of disguise – but he's not sure he'll *ever* get used to the food!

SPACEDOG AND ROY

Roy is quite surprised to find an alien spacecraft in his garden – but that's nothing to the surprise he gets when Spacedog climbs out.

ISBN 0 09 983650 5   £2.99

SPACEDOG AND THE PET SHOW

Life becomes unbearable for Spacedog when he's entered for the local pet show and a French poodle falls in love with him.

ISBN 0 09 983660 2   £2.99

SPACEDOG IN TROUBLE

When Spacedog is mistaken for a stray and locked up in the animal sanctuary, he knows he's in big trouble.

ISBN 0 09 983670 X   £2.99

SPACEDOG THE HERO

When Roy's father goes away he makes Spacedog the family watchdog – but Spacedog is scared of the dark. What can he do?

ISBN 0 09 983680 7   £2.99

Other great reads from **Red Fox**

Giggle and groan with a Red Fox humour book!

Nutty, naughty and quite quite mad, the Red Fox humour list has a range of the silliest titles you're likely to see on a bookshelf! Check out some of our weird and wonderful books and we promise you'll have a ribticklingly good read!

MIAOW! THE CAT JOKE BOOK – Susan Abbott

Be a cool cat and paws here for the purrfect joke! Get your claws into this collection of howlers all about our furry friends that will have you feline like a grinning Cheshire Cat!

ISBN 0 09 998460 1   £1.99

THE SMELLY SOCKS JOKE BOOK – Susan Abbott

Hold your nose . . . here comes the funniest and foulest joke book you're likely to read for a while! Packed with pungent puns and reeking with revolting riddles, this one is guaranteed to leave you gasping for air!

ISBN 0 09 956270 7   £1.99

TUTANKHAMUN IS A BIT OF A MUMMY'S BOY – Michael Coleman

Have you ever dreaded taking home your school report or a letter from the Head? You're in good company! Did you know that Shakespeare was really "hopeless at English" and that Christopher Columbus had "absolutely no sense of direction"? There's fifty other previously unpublished school reports which reveal hilarious secrets about the famous which not many people know . . .

ISBN 0 09 988180 2   £2.99

THE FISH AND CHIPS JOKE BOOK – Ian Rylett

This book comes complete with a fish-and-chips scratch and sniff panel so you can sniff while you snigger at this delicious collection of piping-hot pottiness! Your tastebuds will be tickled no end with this mouth-watering concoction of tasty gags so tuck into a copy today! It's a feast of fun!

ISBN 0 09 995040 5   £2.99

Join the RED FOX Reader's Club

The Red Fox Readers' Club is for readers of all ages. All you have to do is ask your local bookseller or librarian for a Red Fox Reader's Club card. As an official Red Fox Reader you will qualify for your own Red Fox Reader's Clubpack – full of exciting surprises! If you have any difficulty obtaining a Red Fox Readers' Club card please write to: Random House Children's Books Marketing Department, 20 Vauxhall Bridge Road, London SW1V 2SA.